Can Amanda find the strength to take back control of her life?

Breaking Eggshells

LIV ANDREWS

Copyright, ©Liv Andrews, 2021

The moral right of the author has been asserted.

This is a work of fiction. Names and characters are the product of the author's imagination and any resemblance to actual persons, living or dead, is entirely coincidental.

Published by Words On Toast Ltd

DEDICATION

To Stuart, my wonderful husband,
and Andy, my amazing son.

Love you both to bits.

CHAPTER ONE

Amanda

I'm not beautiful like my sister, or bold like my aunt. I may lack their drama and intrigue but I think I make up for that by being reliable and grounded. I believe I am rooted, like an oak tree, to the life I know. Wife, mother, daughter, sister, niece. Those are my roles and I don't just play at them.

Despite the certainty of my position in the world, which was my place as Dan's wife, things started to happen that unsettled me. Small things, but they sat heavily on my mind and made me question everything.

The first was that Dan started wearing a new, expensive looking silk tie. Yellow, with tiny red dots on it that oozed luxury and exclusivity. It was no ordinary tie. I asked him about it because he usually only went clothes shopping with me in tow.

'I saw it in London when I was waiting for George before that meeting. He was running late so I had a look around the shops. It was an impulse buy. Even men are susceptible to that, Amanda.' Smiling, he shrugged his shoulders.

It sounded plausible yet he'd only mentioned it when I asked and he was a bit of a peacock. I was surprised he hadn't show it to me when he first bought it, shown off that it was designer and that it cost a packet. It crossed my mind that it was the sort of thing someone might buy as a gift.

The second thing was that his mobile phone was by then virtually grafted to him.

I've never had the passcode to his phone. It's never occurred to me to look at it. Most of his calls and messages were about work and he rarely used it at weekends but lately, I noticed, although it was on silent, it did still vibrate. It was going constantly, all the time. He'd look at the message, face impassive, then put it back into his pocket.

It nagged at me and frustrated me because I'd never been like that, never been a suspicious person and the thoughts that were going through my head annoyed me.

One Sunday afternoon, I asked, as casually as I could, who was messaging him at the weekend.

'Oh, it's just Martin, you know he's on his own now. I think he just gets a bit lonely.'

I knew Martin was lonely. I knew this because some Wednesday evenings, Dan would take Martin out for a meal.

And that was the third thing.

Dan wasn't that kind of person. I'd never known him to be so attentive to friends and in any case, Martin was more of a business associate. At first, I thought it was kind of Dan to be looking out for someone. I thought maybe he was learning the value of friendship. But I didn't expect he'd still be going out to dinner with him four months later. I thought it would have worn off. Then, when he got home last Wednesday, he told me that he and Martin had gone to Paulo's Italian, a little bistro that he and I used to go to in East London. He'd described the ravioli and said how the wine was very good for the price, that Paulo was looking as handsome as ever, and how he'd nearly missed the last train home, and on and on he went. Too much detail. It didn't feel right.

I kept trying to push these thoughts aside. Dan never gave me reason to doubt him. Everything was fine between us. Absolutely fine. Just last weekend we'd gone out with Steve and Suzie and he'd been talking about how long we'd been married and how next year it would be our twenty-first wedding anniversary. He turned to me and said, 'We'll have to start thinking about what we're going to do for that, love. Think about a special holiday.'

Only recently, he was talking about the future and yet I was imagining all sorts of things. I told myself I was being stupid.

Then, one Friday night when we'd watched a thriller and gone to bed early, I was looking through Facebook on my phone and saw that Eve had tagged me in a memory from exactly six years ago.

'Remember this Amanda?' the caption read, above the picture of the four of us, with glasses raised and big smiles. *Great meal at Paulo's, can't believe it was six years ago! Think we all had a bit too much that night!* @PaulosLondon24

It had been great fun. Eve was my best friend and every night out with her and Marco was good. They were down to earth people, such easy company.

I clicked the link to Paulo's page. He was always posting funny memes and photographs of Italy.

At the top was a pinned post, dated three weeks previously. I read it several times.

'A heads-up for all you Paulo fans! We're going to be closed from tomorrow, May 17th, and will be re-opening on June 28th. BIG refurb going on and we look forward to welcoming you all back at the end of next month!! Same great food, same great service!'

I swallowed back acid as I put my phone away. I'd just gone to bed and was waiting for Dan to finish brushing his teeth.

He whistled as he came into the room, threw the duvet aside and got into bed facing me, reaching out to take my hand. Closing his eyes, a smile of contentment spread across his face.

'That film was good,' he said. 'Didn't think it was going to be the wife, did you?'

'No. Didn't see that coming.' I tried to sound as natural as possible but I had to clear up the discrepancy between what he'd told me about dinner with Martin and what I'd just read. Maybe I'd got it all wrong.

Dan reached over, switched out the light and turned his back to me, getting into his favourite sleeping position.

'Oh, by the way, I meant to ask you. You know when

you went to Paulo's on Wednesday? Did Paulo mention his daughter Gina? Her baby must be due around now.'

I was aware of a sudden tension in the body next to me. A little hesitation while he framed his answer. 'Er, no I don't think he did. He was quite busy though, so who knows? I'll ask him next time I see him, if I remember. Night love.'

I barely slept. I questioned what possible reasons he could have to lie to me. I picked apart every tiny aspect of our lives, everything that could have happened, every person who could have caught Dan's eye.

Was I happy? Was my marriage good? I couldn't fool myself that everything in the garden was rosy, but who can? Don't most couples put on a united front, papering over the cracks so that their outer shell looks impenetrable whatever might be happening behind closed doors?

I was content. Sort of. Dan could be moody and I wondered if his moods might be extreme, but I daren't ask anyone what they thought. I couldn't hold our problems up to the light in public and examine them, compare them to what other people considered the norm. He's the type of man who believes that what happens behind the closed doors of a marriage should stay completely private.

Could he be having an affair? It seemed unbelievable even though there were so many signs pointing to it. Then, of course, if he *was*, who with?

One name did float through my mind.

The woman from the village who had been on her own for

a couple of years. The quiet divorcee, who everyone said was so *nice*, so *kind*, such a *shame* she was on her own.

He'd mentioned her in passing once or twice. And I'd seen them talking together outside the paper shop one Sunday morning a few weeks back, when I drove past on the way to pick Ben up from football. They were laughing together, very focussed. She was beaming at him. And I remember thinking at the time that she might be flirting with Dan a bit, bless her. At the time, I'd smiled to myself because it didn't matter, because Dan wasn't like that.

I got up early and busied myself loading the washing machine and emptying the dishwasher. I grabbed a slice of toast and a coffee and went out to get the papers. It was going to be another beautiful day, the fourth week of a heatwave that lifted my spirits after a long, grey winter. I smiled at people who were working in their front gardens or walking their dogs before the heat got too intense to do anything remotely strenuous.

Pink blossom engulfed the cherry tree on the village green making it look like an enormous ball of candy floss, soft and weightless. Two old ladies sat on the wooden bench outside the shops, laughing and sharing a bag of mints and all the people who queued up at the newsagents smiled. The same old bad news was plastered across the front pages of the papers, yet no-one seemed quite so bothered about that when the sun shone.

Walking home, I wondered if the anxiety of the previous night said more about my own state of mind than the reality of what may or may not be happening in Dan's. He often said I was an over-thinker. That I made a song and dance about things that really weren't the problem I made them out to be. Perhaps he was right. Perhaps this was exactly what it was, and in the middle of the night when everything appears magnified, my imagination had run away with me. Perhaps there was a perfectly good explanation. Perhaps it's all just a misunderstanding on my part.

I decided the best way forward was to simply ask the question. Dan would laugh, he'd explain everything and then I'd laugh too and that would be that.

When I got home, Dan was standing by the kettle in the kitchen, looking at his phone. As I came through the door, he looked up, an awkward expression on his face. Within a second he looked away, cleared his throat and placed the phone face down on the worktop. He scratched the side of his face and ran his tongue over his lips.

My reassuring internal dialogue on my walk back from the shops, which had convinced me that my worries were unfounded and a symptom of my own neurosis, was slammed away from me like a tennis ball into a net.

'Hi love,' he said, before letting out a long breath and picking his phone back up and sliding in into his jeans pocket.

I put the newspapers down on the kitchen table and turned to face him. There was a silence between us so charged that I could almost see it. I stood on a precipice knowing I couldn't stop myself from jumping.

* * *

'Are you having an affair?'

Before he could answer, the darkness in his eyes gave him away and everything shattered.

When he spoke, only a few words registered.

'*Love; sorry; inevitable; powerless; overwhelming.*'

Strangely, his description of his betrayal perfectly expressed my own feelings.

Then came the word that felt like a kick in the solar plexus. The name I suspected was coming but I needed to hear him say.

'Penny.'

There it was. Out there. The woman I'd seen him laughing with, the woman who was deluding herself if she thought there could be anything between her and Dan.

What an *idiot* I was. How had I not seen it? How did it develop around me as if I were just a bemused bystander? I couldn't speak. Dan continued and when eventually my heart began to feel like it was pumping normally again instead of inside an echo chamber, the details began to sink in.

'I didn't go looking for love elsewhere, you know. I would have to say, truthfully, love found me.'

I had an overwhelming urge to tell him how utterly corny

he sounded but when I tried to speak all that came out was a sad, choky little sound.

'I absolutely know it's my fault,' he said, looking me in the eyes for the first time since he'd answered my question. 'But you have to share some of the responsibility for this. Your only interest has been the kids and you're a great Mum but a marriage has to have some spark and frankly I think you've detached from me so much that you've just stepped back and allowed it to perish.'

The slap hurt my hand. It bent my fingers back and at first, I thought I'd broken something. The rush of pain was so fierce that I hesitated for a moment, staring at my reddened palm before I spoke.

'You bastard. You utter, utter shit.'

Tears blurred my vision and I could barely make him out as he stood rubbing the side of his face.

I fired questions at him that I didn't want answers to. How long had it been going on, had she been in this house, who else knew? He answered with a coolness that made me want to hit him again.

It had been going on for about six months. No, she'd never been in our house. Nobody else knew.

He talked about his affair with a faraway, bewildered look in his eyes, as if it had all been a complete surprise to him and not a conscious act.

I asked if it was truly love and he nodded. 'So that's it for us then? I'm being replaced. You have your future mapped out with, with…*her*, and I'll just have to get on with it?' He stared at me and said nothing. His expression reminded me of the pitying look on the doctor's face, when he'd told me my father had died.

I had to get out. The suffocation of being in close proximity to him was becoming uncomfortable. I stepped into the garden and took a lungful of fresh air.

I walked to the end of the stone path and sat down on the wooden bench, the one we'd bought together the year before, when everything was normal.

What was I supposed to think now? What was the correct protocol for women who have just discovered their husband's infidelity? Scream? Throw his clothes out of the bedroom window? Beg him to stay? Ask him to leave?

I sat on the bench staring blankly at the bird table at the other side of the garden, feeling so small and lost. This must be shock. Something inside me had been snuffed out and I would never be more than an empty shell. It made me wonder if in fact I'd been lost for a long time. The world was tilting on its axis and it wasn't my choice. It was Dan's choice but it would be me and the kids who would suffer.

The thought of telling Sammy and Ben that the life they had known had been ripped apart and the future was just a huge, black question mark was too much. I made it to the compost heap in time for my knees to give way before I threw up my breakfast.

I sat back on my haunches, closed my eyes and took some deep breaths. I wiped my mouth on my sleeve and found an old, crumpled tissue in my jeans pocket that I used to blot away my tears.

My head pounded. I had to get through this and somehow fix everything for the children. Fix myself and create a new future without Dan. I knew already that this was where my energies would be directed because my marriage was beyond repair. And the fact that this was immediately clear—that there was nothing worth fighting for—shocked me almost as much as Dan's confession had.

I stood up and brushed grass cuttings from my jeans. Something clicked in my head. Like a camera lens finding the perfect focus, the picture of my life was clear. I'd spent years walking around with my eyes half closed but now reality had arrived, like a noisy, uninvited guest. There could be no more deceiving myself. I'd looked the other way while my life had become a joke, my marriage a sham and I'd morphed into a pitiful creature.

I made my way back into a silent, empty house. I heard wheels crunching on gravel and the sound of an engine fading into the distance.

Of course he would flee. He'd said what he needed to say and would no doubt be off to fall into the arms of Penny. His thoughts would revolve around how hard this had been for him and I doubt he gave much thought to how I was feeling. I wondered if he'd imagine me simply bereft at losing him, or whether he'd recognise the fear and anger that clawed at me.

I picked up my phone and composed a text, suggesting he stay away for now, come and get his things at a pre-arranged time and that I would tell the children. A few minutes later he texted his agreement.

I sat at the bottom of the stairs, wrapped my arms around my legs, rested my forehead on my knees, and tried to comprehend how my life could have been ripped apart in the space of twenty minutes.

* * *

Sammy and Ben both enjoyed a lie in every Sunday. For Sammy, Saturday night out on her rare jaunts back from Uni meant a visit to Vixens, the local club. I'd not even heard her come in. Ben's exhaustion came from all the sports and activities he enjoyed. He'd arrived home late on Saturday, still soaked from a day of sailing. I let him jump straight in the shower, served up a chicken wrap and suggested he turn in early. He was so tired and I was so efficient at fussing over him that he had no chance to wonder where his father was.

Usually I was happy for them to stay in bed but on that Sunday morning I desperately wanted them to get up. I had to get this over. They might have been sleeping like logs but I'd barely slept a wink. I didn't want to be the sort of Mum who broke news like this with a side order of vitriol towards their father. I had to remain neutral, to be measured. This would be hard for them as it was, without having to deal with my emotions.

Outside Ben's room, I took a breath and rapped my knuckles on the door. I heard him stir and make a 'hmmph?' sound.

'Ben, love, think it's time to get up. I'm going to have breakfast on the table in five minutes so get dressed and come straight down. Have your shower later, OK?'

I heard something resembling a 'mmm yup,' and left him to it. Ben was reliable. He always did as he was asked. He was so easy.

Then I went up to the attic room. Sammy's ever-present fog of resentment seeped under the door and draped itself across the small bannister.

'Sammy, are you awake?'

'What? What time is it?' Before I could reply, there was the sound of movement followed by a shriek of disgust. 'Oh, for God's sake! It's eight o clock! What are you waking me up now for? I didn't get in until two-thirty!'

She must have buried her head under the duvet. Muffled words followed which thankfully I couldn't quite make out.

'Look, just get up okay? I need to speak to you and Ben downstairs. Breakfast in five. It's important.'

She didn't answer but there was a sigh of resignation and some movement so I made my way downstairs, laid the table with cereal, popped some bread in the toaster and rehearsed my speech for the hundredth time since yesterday afternoon.

They meandered downstairs and took forever to eat. I cleared my throat, told Sammy to put her phone down and braced myself to deliver the bad news as I sat across the table from them.

'Kids, this isn't easy.' I looked from one to the other, needing to see their faces, wanting to be ready to react, to hold them up and to do whatever I could to minimise the damage. 'I'm so, so sorry that we are in this situation but something horrible and unexpected has happened. Dad has,' I faltered, looked up and saw Ben's sweet face, mouth in an 'O' shape, eyes wide. He swivelled in his chair, looking around the room and registered his father's absence.

'What?' He asked, his voice childlike and desperate. 'What's happened to Dad? Is he alright?'

'*Mum*!' Sammy cut in, with a deepening frown on her forehead. 'What the hell?'

'He's fine. He's absolutely fine, not hurt or anything, really, you don't have to worry.' I held my hands up in front of me to push away their fears and kept my voice as calm and even as I could. I tucked a stray bit of hair behind my ear and stared down at the grain on the wooden table top as if it would give me a clue about how best to proceed.

Sammy narrowed her eyes. She's shrewd for her age and I think that was the moment she got the first inkling of what might lie ahead.

'I discovered yesterday that your Dad has been having an affair. So we discussed things and decided that at least for now, it would be better if he moved out. So that's where we are, and I just need you two to know that everything is fine and that there is…'

'An affair? Dad's having an affair?' Ben's voice was loud, for him. His face crumpled with shock and anger. I wasn't sure if the anger was aimed at his father or at me for bringing him such unbelievable news. 'Who with? Who is having an affair with my Dad?'

I took Ben's hand. His eyes were downcast and he shook his head. 'No, I don't believe it,' he whispered. 'Not my Dad.'

'I'm so sorry love. I can't tell you how much it upsets me to know what this must be doing to you and your sister.'

I glanced at Sammy, who sat back in her chair staring at me, somehow detached from the whole thing. It was impossible to tell what was going through her mind.

'So, come on then Mum,' she asked. 'Who is it? Who's the bitch that decided it would be completely okay to wreck our family? Who is she and where does she live? Because I'm going straight round there.'

I think the words were out of her mouth before she'd even processed the thought.

'Yes, that's what I'm going to do. Do you know who she is Mum? If not, I bet we can soon work it out. If you know her first name and where she lives, I'll look on Facebook. We can track her down from there.' She grabbed her phone and immediately started tapping away with both thumbs and a concentrated look on her face.

'Sammy, I know who she is. I've met her once or twice, so put your phone down, and you are *not* going to anyone's house and causing a scene. Do you understand? I mean it Sammy. Just leave it.'

She looked at me, shook her head and threw her phone down on the kitchen table before sitting back and folding her arms.

Ben's elbows were on the table as he rested his chin in his hands, still shaking his head slightly, as if the movement would take away what he'd just heard. My poor, darling Ben.

We sat in silence for a moment or two. The new reality of our lives had to settle around us, as much as it could. They needed to re-calibrate, to understand that their future was not the next step on the path they'd been treading since the day they each were born. This was unknown, rough terrain, and none of us were equipped for it.

'So! You're just going to let her get away with it, are you?' Sammy frowned.

'Excuse me? *Let her get away with it*? Sammy, it's happened. We are where we are. It's complex. She's not stolen a Mars bar from the corner shop.'

'Mum, are *you* alright?' Ben got up and came around the table and hugged me awkwardly. Fresh tears cascaded down my cheeks and despite the sick feeling I had in my stomach, my heart made a little leap. Since he'd hit puberty, Ben had withdrawn his hugs and cuddles with me in a bid to assert his independence. This little show of compassion warmed my soul.

'Don't worry about me. I'll be fine. I just need you both to know that it will all work out. You just carry on as you are. You'll still be seeing Dad and you'll adjust to it, you will. In years to come it will seem completely normal.'

'Well, that sounds pretty final then,' said Sammy. 'That doesn't sound like he's moving out just for now, or whatever you said. That sounds like it's all over. Bit feeble though, isn't it Mum?' Her tone was bitter.

Ben slumped back down into the chair next to his sister, casting a despairing look in her direction.

'Adult relationships are complicated, Sam. Dad probably thinks he's doing the right thing,' I said, trying to keep the sarcastic edge from my voice. 'He probably thinks he's not being feeble, he probably...'

'Not him, *you*!' Sammy cut in, her voice high pitched and strained.

'What? Sam, why are you accusing me of weakness?' Anger rose toward Dan for putting us in this situation. I imagined him in the arms of miss fancy-pants, blissfully unaffected by the carnage he'd created at home. A vision of the two of them gazing into each other's eyes without a care in the world made me shudder. I needed to steady my thoughts before trying to control where this conversation was going, to keep my family on an even keel.

'Well, you've just let another woman come along, flirt with Dad, shag him and take him away and you're just like, "Oh don't worry! It'll be fine. It's all normal". She wiggled her head as she spoke, putting on a child like voice; obviously how she saw me.

'Stop it Sam!' Ben shouted. 'I don't want to hear what they've done, what he's doing with that other woman. And don't take it out on Mum!'

Sammy sat back, arms still folded and eyes studying the table, bottom lip jutting out slightly in defiance. But she couldn't stop the tear that snaked its way down her face, couldn't stop the fact that her feet were jiggling up and down under the table. I had so much I wanted to say to her but I had to be careful. She was hurting and at nineteen, she'd just had her entire understanding of relationships, marriage, loyalty and love turned on its head.

'It's okay. It's okay.' I spoke quietly and allowed a few moments of silence so that everything could calm down. But I couldn't let what Sammy had said go by without comment.

'Sammy, I know how upsetting this is, but please, sweetheart, don't ever fall into the trap of thinking all men are just poor, unwitting victims who only cheat because some evil temptress has come along and mesmerised them. I happen to know the woman Dad's with is single, so she's done a wicked, selfish thing, no question. But he's the one who was married.'

Sammy sniffed and more tears came, heartbreak replacing anger. She covered her face with her hands and doubled over, sobbing freely.

Ben moved his chair closer to hers and put an arm around her, his face red and puffy with the tears he was trying not to shed. I got up and went around the table, stood behind them and wrapped them both in a hug, wishing I could absorb the pain their pain for them. But I did feel a huge flood of relief. I would never have to do this again. This worst and terrible thing had been done.

CHAPTER TWO

Amanda

Now I'd have to tell everybody. The idea of dragging myself around the village and seeing the shock and pity on people's faces was unbearable. But the sooner I got it out of the way, the sooner I could begin to regroup, to find my footing again. The sooner I could begin the new life I hadn't asked for.

I was braced for a dose of schadenfreude. The smug, *that wouldn't happen to us, we're solid as a rock* looks from certain couples, who would instantly start dissecting my marriage and my personality, just to prove to themselves that it was inevitable. I'd let myself go; not paid him enough attention; we were never right for each other. I'd seen it before. The shock of a long married couple splitting creates ripples of fear that such a thing really can happen to anybody.

Picking up my keys, I glanced in the hall mirror. My eyes were swollen and blotchy, hair frizzy and I realised that I had slept in the tee shirt I was wearing. It looked like it too. I threw the keys back down and ran up the stairs to my bedroom. Tying my hair into a pony tail improved things slightly, as did a quick swipe of mascara. I pulled on a clean top and looked in the full-length mirror. Not exactly stunning, but it would have to do.

Back downstairs, I took hold of my keys once more and rested my hand on the front door handle. Taking a deep breath, I closed my eyes and tried to prepare for what lay ahead. This was not humiliation, not failure. It was about what had happened to me, not about who I was. I almost believed it too.

My first stop was Eve and Marco. Of all my friends, I knew I could rely on their support the most.

Eve opened the door and her smile dropped instantly. Our connection was so strong that one look gave me away.

'What the bloody hell's happened?' Typically, Eve cut straight to the point.

'Dan's having an affair. He's in love with Penny Webb and he's moved out to be with her. We're finished.' Without thinking about what I'd say, the words just formed themselves and popped out. Like those women who don't know they're pregnant and suddenly give birth to a seven-pound baby. Fully formed. And they wonder where it came from.

Eve reached both arms out and drew me into a bear hug.

'Bloody hell mate! Bloody hell, what a bastard. Jesus, what a bitch!'

She pulled back and stuck her face into my face, nose to nose.

'You're not messing with me, are you? This isn't a joke?' She didn't need me to answer.

Cupping my cheeks in both hands, Eve was silent for a moment as she looked into my eyes and I saw she had tears in her own. Both of us were slightly shaking.

'Right, OK. Let me tell you this. You, my lovely friend, are going to be fine. You are going to be better than fine. We are all going to be here for you and it will all work out, you hear me?'

I nodded, tears seeping out despite my best efforts at a brave face. Eve pulled me inside and slammed the front door with such force that the house shook.

'Marco!' She hollered out into the back garden. 'Marco! Come in here! This is important!'

I could see through the dimness of the hallway and the kitchen to the sunlit back garden and the silhouette of Marco obediently responding to Eve's command.

Before he had chance to ask what the problem was, Eve launched into a foul-mouthed tirade about Dan and Penny, becoming more animated and furious as she spoke. Her fury somehow drained some of my own anger and rage. It was temporarily calming.

'Oh my darling Amanda, I'm so sorry.' Marco walked over and gave me a gentle hug and kissed me warmly on the cheek. 'I'm so shocked. I just would never, nobody would. Nobody would have thought you and Dan of all couples, it just seems, I don't know…'

Marco trailed off, staring into space and shaking his head as he wiped his hands on a cloth, over and over, in a trance.

We made our way to the kitchen. I told them both what had happened, about my suspicions and his confession. Eve said nothing, just nodded her head from time to time and frowned. She flicked the kettle on and off again instantly, and instead reached into the fridge and retrieved a nearly full bottle of Pinot Grigio.

'You know, I'm going to tell you this now, now this has happened and there's not much more that could hurt you,' she said, taking three wine glasses out of a cabinet.

'He made a pass at me once.'

Marco looked up, wide eyed and opened mouthed. 'Did he really? Good Lord!'

'Yep. That party for Sally Proctor's 30th at the village hall, oh blimey, years ago. Sammy was a little kid. Do you remember her running around after scoffing loads of sweets and then chucking up in the middle of the dance floor?'

'How could I forget? Sally Proctor certainly never let me forget.'

I dreaded to think what I was going to hear. The shock of finding out about Penny yesterday was quite enough to process but hearing that he'd made a pass at Eve made me wonder if there had been others. If she was just one in a long line.

Eve splashed the wine into the glasses, streaked white from too many runs in the dishwasher.

'So yes,' she continued. 'He was still smoking at the time and he'd gone out the back for a quick cigarette. I was helping a bit, clearing away paper plates and stuff and I went out back too, to the bins. So he starts talking to me. He was pissed as a newt to be fair, and said something about how great I looked, all that old flannel.' Eve paused as she sipped her wine and signalled to me to follow her outside into the garden. The three of us sat at the grubby old plastic table.

'Then he sort of, well, cornered me. Starts running his hands up and down the side of my body. I'm still holding on to black bin bags at this point, so I dropped them and pushed his hands away and told him not to be a dick. I still just thought he'd had too many I wasn't that bothered but then he sort of lunged at me and actually grabbed my boob! Can you believe it! Then he starts saying all this stuff…'

'What I can't believe is that you never told me any of this! Honestly, Eve, I mean what the hell?' My heart thumped. I had no doubt that Eve would not have let this continue, that she wouldn't have encouraged Dan to even think she might be interested in him but why had she never told me? Why had I been kept in the dark? Was I that insignificant?

'I'm wondering the same thing,' said Marco, sitting back and folding his arms, a sad little frown on his face.

Eve glanced briefly in Marco's direction, rolled her eyes and turned back to look at me. 'Yes, I know I should have, but why hurt you? It was probably just drink and at the time, what he said, I kind of thought it was just bravado, a load of bull. Now of course, I wonder if there was something in it.'

'So what else did he say?' asked Marco.

'After I'd smacked his hand away from my boob and told him to do one, he started muttering something about having a little fun, that he liked to have fun. Then, I guess because I'd rejected him, he got all sulky and said something like, "Some women are so uptight, nothing wrong with a little secret fun, nobody needs to know." So I walked away. I think I called him a tosser.'

My head started to hurt. It was partly down to a combination of wine and hot sun but mostly the shock of hearing Eve's revelation about Dan. Yes, it could have been drink, male bravado. But maybe somewhere deep inside my subconscious I had picked up on his behaviour. Eve's story was about something that happened fifteen years before, in the middle of a drunken party. Yet my instincts screamed that his clumsy pass at Eve was not an isolated incident.

'So, did he ever refer to it again? To that night, I mean. Did he seem embarrassed the next time he saw you? Did he apologise or anything?' I studied Eve's face. She wouldn't deliberately lie to me but she might lie by omission.

'That's the thing,' said Eve with a small shrug. 'There was nothing. No awkwardness, no apology, he wasn't aloof or anything. It was as if nothing had happened. And that's mainly why I never told you. I thought he must have been so hammered that he genuinely had no recollection of it. I didn't want to embarrass or upset either of you bringing up something that was probably nonsense.'

'Well, you could at least have told me,' said Marco, sounding mildly offended.

Eve rolled her eyes again and let out a big sigh dismissing Marco's comment. As much as I love her, I do sometimes wonder how he puts up with her.

'So, you're telling me this now to make me feel better?' I asked, raising my eyebrows.

'Don't be daft. I just wondered if there was something in it. Do you remember those rumours that went around a few years ago? That the girl from the car showroom in town was messing around with a married man from the village?'

I did remember. It kept the gossips entertained for months. The girl, probably only in her early twenties, had been seen driving through the village in her flash company car. She had blabbed in the local pub one evening about how she'd been 'seeing some married bloke from around here.' He'd dumped her and she was threatening to spill the beans but then she moved away and the gossips found a new victim.

'Us four were all laughing about it one night over a curry, and I remember thinking at the time that when we were all guessing who it could be, Dan went quiet. Some of his friends' names had come up so I wondered if he knew who it was and didn't want to let the cat out of the bag. Now I'm wondering if it was Dan himself who was messing about.'

The pain just kept mounting up. It may not have been Dan, but now I knew what he was capable of, every memory, every recollection of something being out of place would make me suspect, make me question.

Eve gulped the last of her wine and switched into practical mode. She began listing all the things I would be wise to do and offered help with solicitors (even though I hadn't even considered divorce just yet), promised to cook meals, run the kids about, take me for a girls' night out, gather Dan's stuff together so he never had to set foot in the house again and 'dump the whole bloody lot on that bitch's driveway.'

I was grateful for her energy but my head was still like a snowstorm and I was completely incapable of making decisions just yet. But it felt good to know I had Eve and Marco in my corner.

I thanked them and had another bear hug from Eve, urging me to call whenever I felt down, even if it was in the middle of the night.

I got home and hit a wall of exhaustion. I hadn't the energy to see anyone else and tell them face to face. It was painful to do and I feared what other revelations I might hear. How many other friends might tell me something about Dan that had been kept hidden from me?

I fired up my laptop and emailed everyone who needed to know with the same brevity and directness I'd used when I told Eve.

Hi.

Just to let you know, before you hear on the grapevine, Dan has been having an affair with Penny Webb. They are apparently 'in love' and he has left me and the kids to move in with her. Our marriage is over.

I stared at the blinking cursor for several minutes. Then added:

I will be filing for divorce.

Amanda xxx

I pressed *SEND* and sat back in my chair as the old, familiar facade of my life disappeared into the ether.

***

Three days had passed since Dan's revelation and I'd not yet said a word to Mum or Maddy. I knew they'd hear it all from the local gossips eventually but I couldn't face them straight away, especially Mum. I wasn't sure if I could cope with her self-pity and even less sure that I would control my temper.

I knew I must grit my teeth and call a family meeting. When they arrived at the front door, Mum looked worried and Maddy looked cheesed off that I'd interrupted her day. My face contorted as I tried unsuccessfully to control my emotions. I couldn't speak and ushered them into the lounge.

They sat opposite me, in the same pose. Heads tilted, furrowed brows and right leg crossed over left. Maddy played with her car keys, Mum with a bunched-up tissue. I noticed the likeness between mother and daughter. I felt completely outside of them.

'So, are you going to tell us what's going on?' my sister asked. 'Must be pretty serious to get us over here out of the blue.'

'Yes, come on darling, we can't help unless we know what's wrong and it's very distressing to see you like this.' Mum was already looking teary and she bit her lower lip and did a little wobble of the head.

'It's Dan. He's been having an affair. He left me on Saturday.'

'Oh Amanda!' Mum gasped and brought a cupped hand up to her mouth. Maddy patted Mum on the arm and she visibly relaxed. 'Are you sure?' Mum leant forward, her hand now splayed across her chest. 'Is he really having an affair? Has he really left?'

'Of course I'm bloody sure!' My voice was raised.

'Amanda!' A warning shot from my sister.

'Yes, Mum, yes I'm sure.' I spoke gently, reminding myself that Mum is in her late sixties now and she's not young-at-heart either. She and her sister, our Aunt Julia, are poles apart. Julia is still young in outlook and appearance. Mum has always been a bit of a stick in the mud, a bit unadventurous, a bit safe. 'It's a woman from up the road, Penny, apparently they've been—'

Maddy cut in. 'Penny? What, Penny Webb?'

I nodded.

'I vaguely know her,' she continued. 'Sanctimonious bitch.' Maddy pulled a face, wrinkled her nose up and leant forward. 'Well, I'll be damned. How long has it been going on?'

'He's admitted to about six months. But who knows?'

Mum uncrossed her legs and linked her hands across her knees. 'So, what's going to happen now then? Has he said if he intends to come back? Is this a silly middle-aged fling?'

'If he intends to come back? Mum, seriously, I'm not sitting here hoping that Jolene won't take my man. It's not about what he intends to do. It's about what I do, what me and the kids do now.'

'Do the children know?' Mum seemed horrified.

'Yes, of course they do. I think they might have noticed that their father hasn't been here for the last few days, don't you?' I told myself to dial down the sarcasm in my tone. But it was hard.

'You could have made an excuse. You could have said he was away on business. I mean, if this sorts itself out and he comes home, then there wouldn't be a reason for them to know, would there?'

Maddy rolled her eyes and looked away. I could imagine the fuss if Max ever cheated on Maddy and left. The whole world would know about it. Max's name would be dragged through the mud and she wouldn't rest until she'd destroyed him.

'Mum,' I paused to steady myself, to try to explain it all as calmly and reasonably as possible without showing my frustration. 'The thing is, firstly, I doubt very much that Dan will be asking to come back. Secondly, if by some weird turn of events he did come crawling back asking forgiveness, I can tell you now, there won't be any. The trust has gone. A few days before I found out about it all, he was still talking about holiday plans for the summer. His ability to fool everyone is breathtaking.'

I thought back over the last year and couldn't remember a time when he'd said he was unhappy with our marriage. He had his temper tantrums, would give me his silent treatment but that was just how life was. It was all fine for him because he controlled it but I was the victim. Now I wondered why I'd allowed this situation to go on for so long. But I wasn't ready to look into the eye of that particular beast yet—it had been hard enough acknowledging its existence. I'd spent years brushing everything that was wrong under the carpet and it was going to be a while before I could own up to the part I'd played in my own downfall. Dan never said he thought our marriage was failing, or that he wanted me to change. I'd seen other people devastated at their partner's infidelity. But only now did I understand that the shock and the pain was complex and didn't just come in one hit. It keeps coming in waves, so that just as you process what has happened, another revelation or realisation hits you. It knocks you off your feet and brings you crashing down.

I sat back, staring at my hands folded in my lap.

'What an absolute cock,' said Maddy, bringing me back to the moment. She stood up and threw the car keys down on the sofa. 'I'm going to stick the kettle on,' she said. 'Think we could all do with a cup of tea.' She went off to the kitchen.

'So you're saying that's it then? No second chance? I do know it must be awful, *awful*, to have heard this. Perhaps the two of you just need to sit down and talk and see if you can re-build. Do you really want to throw away twenty-odd years of marriage for one mistake?'

I hung my head and closed my eyes. Was this woman ever going to actually listen to what I was saying? Did she have any idea of how hypocritical she sounded?

'Ok Mum, so, Dad used to talk about how GranDad William left him and his Mum and went to America with another woman and you both wanted nothing to do with that other family. That it was disgraceful how poor Granny Ivy had been treated and William Saxby was a disgusting individual. Yet you tell me Dan deserves another chance, that we should rebuild, like he's not such a bad guy. Yet William is a pariah, persona non grata. I suppose you think that was different, do you?'

A blush crept up Mum's neck. I knew this was a difficult subject. To even be talking about it felt disloyal to Dad's memory.

'I think it's slightly different, yes.' Her back straightened but she wouldn't look me in the eye. 'Women throw themselves at men these days, and men are weak. They can't resist. You can't always blame the men. But things were different in those days. Life was slower, people weren't fed all this,' she shook her head and made a little royal wave with her hand, 'this sex, on television and in the papers and social media. Temptation is everywhere now. William Saxby's behaviour was quite different. He was a womaniser, pure and simple.'

She paused and I could see a shadow of deep sadness cross her face.

'Poor Ivy was distraught when he upped and left. To go off to America and leave them behind, well. It was just terrible.'

The grandfather I'd never met, William, had started Saxby Marine with a small strip of land in The Bahamas with a tiny pontoon. He cleared the land himself and gradually built on it, initially so that a handful of boats could moor up and make use of a few basic services. By the 1990's, Saxby Marine had evolved into one of the largest marinas in The Bahamas and William became wealthy. His charisma helped. The press loved him. He dined with Presidents, rubbed shoulders with film stars and at some point in all of this, he must have quietly divorced Ivy and married Christine, the woman he'd run away with. They'd had two children and three grandchildren. William's son, Robin, eventually took the business over.

There was no point in trying to change Mum's mind. She wouldn't agree and, in any case, it would make no difference to the outcome. I would never be persuaded that Dan was some poor innocent man, seduced by a floozy.

'Alright, Mum. Well, let's agree to disagree. I know Dad struggled with it all and as you say, times were different. But please understand, Dan and I are over and I will make sure that Sammy and Ben still have a relationship with him and that we handle it the right way.'

Maddy returned with our teas. She looked slightly uncomfortable with all this, although I doubt she would ever imagine being left for another woman. That sort of thing only happens to worn-down 'Mumsy' types like me.

The three of us talked for another half an hour. Whether I'd need to sell the family home, how my finances stood, about the law, how much Dan would be required to pay in child support and what he would be prepared to do.

Mum and Maddy tried to help. I'm sure they were doing their best but I now felt even more uncertain of the future.

And exhausted. It was only four o'clock but I was completely drained.

Ben would be at his archery club until at least seven. Sammy had already gone back to Uni. So, after Mum and Maddy left, I tidied around and decided to have a lie down. An hour or so in bed with a book wouldn't do me any harm and I'd be refreshed and up in time to knock up some dinner for Ben.

I had a shower and climbed between the cool cotton sheets, feeling immediately relaxed. I glanced at the book on my bedside table but thought I'd close my eyes for a while. Just give my mind a chance not to think about anything. To untangle itself. Maybe if those knots worked themselves free, I wouldn't feel the tension of them so acutely.

I wanted to wake up and be a strong woman, capable and optimistic, like I used to be many years ago when I was Amanda Saxby, instead of Amanda Phillips, a faded and rather useless waste of space.

CHAPTER THREE

Maddy

Well, you could have tied me to a lamp post and called me Delilah.

I could barely believe that my sister and her husband had split. I thought Dan fancied himself but I never had him down as an adulterer.

Mum and I were summoned. Amanda was distraught and I thought that she, or Dan or one of the kids, was seriously ill. I sat next to Mum on the sofa waiting for Amanda to speak. Mum would have fallen to bits if she thought there was illness in the family.

So in a strange way, it was almost a relief when she told us about Dan's affair. A girl can get through that. Although poor old Amanda doesn't have fire in her veins like I do so she's collapsed in a heap. I'd probably have attacked him with a machete.

Worst of all, I'd spent the previous week building myself up to tell her what was going on with me.

I knew it would need careful handling. My sister can be so superior sometimes, but this business with Dan and the slapper from up the road had made it a hundred times worse.

Not that I was proud of what I'd done but sometimes the planets align and throw you into a situation that you can't help. That's how I saw it with me and Paul.

Max, in lots of ways, was the perfect husband. He looked after me well and I didn't want for anything and we were both complicit in this silent arrangement whereby I pushed him to his limits but he always forgave me. He didn't know about Paul, thank goodness but I did test the boundaries all the time. But that was us. It's who we were, and when I went too far he would say, '*enough*' but sometimes (and this might sound odd) he put up with too much and frankly, that was just lazy. You don't have a pet tiger and let it roam about doing what it wants. You have to respect its need for some freedom but you must also work to make sure it abides by the rules.

I got attention from Paul and soon became aware of the pulse of desire he had for me. It was exhilarating to be wanted again. I hoped Max would get an inkling that I was up to something; not to find out what exactly, but to imagine that he risked losing me if he didn't focus and show a bit of interest.

The trouble was, he was so wrapped up in his work that I doubt he noticed any change in me. So what was going to be a flirtation with Paul just to boost my ego evolved into full-on adultery and it all moved on from there and in just a few weeks, he fell head over heels in love with me. I was quite fond of him, in a way. I felt a bit sorry for him, for the situation he was in. It was all a bit of a mess really. But for a while it was flattering having someone who clearly had me on a pedestal so I had no intention of stopping until I had to. If something had forced my hand, I would have quit this thing with Paul in an instant. I was pretty sure I could handle it.

* * *

Max had decided we needed a gardener and interviewed Paul for the job, to do just a few hours once a week. We only have a couple of acres but we like it to look good. Our home is a material expression of our success and that means I want to see well-manicured lawns and beautiful plants. Paul was an experienced gardener and quite sweet. He'd been working for us for about three weeks when I noticed him properly and something about him intrigued me.

I watched him from the bedroom window one sunny day. He was younger than me and I knew he was from one of the families at the other side of the village. The people who had lived here for generations in the old farm cottages. They were insular, suspicious of newcomers and of those of us who had done well for ourselves and that included me and Max, even though I was born here.

Friends and family find ours to be an odd marriage. He's quieter, more thoughtful than I am. Even the simplest question posed to Max would result in a pause, a gaze into the middle distance before he gave his definitive answer. I'm not like that. I prefer to make a wrong decision than dither endlessly.

Max has always kept himself in good shape but he sits behind a desk each day drinking too much coffee and deepening his frown lines. Bless him, he's such a perfectionist. I've never doubted his love but I don't get his full attention and somewhere along the way he's lost any sense of spontaneity he had. When we get invited to parties, Max is always the first to want to leave and I usually end up being dragged off the dance floor at three in the morning. It's hardly surprising that some people think that Max is a bit dull for me.

I sometimes think that myself.

Paul was digging compost into the new veg patch, working hard. His t-shirt was damp with sweat. Enough to be slightly clingy. My imagination fired up.

I went downstairs to the kitchen, grabbed a diet coke from the fridge and made my way to the end of the garden.

'Here, you look hot,' I said passing the can to Paul.

'Oh thanks, I could do with that.'

Paul ripped open the can and took several large gulps. A few drops ran down his chin and onto his chest.

I played with my hair, piling it up on top of my head and weaving it through my fingers, tilting my head back.

'I love heat.' I brought my head forward and looked straight into Pauls eyes.

He looked away quickly and I noticed that his hands were shaking. Christ, he's so bloody humble.

'I don't like it too hot,' he said. 'Ground can get hard if we don't get much rain, then you've got to spend hours watering.'

He took another swig from the can. I wanted to get him talking, establish some sort of rapport.

'So take a break and let's look at the plants you've already got in. You can educate me a bit, tell me what the plants are called and why you've put them where you have.'

Together we made our way to the shadier part of the garden and Paul began to reel off the names of plants and shrubs and all sorts of tips about their preference for sun or shade, what type of soil they thrive in and when they flower.

I feigned interest. Some of it was useful to know but after all, that sort of detail was why we'd employed a gardener in the first place.

It did make me notice that the planting was a little sparse though.

'So, Paul,' I interrupted as he extolled the virtues of Azaleas. 'It strikes me we could do with a whole lot of new stuff in the garden. Obviously, that's going to mean some extra work for you, so do you think you could do a few hours on a Friday too?'

'I suppose I could do from two onwards, if you like.'

'Oh brilliant!' I smiled. 'Can we start this week? Only I was thinking, if you could take me to the nursery in your truck you could help me choose the right plants and we can get them there and then.'

'Can do if you like. Or you could just give me a list.'

I insisted that I should be involved and arranged that Paul would collect me that Friday afternoon.

At last, a little flirtation was going to liven up my life.

* * *

As Paul drew the truck to a halt that Friday, I caught him looking me up and down and felt a flush of satisfaction. I'd never met Paul's other half. What was it? Toni? Tracey? Whatever, Paul's obvious interest in me was a little harmless fun for both of us and anyway, I loved this. I loved the game.

The day was a hot one. According to the weather station Max had installed in the kitchen, it was twenty-six degrees.

'Afternoon,' called Paul from the cab. As I climbed into the seat next to him, he said, 'Are you sure you don't just want me to go and pick some plants up for you?'

He looked like a frightened rabbit. For a moment, I found it off-putting. Generally speaking, I prefer confident men. But this was different. This was fun, and it might add to the enjoyment having someone I could play teacher with.

'Absolutely not, I really want to come with you. I might like the look of something I see.' I placed my hand on his arm. 'But you are the expert. You can tell me if I've made a good choice.'

I saw a brief blush again, took my sunglasses out of my bag and faced forward as Paul moved the truck into first gear and pulled away.

That evening, when Max came home from his client visit, he began a monologue about how the new sports complex project was proving difficult because of too many stakeholders, and how the council were arguing among themselves over the ecological aspects of the design and blah blah blah. I stopped listening after about ten seconds.

My mind drifted and I thought about my afternoon with Paul. We'd walked around in the heat looking at plants and I'd pointed to some I liked and eventually I spent what for some people would be a month's wages on new planting and slate and a contemporary water feature.

Paul relaxed a little when we got back to the house. He unloaded the truck while I went inside and got a chilled bottle of wine and two glasses.

Calling Paul over, I poured a large glass and held it out as he approached.

'Oh no, no thank you,' he said, his hands up in front of his chest. 'I've got to drive and I don't drink much anyway. In this heat it will just go straight...'

'Oh Paul, just one glass,' I tilted my head to the side. 'Now you've unloaded everything, it's too hot to dig the new plants in so have a rest. There's no point watering everything until the sun goes down. I'll water them all this evening. Come on, please. It's only a glass, it won't put you over the limit.' I gestured towards a chair.

He had a glass of wine with me. I had to smile to myself. He wasn't kidding. Just that one glass seemed to have an effect on him. He became chattier, and didn't blush when during the conversation, I occasionally laughed and rested my hand on his arm.

He even mentioned his wife, a veiled reference I thought, to not having a great sex life. He'd said something about the baby getting more attention than he was, all said with humour but I know such flippancy often hides the truth of the matter. He muttered something about how his wife was always tired, and even though he was tired too, she never seemed to have any time or energy for him.

I made a point of touching his leg, briefly at this point, and saying, 'Oh Paul, we all need fun. Work hard, play hard I say.'

We finished our drinks and Paul went to dig in the new stock.

That night, sitting with Max, I drifted off into a fantasy about what Paul and I might get up to. I've always had a vivid imagination, and so while Max was mid-sentence, I leant across, took his hand, and gave him a look that he instantly knew the meaning of. His serious expression melted away and a smile spread across his face.

'Oh right, like that is it?'

He was still smiling as he followed me upstairs.

CHAPTER FOUR

Amanda

No wonder Maddy looked so uncomfortable the day I told her about Dan's betrayal.

I found it incomprehensible that she could assume a protective sister role with me, watch how devastating Dan's behaviour had been not just to me but to Sammy and Ben, and then announce that she had been messing around behind Max's back.

Worse still, the man she'd been seeing was married himself. He was younger than Maddy and had only been married five years. They also have a baby son.

At least she had the humility to look embarrassed when she told me. Absolute rage bubbled up inside me but I've been so accustomed to tip-toeing around Maddy my entire life that I suppressed it. I allowed her to speak without expressing how bad her ill-judged affair made me feel, even though she didn't deserve that consideration.

I didn't ask anything else about it. I didn't really want to know the details. She's always been a diva and everyone knows what a flirt she is. She can barely function without people telling her how gorgeous she is. Her vanity knows no bounds but I didn't expect her to actually have an affair. Naturally, she swore me to secrecy and was worried about Max finding out. I could tell she didn't expect it to last.

'Don't go shooting your mouth off to Mum either,' she warned 'She'll get in a state and even if she doesn't actually tell Max it'll be pretty obvious something's going on,' she'd said, pulling a face. We were sitting in my garden eating cheese on toast. She took another bite and curled her tongue around the strands of melted cheese that clung to the rest of the slice.

'Of course I won't tell anyone! I don't want to be the person who breaks Max's heart and in any case, I'm hardly proud of what you've done. It's embarrassing, frankly.'

She looked at me sideways, finished her toast and noisily licked her fingers.

'Look, it will probably fizzle out in the next week or so. I wish I hadn't told you now.'

Maddy put her plate back on the garden table. She sat back and drummed her fingers on the arms of the chair, staring off towards the end of the garden.

'I don't see why you have to wait for it to fizzle out. That makes it sound like you have no control over it and obviously you do. Why don't you do the right thing, just call him or text him and tell him it's all been a mistake? Make up some story to Max about why this man can't work for you anymore and that will be that, it will be over and done with. At least if he's married himself, he's unlikely to create a fuss. And you should be doing that anyway without any prompt from me. I can tell you from first-hand experience that being cheated on is a body blow that can't be described. You have to experience it to really understand and despite what you've done. I hope you never get to feel what I'm feeling now.'

I picked up our plates and teacups and took them inside, leaving Maddy to mull over my suggestion. Not that I was fooling myself that she might sit up and listen, but if the idea of ending it all now had been in the back of her mind, this might just impel her to take action sooner rather than later.

After I'd finished washing up, Maddy followed me back into the kitchen. She looked thoughtful but immediately turned on the TV to watch the news, so I got the message that the conversation was over. I wasn't going to mention it again. I just had to hope my words had hit home and that she might do the right thing.

I made us another cup of tea and when Maddy became bored with the news, she flicked the TV off again and turned around to look at me.

'So. What about you? I know you told Mum that you'd not take Dan back in a million years, but have you changed your mind? Have you really thought it through?'

'Are you suggesting that I take him back for an easier life?' I slid the biscuit tin in her direction and felt a stab of jealousy that she could probably eat several and still stay slim. The only thing keeping me slim was my complete lack of appetite. All I'd eaten all day was cheese on toast.

'No, I'm not suggesting that but there is another way to look at it. To make sure you come out of this in the best possible position.'

Maddy had always been as sly as a fox. Trust her to come up with a way of turning a disaster to advantage.

'Let's hear it then. Although I doubt it's anything I would consider.'

She wiggled her bottom on the breakfast bar stool, getting herself comfortable in readiness to impart her wisdom.

'So, I always say, there are two types of women. Those who crumple up like a used tissue when their men start shagging around, and those who step up, take control, and put themselves and their financial security first. Don't be the first sort!'

'I can imagine exactly what category you'd fall into,' I said, grabbing the biscuit tin and sitting next to her. I offered her a chocolate digestive but she wrinkled her nose and shook her head.

'This isn't about me, Amanda. It's about you and the kids. So, I would say, your other option is to beg him to come back, play the old "I can't possibly live without you and the children need their Dad" card. Even tell him he can carry on with old golden tits on the side, if he wants. Then syphon off as much of his cash as you can, get a Rottweiler solicitor on the case and when he's least expecting it, *bang*! Divorce papers!'

At this, Maddy thumped her fist down on the breakfast bar, with a look of triumph on her face and a broad smile.

'Maddy, I know that's what you would do. It's not me, though. I just want to re-build now, start my new life. I've got to try to piece together what was going on below the surface and make sense of it all. I'm looking at things in a different way now and it's exhausting. I need to move on and it's not just about being the wronged wife. Believe me, that's just the tip of the iceberg.'

Maddy watched me for a while, I could almost hear the cogs turning in her head. She may be a nightmare in so many ways but there was no doubting her intelligence. We were so very different and it's true, most of the time her view on life was incomprehensible to me but that sharp mind does sometimes hone in like a missile, to the very nub of the matter. She said no more and looked away, studying the picture of the dog on the side of her tea mug.

'So, back to you Maddy. Do you want a new life? I know you don't want to part from Max but if you've jumped into an affair, it must mean things aren't quite right between you. What do you wish was different about your marriage?'

Maddy shrugged her shoulders. 'Don't know. I can't change Max. I do know that. But he sometimes seems to be floating above everything, disconnected somehow.' She shrugged again and stared out into the garden. 'I do love him you know, and I know he looks after me brilliantly and I have a privileged life but there's something missing. There always has been, but I've never figured out what it is. It's not Max's fault.'

I watched her as she considered it all. I thought back over our childhood, wondering why she has always created havoc wherever she goes. Wondering why I have put up with her behaviour when many people in my situation would have cut her out of their lives. Yet everyone seems to accept Maddy, no matter what. Despite the terrible things she's done, there is something just out of reach, a frailty and tiny spec of helplessness that sucks us all in and means she is forgiven time after time. She's always been the type to get away with things.

Yet I had a feeling that this time would be different.

CHAPTER FIVE

Maddy

Things sometimes just gather momentum and the rush is too exhilarating and that feeling stops you from putting on the brakes, even though you know you should.

I can pinpoint exactly when our flirtation moved from a fun diversion to an inevitable, unstoppable force.

The laughing together and the banter had become a commonplace part of our interaction. Then, one day, Paul was talking to me by the summerhouse when a bumblebee started weaving lazily around my yellow top. I jerked away from it, this way and that but it was unperturbed and landed just below my ear.

I'm not that scared of bees. But as part of our little game, I pretended to be terrified, to give Paul the chance to be my hero.

'Oh no! Help! Get it off me Paul, please!' I looked up at him wide eyed, breathless and pleading.

He calmly leant forward, and slowly cupped the little creature in his hands. He was being so careful not to cause it any harm, or panic it into stinging me, that concentrating with such seriousness meant he had to lean his face in close too. As the bee became enveloped in his hands, his eyes flicked up, looking into mine just a couple of inches away. It was just a second, that look, but it contained a lust for something that Paul might never have imagined, until he met me.

He lifted his hands away and took a few steps to the right before releasing the captive bee by a climbing rose. He wore a worried look and folded his arms in front of him defensively. The moment had unsettled him. I hesitated about my next move. I understood that this was all an amusing interlude to me but an unknown and frightening aberration for him and it almost made me stop. My moral compass briefly swung into life and the possible consequences of pushing on further raced before my eyes.

But it didn't stop me.

I walked slowly towards him, unfolded his arms and leant up to kiss him on the lips. I justified it to myself as being *only a kiss* but the delivery of it wasn't *only* anything.

'Thank you,' I said, still holding on to his hands.

He glanced away, pained and I stroked his fingers with my thumbs, staring straight at him before taking a breath, releasing him and turning away.

It had all changed. Just like that. I was now aware of the absolute power I had over this situation. I wasn't just an attractive woman who had teased someone and tacitly suggested a fling, a temporary diversion from his mundane life and the demands made on him by his family.

I had mesmerised him. I knew that I would be like a drug to him now, coursing through his veins.

The compass flickered again, sending me a warning to back away.

But I've never been too good at following orders.

* * *

Max often took me to hotels and they were always five-star, luxurious places.

In fact, because of the circles I mix in, classy hotels had become quite ordinary.

But there I was, with Paul in a cheap RoadStar motel, one of a huge chain of identikit, cheap stopovers for travelling salesmen and illicit couplings up and down the country. It felt naughty, and I liked it.

We'd had sex in my garden, in the park early one morning, in the Wallington's orchard in broad daylight, and in the back of my car. I was yearning for sex on an actual bed so I booked us a room.

We were lying in the tangled sheets and I could sense Paul's mind starting to drift. I knew he always felt guilty afterwards and I also knew how to pull his attention straight back to me. I lifted my body, smiled at him and began kissing his torso, moving down and sliding my hands between his legs, hearing him groan.

Then his mobile rang. He sat up, nearly tipping me off the side of the bed.

'What the hell, careful!' I said.

'Sorry, sorry, that might be Tanya. She'll be suspicious if I don't take it.'

He reached across to his discarded jeans and thrust his hand into the pocket.

'Hi love.' He tried to sound as casual as possible and started to walk, phone in hand, to the bathroom.

I could hear shouting at the other end of the phone. High pitched, frenzied shouting, and watched as Paul turned ashen, saw his eyes bulge and heard him start to whine, catching his breath.

'No! No, that's not true, don't be silly, I wouldn't do that to you! Tanya, don't listen to stupid rumours…no, she's just a customer I just do her garden, I don't even fancy her…no, no it's not…'

I sat up, alert now, snapping my fingers to get Paul's attention but he was lost in his highly emotional state.

He tried to speak again but the volume from the other end of the phone increased and continued for several minutes. Then before Paul managed to say anything else, it went quiet.

He stared at the phone in his hands for several seconds before slowly turning towards me. His mouth was wide open and he looked like a child, helpless and paralysed with fear.

'Ah.' I said calmly. 'So we've been rumbled, I take it?'

'Oh God, oh God!' Paul actually started to cry. Then snapping out of his dithering, he grabbed his clothes and fell over as he tried to get his legs into his jeans.

'Calm down,' I said, getting off the bed and putting my hands on his shoulders. 'Look, just deny it. Someone has obviously seen us together somewhere and said something but that's not proof of anything. The more you panic the more guilty you'll look.'

He pushed my hands away and began looking around the room for the keys to his truck, with tears still seeping from the corners of his eyes.

'I'm going straight home,' he said, finding his keys next to the kettle on the tea tray. He sat on the end of the bed, trying to get his trainers on but he was in such a state he looked like a drunk.

He was being horribly dismissive of me.

'Did you hear what I just said?' I asked, completely naked and standing with my hands on my hips at the side of the bed. 'Deny, deny, deny. She'll try and trick you but just keep telling her she's wrong. Eventually she'll believe you and it will all be…'

'She *KNOWS*, Maddy. She knows!' He'd succeeded in getting one trainer on and done up and was still trying to tie the laces on the other one. He stopped what he was doing, sat up and looked me in the eyes.

'She's not heard a rumour, she's seen a photo. The whole bloody world knows. When you dragged me down to that orchard last week there were some kids around by the shed where they keep the trailers. I bet it was them. I told you! I told you I'd heard something!' He sounded angry now.

'Oh, for Christ's sake, it could be a photo of any couple

shagging in the orchard, it's a well know spot. I was surprised there wasn't anyone already there when we rocked up. Anyway, why would they send it to Tonya?'

'Tanya. *TANYA*. And they didn't. They put it on Facebook. It was so bloody clear Facebook took it down. But not before someone screen grabbed it for her.'

I suddenly felt less confident.

Shit. Shit.

'So it's definitely not still on Facebook? It's just Tanya and whoever sent her the screenshot that know about it then?'

Paul now had his other shoe on and his truck keys in his hand.

'I don't know Maddy,' he said. 'She didn't give me a run down on how many likes, comments and shares it had. She just said it made her feel sick to look at it and that she has started packing my stuff into bin bags.' He opened the door and then stepped back in for a moment to say, 'I'll text you later.' Then he was gone.

As the door shut, I started running through all possible scenarios in my mind. The best that I could hope for was that Tanya wouldn't want anyone else to see the photo, that whoever had sent it to her wouldn't send it to anyone else and that the kids who took it had moved on to catch the next unsuspecting couple.

I found my bra and knickers, put them on and pulled my little cotton summer dress over my head.

I ran through damage limitation techniques in my mind. How could I keep this away from Max? Not too difficult as he didn't do social media; he thought it was a waste of time. But I needed to get to work on a story just in case.

I picked up my bag and as I fumbled inside for my car keys, I heard the gentle 'ping' of a text message coming through.

It was Max.

I want you to come home now and explain this

A second later, a photograph appeared. Paul on top of me, his jeans halfway down his legs while my skirt was hitched up to my waist. My top up around my neck. My hands on his buttocks, his right hand cupping my left breast. Both our faces turned towards the camera, eyes shut and mouths open at the point of ecstasy.

It was a bit blurry. But there was absolutely no doubt who we were. And no question whatsoever as to what we were doing.

* * *

Max completely wrong footed me.

His voice wasn't just raised it was strangled. The ferocity of his movements made him look like a madman, a violent being with no control.

I wasn't used to seeing him in a rage. His mood was always on such an even keel it was barely human. In fact, I always joked that if Max won millions in the lottery, or was told his house had burned down, he would give the same reaction. Raised eyebrows, slight tilt of the head and a quiet, 'Hmmm, I see.'

Now he was pacing up and down, constantly shaking his head, picking things up and putting them straight down again.

'Tell me,' he said, 'just tell me one thing that I've done to deserve this? Nobody's perfect and I'm not saying I am but from where I'm standing I'm failing to see why this has happened. You've not told me you're unhappy, you've not asked me to do anything different have you? *HAVE YOU*?'

'No. No I haven't Max.' I studied the floor. I was subdued, keeping calm and letting him rant. It reminded me of all those occasions years ago when I was hauled before the headmaster over one of my many misdemeanours.

'Look at me. *LOOK AT ME*!'

I looked him in the eyes. There were tears in them.

'I have done everything I possibly can to make you happy,' he said. 'I knew you liked the finer things in life and I've done my very best to provide you with those.' He turned away and stood with his back to me, shaking his head again and running one hand through the back of his hair. I returned to my study of the floor tiles. This was just something to be got through. It would all calm down in a while. I just need to let him get it out of his system.

'I've not looked at another woman since I've been with you. And don't think I haven't had my opportunities, because there have been plenty.' He spoke quietly now. More defeated. 'But it's not in me to cheat. Even though I've sometimes felt I'm the only one making any effort in this relationship. Even though I've felt lonely sometimes, I've kept plugging away, working to make it better.'

It was true. I couldn't deny that. I knew my behaviour was that of a spoilt brat and though I have many faults, I am intelligent enough to acknowledge my own shortcomings.

'Max, I'm sorry, but I just, I don't know, I get bored sometimes. That's no excuse I know.' A few tears ran down my face. 'I just don't know what's wrong with me sometimes. What's wrong in my head?' I covered my face in my hands now, audibly sobbing and expecting, any moment, to feel Max's arms around me, comforting. Instead, there was silence and when I eventually dropped my hands and looked up, Max stood with his back to the sink, arms folded, regarding me with contempt.

'You can drop that act, Maddy,' he said in a chillingly reasonable tone. 'You know, there are people in this world who really do suffer with their mental health, who really can't help their behaviour. You are not one of those people and it's an insult to them that you pretend to be.' He uncrossed his arms and leant back with his hands against the edge of the unit.

'Not only did you hurt me, but you've completely wrecked another family. That man's wife is devastated. They have a baby son who may now grow up without his father present. All so you could have a bit of fun.'

That hurt. Not because I had any particular sympathy with Paul's family. As far as I was concerned, it was Paul's choice to have an affair and it was equally his wife's choice to let herself go and allow the physical side of their relationship to slide.

But this situation was too close to home. I had seen how devastated Amanda had been over Dan's affair, and it had taken the wind completely out of her sails. There could be no doubt how much she was suffering.

'I'm going up to the study to do some work,' said Max. 'Perhaps when I come downstairs, you could be gone, yes?'

I looked up in surprise.

'Gone? What? Do you want me to stay at Mum or Amanda's tonight? That's probably a good idea actually, I'll come back tomorrow morning and we can talk all this through.'

'No, I mean go. Leave. Get out. For good, as in, don't come back.' Max said this as he made his way past me to head upstairs. He didn't even look at me as he spoke.

'I really think we need to actually talk about this, you know,' I said, turning to watch him leave.

'Nothing to say,' Max's voice trailed behind him as he walked through the kitchen door and into the hall. 'Take what you want tonight, you can come back and get the rest tomorrow morning.'

I strode into the hall in time to see him disappear up the stairs.

'It's my house too, my home!' I shouted after him.

Then the door to the study slammed shut.

What now? When I'd come back to the house, I knew, of course, that there would be a scene, there would be anger and hurt but I hadn't expected this.

Max had never found out about the couple of brief indiscretions I'd had previously. But both occasions had been one-offs with men who didn't want anymore than I did, a bit of fun, a diversion from everyday life. I never expected to have to cope with being found out but even so, it hadn't occurred to me that it could spell the end.

Come on now, Maddy, I told myself. He'll calm down. I'll stay away for a day or two and then we'll talk. Maybe I'll make the first move or maybe not. I'll play it by ear but I know exactly which buttons to press.

I tiptoed up the stairs, grabbed a bag and a few essentials and then headed down to the car, pausing at the bottom of the driveway, trying to decide whether to go left towards Mum's or right towards Amanda's.

CHAPTER SIX

Julia

Surely there was a mix up at the hospital all those years ago?

Whenever I go 'home' to the family, I feel guilty. Guilty because I have to appear to be delighted to see them and because I have to bury the ever-present temptation to leave again as soon as possible. I struggle to believe that my sister Diana and I are actually related. Our values and ambitions (if you could call Diana ambitious in any way) couldn't be more different. Sadly, my sister is a stranger.

She called me while I was staying with an old friend, Fiona. I often used her place as a base when I returned to the UK after one of my long-term projects abroad.

I knew instantly that Diana was ringing to tell me about a bereavement, to ask a favour, to gloat, or because there had been some kind of drama that she was unable to cope with by herself.

I took a breath as I rang the doorbell and applied a well-practised smile. This little game was predictable and awkward. Diana would have been in the kitchen, would have seen my car pull up. She knew that I'd be there just after lunchtime. But still, this little charade where Di would open the door, feign surprise, and say something like, 'I hadn't expected you yet, you're always flitting around here and there I wasn't sure when you'd get here,' before hugging and air kissing and filling the gaps with, 'Oh you look so well, is that a new necklace, have you had your hair done?' All nonsense. But I go along with it because it's what we do.

Sure enough, Di came to the door and after the standard greeting, my bags were retrieved from the car and I was immediately ushered into the garden where afternoon tea was already laid out on the wooden table beneath a tattered parasol. I would have preferred a gin and tonic, but now wasn't the time for that old chestnut.

It was actually quite a surprise to see my sister looking so bright. On the phone the previous week, she'd mentioned, in very dramatic style, that something had happened, something 'dreadful' and that it was all 'terrible.' In fact, it was so shocking that she refused to say exactly what had happened, or to whom.

The little water feature was babbling away at the end of the patio and birds darted in and out of the feeding station John had built years ago, before he'd left Diana alone to wear the cape of widowhood and an aura of hand-wringing nervousness. I waited for her to stop swiping at the wasps weaving drunkenly around the jam pot, to pour the tea and to relax as much as she ever could.

'So. What's the big news?'.

Diana's face immediately became serious. A sharp intake of breath and shake of her head betrayed her worry.

'The girls. The girls are what is the matter,' she said. 'Dan and Amanda have split up. He's gone off with another woman. And Maddy, well. Well!'

I could see her struggling. I really shouldn't be so hard on her. She may be weak in many ways but I still try to believe she's a good person despite everything. Her family are so important to her. Whatever Maddy had done would hardly surprise me. Maddy was a spoilt brat. But Amanda, that was different. Amanda was supposed to be the sensible, settled one. She must have been completely knocked for six.

'Poor Amanda! That's so terrible. What an absolute sod that Dan is. Never did like him.' I got a threatening look from my sister. I'm always expected to mind my language and heaven forbid I should say anything approaching the truth in a situation.

'It's been awful. He's gone off with a girl from the village too, someone local. So it's in my face all the time. But Amanda has always been focussed entirely on the children. I do wonder if perhaps she couldn't have done more to keep him.'

'More to keep him! Did you really just say that Di?' An image popped into my head of a 1950s housewife, dinner on, kids put to bed, waiting by the door with hubby's pipe and slippers.

'Oh, it wasn't meant to sound the way you think, but Amanda hasn't taken much care of her appearance since the children came along. She's so involved with their lives, I wonder if she even noticed Dan starting to look at another woman. And that Penny is quite attractive, always dresses nicely.'

'That's very disloyal.'

Diana took a sip of her tea. Her chin jutted out ever so slightly at my remark.

'And what has Maddy been up to?'

'Oh dear, well I think Max hasn't been attentive enough towards her and she's had her head turned by some gardener or something,' she said with a dismissive wave of the hand. 'Anyway, Max found out and told her to get out! I mean really, she has as much right to be in that house as he does! So, she's living with Amanda but might move in with this chap, Paul something, in a rented flat. It's all rather sad.'

'He's single, is he? This Paul chap? No commitments?' I asked.

'Well, no, he's married with a baby.'

'Jesus Christ.' I placed my cup down and decided I needed a drink if I was going to get through the next few days of this. To my surprise, when I announced my intention to pour a gin and tonic Diana asked if I could make her one too, so I knew she was in a state.

She followed me back into the house.

'The thing is, Maddy says that his marriage was all but over anyway. His wife, you see—she's another one—his wife has got very tubby, slops about the place in leggings, is grouchy all the time and apparently there's no communication in the bedroom department.'

I felt my shoulders collapse. 'You mean, his wife has a small baby…'

'Nine months old!' interjected Diana.

'A nine-month old baby. She's put on some weight, the baby is a priority and she's probably tired and sore and maybe a little depressed, and her idiot of a husband hasn't had his leg over for a while so when Maddy offers it to him on a plate, he decides to get his rocks off with her does he? Is that pretty much the long and the short of it?'

Tears welled up in my sister's eyes. I knew that Di's relationship with Maddy was completely different to the one she had with Amanda.

'Oh, I'm sorry love,' I said, drawing her to me. 'I know this must be awful for all of you, but you have to look at the situation with honesty. Things don't just happen to Maddy. She manipulates everything.'

'You think I've spoilt her, don't you?' she asked, wiping away a tear and sitting heavily on one of the stools by the breakfast bar.

'You've done your best for your girls but a person's character isn't all down to their upbringing or their genetics. Maddy and Amanda are sisters and yet you couldn't get two more opposite characters, even though they were brought up the same.'

This was a lie. They were not bought up the same, not

in any way. And my comment just drew attention to us. To myself and Diana and the unspoken gaping hole between us.

This spectre at the feast, this distance that we both knew could never be crossed, was becoming a little easier to deal with each time we met. Since John died several years ago, I've made a real effort to keep in touch. I've tried to be a proper sister and not just appear for weddings and twenty-firsts and the occasional Christmas and of course, funerals. But it's not a natural relationship.

Something in Diana's eyes told me that she felt a tug on that same thread, snaking back in time, forever reminding us how fragile and damaged our connection is. She recovered quickly, took a breath and re-focussed her eyes on me, smiling now to show that the moment had passed, that we should move on.

'I know. I must allow Amanda and Madeleine to sort their own problems out. I just worry so much and that's why I wanted you to come and see me.'

She laid a hand on mine.

'I said to myself, I said, "As soon as Julia's here, I will feel better." And I do, already. Thank you for coming.'

I smiled at her, said I would do everything I could to support everyone but that she was right, there would be little she could do to sort the girls out. I, however, had an idea forming of how I might help Amanda. Even though it would probably cause a further rift between myself and Diana.

CHAPTER SEVEN

Amanda

I read the text from Maddy several times before it sank in.

Have left Max. We're done. On my way with overnight bag xxxx

She couldn't possibly have left Max to run off with her bit on the side, could she? We'd not spoken in any great depth about Maddy's affair with Paul. She'd made several veiled references to it but thankfully, no gritty details had been shared. I'd never once considered it to be serious and I was still hoping she would just end it.

Now, with Maddy sitting at my kitchen table, having put her bag in the spare room, kicked off her shoes and generally made herself at home, the small talk was beginning to dry up.

'So, tell me what's going on. Have you completely taken leave of your senses?'

'Oh, don't be like that,' said Maddy, sipping her coffee. 'I might have known you'd side with Saint Max over this. Nobody ever sees my point of view.'

'I'm not siding with anyone. I just don't understand why you risked your marriage and don't care about hurting Max. What is it about this man you are seeing? He doesn't sound like your sort at all. Are you in love with him?'

Maddy shifted uncomfortably in her chair and couldn't look at me.

'Not in love, no,' she said. 'Obviously, there is something there, something, oh I don't know, different about him. I don't want to be with him though, not permanently.'

'So, in other words, you wanted a bit of fun. The life Max has worked hard to create for you wasn't quite fulfilling enough and you thought, sod everybody else, and to hell with the consequences.' I threw my arms up in despair. 'That about right?'

'Don't be so superior,' said Maddy, looking directly at me now, frowning and shaking her head. 'You've always had that attitude. You've always been so smug, so, "Look at me with my long term marriage and my two lovely kids." Not so smug now, are you?'

I gulped a breath. I couldn't speak but I could feel tears stinging the back of my eyes.

'Oh God, I'm so sorry, I really didn't mean that, I'm so, so sorry.' Maddy jumped off her chair and walked over to me and her hug released a torrent of tears. I was overwhelmed with the strength of the emotion.

I cried for some minutes, being gently stroked and soothed by my sister. The ferocity of the sobs had left me feeling almost punch drunk and I realised it had been the first time since Dan left that I'd completely let go. I felt wretched and cleansed at the same time.

Eventually I straightened up. Maddy took a step back and regarded me with a quiet 'You all right love?' I nodded and grabbed some tissues from the box. We sat back in our seats and allowed a few moments of quiet to calm the atmosphere.

'Do you really think I've been smug?' I asked, blowing my nose and wiping the streaks of tears away with the back of my hand.

Maddy's face crumpled and she held up a hand, starting to say 'No, of course I...'

'Maybe you're right. I probably have been. But that means you assume I've been happy all this time. If someone is smug, surely that means they think their life is perfect. That everything is just ticket-y-boo, right?'

Maddy was staring at the fruit bowl, tracing her fingers slowly around the edge, trying to process what I'd just said.

'Well, you were, weren't you? Not smug,' she added hastily. 'Happy, you were happy.' She stopped and looked up at me and raised her eyebrows. 'Weren't you?'

'Content, sometimes. Full of worry, anxiety. Doubt. And I felt I was living a half-life.' I nodded my head. 'Yes, that's it, a half-life. An empty, shallow excuse of an existence.'

Maddy looked at me, mouth slightly open, leaning forward as if being closer would confirm what she was hearing.

'Why do you say that? What are your worries and doubts about? I know you'll always fret over the kids, that's normal and let's face it you can't be any worse than Mum faffing about over us. But empty and shallow? A half-life?'

I welled up again, but with gentle tears this time.

'It makes me feel dishonest to say it. God, I'm such an idiot. Just look at me Maddy, just look at me.'

I put my head in my hands and let out a long crackly sigh. Maddy leant forward and stroked my forearm.

'I look at you and I see my lovely, kind-hearted, generous sister,' she said. 'Definitely don't see an idiot.'

I raised my head and rested my chin on my upturned palms.

'Thing is, I've become so adept at pretending we were fine, so talented at making sure the kids believed we were the perfect family, that I pretty much forgot I was lying, forgot it was an act. I kind of just absorbed the life I was leading and persuaded myself that everything was how it should be. What idiot does that? How did I allow it all to carry on like that for year after year?'

'No marriage is perfect; I know that better than anybody. But you two have always looked like the sort of couple who would be together for life. You two are *AmanDan*. You're a package.'

I felt as if I had a block of concrete in my heart. I glanced up and saw the look on Maddy's face. Watched her try to comprehend what she was hearing.

'How long have you felt like this? How long have things been so bad?'

'Oh, definitely for the last ten years. God, I fantasised about leaving so many times. But you know the kids…and I kept telling myself it must be me, there was something wrong with me. Then you know, it sounds bizarre but I said to myself, it could be worse, he doesn't hit me, or gamble, he's not an alcoholic and—this is the funny bit—,' I said with a false smile, looking straight at Maddy 'he wasn't a womaniser. Ha!'

'So, what happened ten years ago? What went wrong then?'

'The last ten years were the worst, but actually, looking back the signs were there right from the start,' I said, trying to sound matter of fact.

'You know that day I told you about me and Paul? I remember you said you just wanted to start a new life. I thought at the time it sounded like there was more going on than just Dan just having an affair. Why the hell didn't you say anything?'

'Because I'm an idiot?'

'Seriously, no one should live like that. But why? What made you feel it was a half-life? I mean, I must admit you did seem to become, I dunno, settled and domesticated very quickly and I wondered what happened to the old adventurous Amanda, but I just thought it was the life you'd chosen. I guessed it was what you wanted. You had Sammy straight away and you seemed so happy with how everything was.'

'Everything revolved around Dan, everything. I was walking on eggshells every day. We went out when he wanted to go out, stayed in when he wanted to stay in. If we went on holiday, he would decide where and when. I'd have to do all the work of course. Booking it, all the packing, working out how we'd get to the airport, that sort of thing. All the childcare fell to me but as they grew up, if one of the children did something wrong, I was blamed for not having mothered them properly.'

'Yeah, but Amanda, lots of women have that sort of shit to put up with,' said Maddy. 'Not that I'm saying it makes it right but most women do end up keeping the old man happy, doing all the domestic stuff.'

'Except you. That's the irony,' I said, shaking my head. 'To think that your life was what most women would give their right arm for.' I held up a hand to stall Maddy's interruption. 'And yes, I know he wasn't perfect but whatever you did as a couple, wherever you went, was driven by you. It was always the flash hotels and luxury resorts you wanted and it was the other way around. You'd click your fingers and Max would get it all booked, make sure you always got exactly what you wanted. I can't believe you've just thrown all that away.'

Maddy said nothing. I'd rarely seen her looking quite so fragile, so forlorn. I often lost patience with the brittle, self-absorbed version of my little sister, the girl whose behaviour I often secretly compared with Dan's. But seeing a chink in the armour was highly unsettling.

'Anyway, with me and Dan it wasn't just about the laziness and him expecting me to do everything. He had a nasty side.'

'He didn't hit you?' Maddy was wide-eyed.

'No, nothing like that. But if we fell out about anything, even something trivial, he would be vicious in his dressing down. I was left in no doubt that I was a useless individual, and uncaring too. Then he would sulk for days, weeks sometimes. Literally not say one word to me, unless it was in front of the kids or if someone popped over. Then he behaved as if nothing was going on. But they'd leave and he would go back to how he was. After a few days, he'd snap out of it and we'd just carry on.'

'That's just awful, awful, I had no idea. I mean, I wasn't that fond of Dan but I thought he was alright. I had no idea he had another side to him.'

'He had a fake persona, that's why. It worked like a charm. He was clever too. This may sound crazy, but sometimes I used to wish he *would* hit me. Or do something really over the top, like lock me in the house for days on end, or something so extreme that I couldn't even question whether it was acceptable behaviour. But he always stayed just the right side of normal, or at least enough that I believed it was *me* that was being silly. I doubted my own reactions and, in the end, decided I was in the wrong, so I just got on with it.'

Saying all this out loud made me feel vulnerable. Revealing the poor state of my relationship exposed my own failure at least as much if not more than Dan's. Yet at the same time, it was like opening a door and letting in fresh air, blowing away the cobwebs and the stale, musty air, allowing me to take a clean breath. And it occurred to me that starting anew, in some respects, was easier than dealing with what Maddy had ahead of her. She'd have to use every ounce of her cunning to try to fix things with Max because we both knew that her fling with Paul had disaster written all over it. She would have games to play, she would be living on tenterhooks so it was just as well she's good at that sort of thing.

At least for me, I knew that the pain of spotting Dan and Penny walking through the village hand in hand would eventually ease. I knew our finances would be settled and that the children—although suffering now—being adaptable as young people are, would accept their new situation and go on to lead their own lives.

All I have to do is create a completely new and happy life for myself. That didn't sound difficult at all.

* * *

Living with Maddy was not easy. Of course, I'd absolutely forbidden her boyfriend from coming over, so she spent quite a bit of time out and about meeting him. I refused to hear about it. It was enough of a strain for me to be dealing with Dan, negotiating our settlement and arranging times for him to see Ben, and Sammy when she's back from Uni. Neither of the kids would talk about what they did when they saw their father, and they never mentioned Penny. It tore me to pieces because on the one hand I was glad not to have to hear about it, yet on the other hand it made me feel so out of control.

Mum invited us all to Sunday lunch. Sammy was staying with friends, Ben was off kayaking and Maddy, fortunately, was otherwise engaged, presumably with Paul.

I suggested we invite Max.

The house was unbearably hot. Mum seemed to think that a full Sunday roast was imperative and both me and Julia begging her to just make a chicken salad instead had no effect.

I was still feeling wound up after a conversation I'd had at the cafe with Maddy the day before. That girl has always been *me, me, me*, but I did—still do—love her. She's my sister. When we were younger, she could be infuriating and managed to inflict severe pain and embarrassment on me. But there were many days when we connected and had the best times together So I would bury the hurt she'd caused and focus only on the fact that she was lively and that life was always more fun when she was around. I'd had such a mixed experience growing up with Maddy as my little sister. Being at the cafe down by the river bought back lots of memories.

It highlighted how selfish she'd become. She seemed to have no real compassion for Max, for Tanya or even Paul, for that matter.

Max had been quiet at lunch. That's not unusual but there was something about his demeanour, something about his posture that to me was as loud a cry for help than anything he could have said.

Shoulders slumped, eyes cast permanently downward, he'd barely managed a smile when he thanked Mum for dinner. When we'd all laughed about being the only family in the country to be sweating over roast beef and Yorkshire pudding in twenty-eight degrees, he hadn't joined in. He just remained still, staring ahead, lost in thought.

Mum asked him about his architecture practice, not that she was in the least bit interested in his replies. He had only been invited because Julia and I had insisted. She still felt that Maddy, though not blameless, had been neglected by Max in some way and therefore he had dropped in her estimation.

Julia, bless her, started collecting plates and as I stood to help, she gently placed her free hand on my shoulder.

'Why don't you two get some air in the garden?' she said, nodding in the direction of the French doors. 'I'll help Di load the dishwasher and clear up. No point in all four of us dying of heat exhaustion.'

'That sounds good,' I said, knowing better than to argue with Julia. 'Come on Max, grab your drink. Let's go and sit by the pond.'

Max managed a smile and followed me out past the patio, along the weaving pathway to the pond at the bottom of the garden and the shaded swing seat.

We sat in companionable silence for a while, watching dragonflies dancing above the water.

'I suppose asking how you are is a bit trite?' I said.

He turned to me and smiled.

'Well, yes. But I appreciate you asking,' he said. 'You're probably the only other person who has any idea of what this feels like, so you're allowed to be as trite as you want.'

My legs were crossed beneath the swing seat. I curled my

toes and began to gently rock us back and forth, just as I had done when Maddy and I were little. The rhythm soothed me.

'I suppose I'm a couple of months further down the road than you,' I said. 'You are still in that state of disbelief, I've moved on a little to the *Oh My God What Now* phase.'

Max tilted his head back and managed his first proper laugh of the day.

'Perhaps you could enlighten me. What joys do I have to look forward to? What further states of misery await me?'

I laughed too. It was so good to talk with someone who understood, someone who didn't have an angle on my situation.

I settled back into the cushions and relaxed some more, my wine glass held with both hands resting on my tummy.

'Well, the disbelief kind of hasn't gone yet,' I said, turning my head to look at him. 'I don't know when, or if it ever will go. It's just not uppermost in my mind like it was in the first couple of weeks. Like it is for you, now, I imagine.'

Max was still watching the surface of the pond, the insects landing briefly on the lily pads and taking off again.

'Yes, it still seems like it happened to someone else. I wake up every morning and it takes my head a few minutes to adjust to the fact that nothing is as it was.' He shrugged his shoulders. 'But then, well I have no choice. I just have to get on.'

'Oh yes, been there, done that. Eventually the disbelief only really hits when you stop and think about it but the anger's never far from the surface. Give it air and it will overwhelm you. That's what I found anyway.'

'Are you most angry at Dan or at the woman he went off with?' asked Max.

I thought for a moment. When my anger was truly ignited, there was little difference between Dan and Penny. Those two individuals became the *they* that my fury was directed at. Dan had made the choice. He had been married while Penny was single. But neither one could have inflicted this much pain on me without the other.

'It depends on the day. But you know, I control it now. It doesn't control me. I still feel anger but I channel the energy into other things, like trying to find work.'

We spoke of the mundane for a while. Max trying to work and run the house, me trying to make my CV sound as if helping Ben with his homework and trying not to argue with Sammy whenever she came home were transferable skills.

I talked about the future. I spoke about divorce, about what would happen to the house, about downsizing so I could afford to live.

Max didn't really mention the future. He didn't talk about what he thought Maddy would do next, or if he had considered divorce. It was probably still too early for him. And I had no doubt that despite his apparent certainty that they were over for good, it would be Maddy who called the shots, Maddy who would control what happened next.

CHAPTER EIGHT

Maddy

We'd been sitting in the cafe down by the waterfront at Bernstone Point. Trying to enjoy a bit of sister time and making the most of the space while the weather was cooler and cloudy, before the place became swamped with tourists again.

Neither of us spoke. We'd watched people down here since we were tiny. We used to paddle in the water, and played hide and seek among the upturned dinghies lined up at the side of the green. We'd sit impatiently as Dad and Mum got everything ready to row us to our little yacht moored out in the channel. There is such history for our family here. But never had I felt more like the black sheep when I sat there with Amanda that day.

After a while, I finished my coffee and hugged my jacket around me. The breeze had got up and I knew we were both remembering those sailing days with our parents. My childhood wasn't perfect. But my worries had been minute. My life had been easy.

'The thing is Amanda,' I said in the most reasonable tone I could muster, 'you all seem to forget, Paul is a grown man who has made his own decisions. I didn't hold a gun to his head. I keep hearing about what a fine marriage he had, what a lovely girl Tanya is, that I'm a home wrecker blah blah blah, but if it had all been so great, why did he jump into bed with me at the first opportunity?'

'Because you made it so easy?' she said, still gazing out to the little sailboats in the channel.

'And why, if Saint Max is so bloody perfect, do you think I risked my marriage to have an affair?'

'Because you didn't think you'd get caught?' Amanda said, downing the last of her tea and putting the mug down on the table with enough of a bang to make Sid look up from the counter and frown.

I could tell that there was nothing I could say that would make anyone see things from my point of view. As usual, they see only what's on the surface and make assumptions.

We'd walked back up the hill in near silence, just smiling and nodding and saying things like, 'yes, it's quite fresh isn't it, nice breeze too,' to everyone we met who was making their way down to the cafe for lunch.

When we got to Amanda's house, we air kissed and said goodbye. I'd got into my car and drove off to collect Paul from his brother's house. I smiled and gave her a quick wave as I pulled away.

My sister and I have not always got along famously, it's true. But this was one of the bleakest, frostiest atmospheres there had ever been between us.

The few weeks living with Amanda were tense, to say the least.

I felt her revulsion whenever I tried to interact with her but she is so holier-than-thou that she was unable to give voice to what she really wanted to say. Rather than ask me to leave and run the risk of appearing disloyal to a member of the family, she preferred to punish me with her all-pervasive sense of disgust.

Paul, who had been sleeping on his brother's couch since Tanya ejected him from their home, told me he had seen a flat to rent. He said that he needed me, that being with me twenty-four seven would somehow make all the awful events worthwhile.

'I know you're not very happy staying with your sister,' he said. 'And Luke and Chloe have been good to me but I know I'm getting under their feet. I can't bear being apart from you.'

He'd gone silent then. I expect he was waiting for me to rush to agree, but no words came out. I stayed quiet, wondering once again how I'd got myself into this. My daily approaches to Max were being ignored and living under the superior gaze of Amanda was slowly driving me insane.

'So, tell me about this flat,' I said finally, and I could hear his voice change. I could imagine him smiling and lifting his chest, filled with optimism at this fantasy he had of spending the rest of his life with me.

'It's only one bedroom, but it has a view of the park and it's not much but it's a beginning for us. It's furnished too so I'm thinking it will be alright for six months, while everything gets sorted and we get on our feet.'

Quite how he imagined this was going to be achieved was disturbing in itself. He had no money. What little he earned was going to Tanya and short of a lottery win, he was unlikely ever to bring a huge amount of money in. Paul was hardly entrepreneur material. Which meant of course that he was relying on me divorcing Max and getting half of everything. This would, of course, set us up very well but it wasn't going to happen. There would be no divorce between Max and me. I was biding my time but I planned to ramp up the pressure on Max and I just knew he'd cave in, eventually.

I wished Paul was only after me for the money but I think he only saw it as an added bonus. If I'd confronted him, he would have been mortified. He believed that if we spent the rest of our days living in a caravan it wouldn't really matter because we were *meant to be*. He was that deluded.

'So shall I make an appointment for us to go and view the flat tonight? The previous tenant has moved out so we can take it straight away, if we like it.'

My attempts to get Max to take me back by flattery, by tears and by begging hadn't worked. Perhaps if he thought I really was moving out of his reach it might force him to take action. In any case, it would be a relief to get away from Amanda for a while.

'Yes Paul, that's a good idea. Let me know what time the appointment is and I'll meet you there.'

* * *

Dreary. That's the word I'd use.

When I was younger, flitting about here and there, doing my chalet maid work for the ski season, I'd not given a second thought to the properties I stayed in. It hadn't mattered back then. In the winter I was either on the slopes, tidying up after guests and cooking, or in a bar with a huge crowd of other staff.

Summers were spent on the beach, with the odd bit of bar work or housekeeping in a hotel in Cornwall or Devon, all supplemented by the huge tips I'd earned back in the winter in the ski chalet in Meribel.

Life was not so much fun these days. Max spent too much time working but his success at least meant having money to spend on making a stylish home and enjoying real luxuries. It was great but I so missed just taking off, exploring, having fun.

Now though, in the rented flat Paul had found for us, that we'd moved into within days, I realised how important material things had become. And how much Max actually did.

We had to change all the utilities over. The gas, electric, water and council tax. The TV license had to be organised and Paul kept telling me he just didn't have time. He was working about twenty-five hours a week now but constantly looking for more work. He said I would have to take care of all that. Of course I did, but I had the feeling that he wouldn't actually have known what to do anyway. I bet Tanya or his interfering in laws used to do all that.

And he spent every Monday evening with the baby.

Tanya hadn't wanted to see him. She'd been all over social media, making a bit of a fool of herself, frankly. Saying what a lousy piece of shit he was, she never wanted to set eyes on him again, she was better off without him, and she finished every post with, 'That slut he's with is welcome to him.' Charming. She's never even met me.

So he spent most of Sunday evening working himself into a state, gardening all day Monday then went to the in laws' house to play with the child and endure being stared at by a grim faced couple who refused to speak to him, except to pass on the odd message about Tanya needing more money for bills, for nappies, for clothes and other stuff for the baby.

The one and only useful tip I ever had from Aunt Julia was that a girl should always have a 'Plan B fund,' as she called it. A running away fund.

So, because Max had been very generous over the course of our marriage, I had quite a nice little nest egg. I planned on getting some decent bedding, new curtains and a TV, and made a huge online order of cutlery, plates, pots and pans and all sorts of paraphernalia.

Just being in the flat depressed the hell out of me, though. There were hideous net curtains at the window, the cooker had one ring that didn't work on the hob and the sofa had some suspicious looking stains that someone had tried to clean up without complete success. There was a throw on order. I wasn't sitting on the sofa without it.

But I let Paul pay the rent and half the bills. I've always felt a man should do that. Despite what my sister might think.

'The poor chap has to pay for his wife and child to live, and he wasn't earning much anyway. Don't you think you should at least offer to pay half the rent?' she had said, wearing that face that tells me she has already decided what the answer is.

'Er, so basically you're suggesting I should look after him, are you?' I said. 'I've bought loads of stuff. I've probably spent the equivalent of six months' rent on nice things so that he has a better life with me.'

'Yes, and when you leave him, you will be taking all of those things with you.'

I had to bite my tongue when she said that. Why did she assume so much? I had a very well-defined picture of how I expected my future to look and though it included Max and not Paul, I knew I could engineer it very effectively, so everyone would come out it with a rosy future. It was a matter of when, not if.

CHAPTER NINE

Julia, 1971

I always felt the weight of my parents' expectations. Expectations that I knew I could never fulfil. My sister, Diana, was the obliging one. She was round faced, angelic. I was the taller, leaner and angular one and I'm sure my mother saw sharp edges on me that she feared would cut her darling elder daughter as well as herself.

When we got older, Diana was all floral prints, curly hair and swirly skirts. I was tailored, my hair was straight and never did I feel the need to appease anyone with a simpering smile just to gain favour. It took me years to understand that the main problem was that I had not been carved in my mother's image, whereas Diana had. Put me and my sister side by side and it would be difficult to believe we came from the same uterus.

At school, I briefly tried to win approval by striving to be the best at whatever I did. And what I did was to excel in languages. Although I was not popular in the sense of having hordes of people around me, I did develop deep and loyal friendships with a close circle of some of the more academically minded girls. Like me, they felt no need to be liked for the sake of it. And that can be very unsettling for people who rely heavily on a large and devoted approval of the masses.

I was frequently chastised for showing off, for *acting superior*. It wasn't fair. My biggest sin by far was passing my eleven plus and going to Grammar School, instead of the local Secondary Modern that Diana attended.

'Are you deliberately trying to undermine your sister?' Mum had asked one day after I brought home a letter from my French teacher telling my parents I was an exceptional pupil and had achieved 100% in a test.

'But this isn't to do with Di,' I'd said. 'Di is good at cookery and needlework, I'm useless at those things.'

'Perhaps you'd better try harder at those subjects then? You come in flaunting that letter; when did you ever see Diana showing off her housekeeping skills? She made that beef stew the other week, which was lovely, but she didn't go on about it did she?'

By then, I think Mother had realised she was trashing my efforts because she back-pedalled slightly. 'I'm not saying you haven't done well to achieve 100% in an exam,' she said in a gentler tone. 'But French? Really, I don't quite see the point.'

'The point is, I'll be able to get work if I get good grades in French and it means I'll be able to travel. Next term, I start learning Italian too, and possibly even another language.' Mother grimaced at this and half turned away from me.

'Most of these places on the continent don't expect us to speak their language,' she informed me. 'English is understood to be the primary language all over the world. When we went to Spain a few years ago for our holiday, we managed to make the waiter understand us didn't we?'

I sighed. The memory of Diana and I trussed up in our 'travelling outfits' and being dragged by our hands up the steps of the aircraft, while Mother tried to stop her hat blowing away in the wind, was seared on my memory. And probably on everyone else's too, as Mum had gloried in describing every aspect of our holiday in great detail, well aware that most of the people we knew had never been abroad and would probably never go.

The year Diana turned nineteen, I was reaching the grand age of sixteen. Our mother threw a party for Diana, with relations and some of Di's friends, who came over laden with presents. It was the early seventies. Mum had grown into a young woman in the shadow of the second world war, a time when females remained little girls until they were deemed mature enough to jolly well pull their socks up and get on with it. They went to work in munitions factories or worked on the land and waited at home for news of the boys who went off to war. They morphed from children to mature women in a heartbeat. I don't think Mum had realised that in our generation teenagers had been invented. As had fun.

So the girls who came to Diana's party were generally dressed to impersonate confident older women. One or two wore hot pants with boots, their eyes heavily and clumsily made up. The rest were dressed simply but the resentment they clearly felt at still being considered children was palpable.

However, Di was not in the least concerned. She wore a monstrous Peter Pan collar dress that Mother had made from a Simplicity paper pattern. It was pink, with large flowers all over and the collar was white. She wore patent black leather shoes on her feet. At fifteen still, I remember being astonished that she went along with our mother on this one. Surely it was her job to be surly and rebellious? Even I knew that, at my tender age. Shouldn't she be paving the way for me? For the next tranche of teenagers with minds of their own, who believed in free will?

So I was dreading the question of how I would like to celebrate a couple of months later, as I approached my sixteenth birthday. I overheard Mum talking to Mrs Hargreaves next door, telling her that she had a birthday party planned for me, with balloons and streamers and a lovely cake, which Diana was going to bake, then ice, with a white and pink flower design. I needed to steer her away from this.

'There's a play on at the Regent,' I said one Saturday morning over breakfast. 'It's on the third, and I'd love to go and see it. Janet and Shelia want to see it too. Please could we go there for my birthday?'

I did want to see the play, a kitchen sink drama, but wasn't even sure that girls of my age would be allowed into the theatre to see it. But the main thing was, it would divert my mother away from subjecting me to a terrible party.

She became flustered. 'Oh well, you know your father and I are not one for plays. We did see that musical a few years back in London but I can't say I really understood what it was all about.' She drummed her fingers on her knee, trying to think of an alternative. 'I know, why don't we all go and see a film?'

I jumped at the opportunity. 'Yes! I think they might be showing Escape from the Planet of the Apes at the Odeon. I think it would be just my sort of thing.'

I was delighted when she agreed. Even more thrilled when she confirmed that neither she nor my father thought it would be their 'thing.' 'We don't much care for programmes about monkeys,' she said. This birthday treat could turn out much better than planned. Dad would drive us to the cinema, drop us off outside at two-thirty in the afternoon and then pick us up at six from the same spot. That would give us time to go into the foyer of the cinema, wait for Dad to drive away and then go to the Wimpy for burger and chips and shakes. Lots of older people we knew from school hung out there. Then came the big disappointment.

'Obviously you'll take Diana with you?' said Mum two days before my birthday.

'Di won't want to hang around with us kids,' I said. 'And the film's U-rated so there's nothing you need to worry about. We don't need anyone looking after us.'

Mother had been peeling potatoes. She turned towards

me and put the peeler down on the counter-top. 'I'm not suggesting that she needs to watch you, Julia.' She sounded aggrieved. 'I would like to think that you want your sister with you. You're lucky to have someone so caring and kind and I think the least you can do is invite her along.' I crossed my arms and leant with my back against the cooker. I'd have to phrase this exceptionally well to avert disaster. There was no way Diana would keep quiet about us sneaking off to the Wimpy and even if she did, I'd cringe if some of the older kids from school met her. She would embarrass me the moment she opened her mouth, if not before.

I bit my bottom lip, thinking of what to say, but Mum continued before I had a chance. 'Well, anyway, you're to invite her, she'd like to go, so that's that.' She turned back to the pile of spuds and the newspaper covered with peelings, picked up a knife and started cubing them. That was it. A done deal.

The next day at school I intended to tell my friends that our grand plans for a burger had been scuppered. But Janet had bought a new top with her pocket money and had borrowed her older cousin's necklace and earring set because she'd heard that David Ringshaw, who was seventeen, always went to the Wimpy on a Saturday afternoon and he looked a bit like George Harrison from The Beatles. He'd smiled at her twice in the playground last week. She was pretty sure it was love.

So I couldn't bring myself to tell them. I'd missed the moment and when Saturday morning came, I thought I'd rather feign illness and cancel the whole thing rather than go through the indignity of taking Diana with me.

Rather than get dressed, I messed my hair up and went into the bathroom and found some Pond's Cold Cream, which I smeared on my face in an attempt to look clammy. I made my way slowly downstairs, clutching at my stomach and walked through into the kitchen, where my mother and father sat with a pot of tea and some thin white toast between them.

'Morning,' I said in my most feeble voice. 'I feel a bit ill. Not sure what's wrong with me.' Rather than any enquiries into my own health, Mum launched straight into some news that unbeknownst to her, was music to my ears.

'Well, I don't know if it's the same thing, but your poor sister has been terribly ill all night. She's been in and out of the bathroom a dozen times. She's gone back to bed now because she feels so poorly so if you have it too, it must be a bug going around. Such a shame; we were going to say Diana won't be able to come to the film with you, but it looks like you won't be going yourself now.'

My eyes widened. I had to manufacture the quickest and least suspicious sudden recovery the world had ever seen. And I mustn't smile. I. Must. Not. Smile.

'Oh no, that's a shame. Poor Diana, I was so looking forward to her coming. I think I'll see how I go, if that's OK with you? I haven't actually been sick or anything yet. Maybe, if I have some toast and a cup of tea It'll settle my stomach, eh?'

I sat down with them at the table and tucked into the toast, aware of my apparent delicate state and chewed as slowly as I could. Mum bought my birthday cards in from the lounge and I opened them as I drank my tea. Then they gave me some presents. There was a cookery book and a book on sewing. I couldn't help raising an eyebrow. But then, I opened an Avon boxed set of sandalwood spray scent with matching soap and hand cream. I smelt very grown up and I was even happier to open my next present. It was a pair of slim fitting brown checked trousers and a classic polo necked sweater. My eyes filled with tears and when I looked up at Mum, so were hers. I hugged her tight. She had put some thought into this and it was so unexpected and made me feel sad and happy in equal measure. Happy because I felt for once that maybe she did understand what made me who I am. Maybe I wasn't such a mystery. And sad because if she did have this intuitive understanding, why did she keep it under wraps most of the time?

During the morning I gradually 'got better.' At quarter past two, dressed in my new outfit and drenched in the overpowering scent of my Avon gift, I stepped into Dad's car and we drove round to Wendham Road then Albermarle Street to pick up first Shelia then Janet. We got out at the cinema, dived in through the large doors and giggled insanely as we watched Dad drive away. We then strode down the road to the Wimpy and went straight to the loos, where Shelia revealed a make up bag secreted at the bottom of her handbag. There was a little rouge in there, some red lipstick and a mascara, which was pretty much dried up beyond redemption, but we still all did what we could with it.

We spilled out of the loo, ordered our food and shakes

and sat down in the window seat. Sure enough, after twenty minutes, David Ringshaw and Robert Wade swaggered in through the swing doors. David nodded in Janet's direction and then followed by Robert, he went up to the counter and placed their order.

Janet was a bag of nerves. She twisted her hair around her index finger and I could tell she was trying to look cool. The boys came and sat on the table next to us, not speaking but smiling and smirking slightly, their own silent code suggesting a conversation that we were not to hear.

The girls and I talked about what we wanted to do when we left school. It made us seem mature we believed, and hoped it would dispel any beliefs the boys had that we were just kids.

As I had been given a little money from relatives for my birthday, I wanted to treat the girls to another milk shake. As I got up to leave the table, I was aware of David's and Robert's eyes on my body.

When I'd dressed that morning, I'd realised how my new clothes showed off my figure and gave me curves, unlike the school uniform everyone usually saw me in that gave me the appearance of a wooden plank. As I made my way to the counter, I became aware that I was slowing down my walk, moving my hips very slightly and standing straight with my shoulders back. I'd no idea why. I suppose it must have been an instinctive response to feeling an attraction and to knowing that a member of the opposite sex was watching me.

By the time I came back to the table, precariously carrying the three shakes, the boys had moved across to our table. I set the drinks down and then looked around, unsure of where I should sit.

'Here you go,' said David patting the seat next to him. 'Slide in here next to me.' I turned to sit but not before I'd caught sight of Janet's thunderous face.

We talked for the next couple of hours and bought more shakes and another two bags of chips, which the five of us shared between us. The time flew. I deliberately gave David the brush off every time he tried to speak to me. He asked me whether I preferred The Beatles or the Stones, and I said I hadn't really thought about it and turned to Janet and ask, 'What do you think Janet? Mick or Paul?' I tried to steer every conversation towards her but even with my inexperience, I could tell that David was more interested in talking to me.

Eventually, the boys left, wishing me a happy birthday and as I turned to watch them leave, David turned too and gave me a wink. Janet was talking to Shelia at the time so she didn't see.

It took another year and three months before David asked me to be his girlfriend. Janet had by then developed an infatuation with Simon Colman which made it much easier as we all grew up, and David and I became closer and our feelings deeper.

CHAPTER TEN

Amanda

The doorbell rang insistently, so I knew it was either a salesperson, or Maddy, or Julia.

I could see dark hair through the patterned glass, a tall, slender figure, hands on hips. Aunt Julia had always been like this. Mother called her 'formidable' but the word always reminded me of a much older woman, a dowager duchess with pearls and a tweed skirt.

The moment I opened the door, I could tell I was in for a talking to and experience told me to just breathe my way through it. And listen. Annoyingly, when Julia gave one of her, 'Here's what I think you should do' speeches, she so often cut through the tripe and her advice would be just what you needed to hear.

'Hello darling,' she said, sweeping past me, all Armani and silk.

'Come in, why don't you?' I said under my breath, shutting the door and following her into the lounge.

Julia glanced around the room, no doubt taking in the pile of old paperwork on the coffee table that I was working my way through, and the three dirty coffee cups I'd not yet taken into the kitchen. She'd not been over to mine since she'd arrived back in the UK. I'd seen her a couple of times at Mum's but resisted extending an invitation for her to come here. She wouldn't mean to do it, but I would feel judged.

'So, how have things been this week?' she asked, throwing an empty tissue box onto the floor so she could sit down. 'Not too good by the looks of things.'

She could have been referring to the state of the house but equally, the state of me wasn't exactly a joy to behold.

I'd lost weight when it all first happened. Then I suppose as people stopped calling me every day, as the rest of the world got on with its life, I started to comfort eat. Whenever Sammy or Ben were out with their mates I just wouldn't bother to cook for myself. It was easier to get a takeaway, or to eat a family bag of cheese and onion crisps and half a packet of chocolate biscuits washed down with the greater part of a bottle of wine. It wasn't good.

The waistbands of my jeans became tight, so I began to wear leggings. All my fitted tops started to strain at the seams so baggy t-shirts became the order of the day.

Then I stopped wearing make up and stopped doing my hair because there didn't seem to be any point. I didn't go anywhere. I didn't do anything. I was invisible so why make the effort?

Now though, in front of Julia—who always made the

effort—it was as if my eyes had been opened and I could see that the old Amanda was gone. She had evaporated entirely.

'So darling, why don't you sit down somewhere and we can have a bit of a heart to heart, hmmm? I know it's sometimes difficult to face the future when things have gone dramatically wrong, but you know I'm simply here to help. You understand that, don't you?'

I flopped down on the end of the sofa closest to Julia and tucked my legs underneath me. I was dreading this. I knew it would be a pep talk. I knew how badly I needed it but the idea of it made me feel exposed.

'Julia, you know, I'm well aware that I've let things slip but I'm planning on coming out fighting again. Don't worry about that.'

'I don't doubt you plan to come out fighting. I don't doubt you plan to turn your life around and I seriously hope you plan on ditching those hideous stained t-shirts. But a plan is nothing; nothing until it is executed.'

It was like being twelve years old again.

'I just need time, Julia. I have to get things straight in my head. I need to find a source of income and I have to map out a future for myself.'

'Yes but that's all mañana, mañana. It's all some airy-fairy plan for the future. It's not very pro-active, is it Amanda?'

I couldn't look at her. It would have triggered the tears I was barely holding back and I felt like a useless mess as it was.

'It's not airy-fairy,' I replied, managing to now sound like a whiny twelve-year-old as well as feel like one. 'I do have a long list of things that I need to do but I have to wait until I'm ready, until the time is right.'

'Oh, for goodness sake the time is never right! If we all waited until we felt ready for anything, bugger all would get done! Don't you see, you have to change your frame of mind and the rest will follow?'

She was making it sound pretty simple. Perhaps that's how her life was. With no children and no husband and a pretty impressive list of contacts, she had nothing to hold her back.

I picked a stray hair from my jogging bottoms. I didn't want to fall out with Julia but I was beginning to feel as if she had no concept whatsoever of what a monumental task I had ahead of me. She had no idea of the weights I had tied around me, dragging me down.

'Yes, that's all well and good but there's another saying: fools rush in where angels fear to tread. If I go forging ahead like a bull in a china shop, well...' I struggled to find an analogy '...a lot of china is going to get broken.'

My clumsy expression broke into the heavy atmosphere and we both burst out laughing. It felt like a natural place to take a breath and it reminded me not to be so resistant. Julia had my best interests at heart and even if she had found it relatively easy to carve her way through life, she had experience to draw on and I would be an idiot not to take advantage of that.

We moved to the kitchen and I took a pizza out of the freezer. Julia immediately snatched it out of my hand, tutted and rolled her eyes dramatically, while shoving it back.

'And one of the first things you can change is your eating habits,' she said, opening the fridge as she spoke.

'Oh, for heaven's sake!' She poked around inside, turning her nose up and making occasional gagging noises for effect.

'Half a packet of bacon that's a week out of date, a couple of mouldy tomatoes and quarter of a pint of milk. No wine, however. I doubt there's any left over to put back in the fridge at the end of the day, is there?'

My face burned and Julia gave me one of her looks. I could cope with the annoyance, not so much the pity.

'You wait there,' she said. 'I'll be back soon.' She flew out of the door and drove away far too quickly, spraying gravel into the road as she went.

Julia didn't return for over an hour. While she was gone, I jumped in the shower, found some body lotion at the back of the bathroom cabinet that I hadn't used in months and slathered it all over me. It was nice to smell like a woman again, rather than my more recent aroma of cheap soap and despair.

I even swiped some eyeshadow and mascara on and found an old dress that I'd last worn just after I'd had Ben and had still been carrying a bit of baby weight. It looked quite nice, surprisingly.

When I opened the door to Julia, she handed me three bulging shopping bags and turned back to the car to retrieve another four. This time, she looked at me, took in my improved appearance and I saw her soften and smile.

Unpacking the shopping in the kitchen, I put things away as Julia pinched various items, heated pans on the hob and chopped garlic and herbs in an impressive whirl of activity.

Within the hour, we were sitting at the kitchen table eating herb encrusted chicken breast with tender stem broccoli, rosemary roasted potatoes and a rich, garlic and tomato sauce. It was delicious. It was the sort of thing I used to cook, when I had a family to care about and not just two children who led a large part of their lives elsewhere. It was the sort of thing I used to cook when I was Amanda. Not the shadow I'd become.

We made small talk over dinner. I was grateful for that. I would have had indigestion if we'd returned to the subject of my future. But I knew that eventually, Julia would circle back to the topic.

'Julia, that was amazing,' I said, resting my knife and fork on an empty plate. 'You must tell me how much I owe you for all the shopping.'

She scrunched up her face and waved my comment away with her hand. It was incredibly generous of her. But I knew better than to argue the point. If I mentioned money again, she would have thought it vulgar.

'Never mind all that,' she said, as she finished eating and moved our plates to one side. 'Tell me what you were thinking about while I was shopping. Don't tell me "nothing". I know your mind has been racing.'

Of course, she was right. I had been mulling it all over and I did get what she was saying. I could wait forever and a day for things to feel right. But it had to be controlled by me, not the other way around. I had to get my act together. I just needed to know how that was going to work.

We chatted about it all for another hour before Julia surprised me with a suggestion that I had the feeling she had been mulling over for a while.

'You know, there's always The Bahamas.'

The mention of our other family always made me tense. It always made Mum tense too, and yet we shouldn't be that way. It all came from Dad, who didn't want to know anything about them.

Growing up knowing that your father had left to be with his mistress and emigrated to America with her was naturally a bitter pill to swallow for Dad. I think I'd have been resentful too.

But Dad's father, William Saxby, was a very old man now. The last we'd heard, he'd had a stroke some years ago and was being nursed at home, unable to walk or speak. I'd seen enough articles about Saxby Marine to know what a go-getter he'd been, what a charismatic person he was. So to be in a such a terrible condition must have been excruciating for him. If Dad wanted some kind of karma, there it was.

It wasn't the rest of the family's fault though. William's son and daughter and their children had, via Julia, consistently extended an invitation to all of us to visit any time. Julia had run into Robin Saxby at a hotel some years ago and they had chatted briefly and swapped contact details.

When Dad was still alive, we didn't even dare mention the

regular invitations and Christmas cards. Since he had died, Mum would say, 'It's nice of them, but no. Definitely not. John would not have liked it.'

So I had always taken the same view. Not because I agreed but because it was kind of expected. It would have seemed disloyal to do anything else, but now, I knew I had to consider all possibilities.

'I should be watching the pennies you know Julia, not spending money on flights. I'd have to pay my way too. I know they all said we could stay with them but it would still cost me. And I'd have to leave the children. And I'm supposed to be looking for work.' I shook my head. The thought of a trip to The Bahamas both thrilled and terrified me, but the scaredy-cat in me won the day.

Julia reached over and took my hand. She gave it a little squeeze before letting it drop. I knew what was coming.

'Right, well here's what I think you should do.'

Bless her. So predictable.

'I think you easily have enough savings to afford the flights and I can tell you that you probably won't be allowed to pay for anything more expensive than an ice cream while you are there. Let's face it, the American Saxbys are worth a fortune. The children will be absolutely fine. Sammy's at Uni anyway. Ben's a little star and I'd happily move in here for a few weeks while you're gone just to keep an eye on him. You know I adore that boy.'

'I know. I know you're right. But there is the job situation. I really should be looking for work.'

'Dan may be an absolute arse, my darling but I'm sure he's left you with a few quid in the bank to keep you going until the divorce is sorted. And to be honest, looking at you, I really don't think you're in a fit state to start applying for work anyway. I certainly wouldn't employ you.'

'Thanks Julia. Thanks for that.'

Julia gave me a sideways look and one of her cheeky smiles. She knows I love her searing honesty.

* * *

I asked Julia later that day if she knew exactly what had happened when GranDad William had left Ivy to run away with his mistress and whether Dad had ever been tempted to investigate the exact circumstances. Whether he'd ever looked through Ivy's papers for love letters and so on or if perhaps he'd found some things relating to that time that may have given him closure. Julia hesitated and seemed to be carefully considering what to say.

'We all poke our noses into places and things we'd be better off staying away from,' Julia said. 'Its human nature. People can't seem to resist the temptation to read diary entries, or other people's letters, when they have no business to. The problems really start when things are vague and we torture ourselves by wondering what might be going on. Then imagination takes over and that's often far worse than the reality of a situation.'

Julia turned her back on me and started unloading the

dishwasher. I felt heat rush to my cheeks as her words brought memories to the surface that had swirled around in the guilt-ridden part of my soul. The part where all the things labelled 'shouldn't have done that' lurked. And because it was Julia, the question that I'd tried to ignore since I was a schoolgirl came in sharp focus.

The summer holidays, a boring afternoon, and a telling off.

Mother had shouted at me, having got back from shopping with Maddy for her new school uniform. I'd been told to wash up the breakfast things, vacuum the lounge and then empty the washing machine and hang everything on the line.

I had done none of those things. I had been off in a dream world, wondering what exciting things the future might have in store for me. I'd been dreaming about getting away from my family when I was grown up. It would be the most exciting move I could make.

'Well, you can jolly well get on and do your chores now. Then go upstairs to your room. And you can start on some of the maths homework Mr Johnson gave you. There's only two more weeks of the summer holiday so you'd better finish it.'

She'd huffed and puffed and declared me a selfish and inconsiderate girl. I said I was sorry and jumped up from my comfortable armchair and did my chores as instructed. Maddy stood at the far end of the lounge, arms folded and smiling at me as I struggled with the temperamental old Hoover. Then she followed me into the garden while I pegged up the sheets and pillowcases I'd just dragged out of the washer.

'I've got lots of new things,' said Maddy. 'My new uniform and PE kit and Mum got me a new dress, a Top of The Pops album and some new roller skates.'

I said nothing. Not that Mum and Dad were ever mean as such. But anything I might ask for, not just material things but things like asking for friends to sleep over, for permission to stay up an extra half hour to watch something special on television, were always a big deal. I was expected to justify my request and would then have to endure a stony-faced silence, as they pulled their mouths to the side of their faces and sighed before pronouncing their decision. Even when it was a 'yes' it was delivered with such a sense of begrudging acquiescence that I often never bothered to remind them of their promise.

I came back inside and put the laundry basket on top of the washing machine. I went upstairs, reluctantly pulled out my homework file and started trying to decipher the symbols and equations that meant absolutely nothing to me.

'I'm taking Madeleine to ballet now,' Mum called out. 'We'll be a couple of hours. If you need to, knock next door, she's always in.'

That summer, for the first time ever, Mum had allowed me to stay in the house on my own. It was just for a few hours at a time, but it made me feel grown up and responsible. And free.

I heard the front door close and as usual, Mum starting the car, stalling it, then starting it again and backing our of the drive. I slammed my maths book shut and decided to play around with my hair, in an attempt to look sophisticated like Kim Wilde.

I remembered that Mum had some heated curlers in her dressing table drawer. I was forbidden from going into her room but I knew they were there and I knew I could have them heated up, used and cooled down before she came home. Then I could tie my hair up in a ponytail so she'd be none the wiser.

As I waited for the little red light on the curlers to stop flashing, I began fiddling with other bits and pieces on her dressing table.

A little soapstone dish full of earrings, plus two safety pins, three hair grips and a perfect little ball of dust. Next to that was a jar of Oil of Ulay. I took off the lid and inhaled deeply. It smelled luxurious and very grown up.

At the back there was a silver framed photograph taken of Mum and Dad on their wedding day, standing outside the church.

I leant forward and traced my fingers around the top of the frame and smiled. Each person's character was so well defined in that single moment in time.

Dad was gazing adoringly at Mum but Mum looked into the camera with a nervous half smile. Granny Ivy stood next to Dad, handbag held across her stomach, grim faced as she too stared into the lens, as if defying those people looking at the picture years later to dare tell her to cheer up.

Aunt Julia stood next to Mum. She looked utterly ill at

ease and I could see why. Her dress was voluminous, with gaudy flowers on a pale background and the whole effect drowned her slight frame. It looked like a pair of curtains that should only be used for wrapping a dead body in. It was truly hideous.

I'd seen very little of Julia until I was about eight years old. Mum had explained that Julia's work in the travel industry took her all over the world and that it was difficult to fit in visits to her family when she had so many things to do and important people to meet.

Then, she'd had to come back to England for a few months and even I could see the frostiness between them. But slowly, over time, a thawing occurred and Julia began to visit more often. I didn't want to like her. Mum's reasoning for why she'd not been around gave me a poor impression of my aunt, and I felt protective towards Mum who must have felt abandoned by Julia. Family is very important to Mum.

But I did like Julia and I could tell that Julia liked me. We must have recognised something in each other that drew us together. Julia was the first family member I felt I could be related to. The first person that I felt was part of the same whole. It made me a little guilty but from early on, I trusted that she would be there and would understand and guide me.

There was also an oak box on Mum's dressing table with a fake ivory inlay. I knew Mum kept her best jewellery in there, an envelope marked *Maddy,* containing a lock of hair, and a photo of Maddy as a very small baby, just a few hours old. There was also a necklace made of pasta threaded onto string and painted. Maddy had made it during her first year at school. Of course, I wasn't supposed to know about the contents of the box, so I could never ask Mum why she had so many trinkets to treasure of Maddy's childhood but not from mine. My baby photos were in an album on a shelf, not cherished, never looked at.

I opened it again as I always did when I sneaked into Mum's bedroom. A part of me hoped to see some small artefact, something I'd created; a card I'd sent her, a picture I'd drawn for her, something.

Nothing new had been placed on top of the pile, so this time, I took everything out, just to be sure.

Then I noticed, for the first time, a lift-tab on the bottom of the box and pulled the little bit of ribbon. Beneath it was an envelope, clearly a few years old and with foreign stamps plastered over it. It was addressed to Mum and marked *strictly private and confidential*.

It did make me hesitate. Not just because of the warning on it but because I shouldn't have lifted the tab, shouldn't have opened the box, shouldn't have even been in the room in the first place. But I was eleven years old. I was curious and feeling slightly wounded so I took the letter out and started to read.

Diana,

I received your letter some time ago and have been wrestling with what my response should be. I had in fact drafted a reply to you when Mother called me and told me the news that has put an entirely different slant on things.

Your letter was very clear about how you felt. On how, should I wish to be a vindictive and vile person, I could cause you as much distress as you have caused me. Typically, you seemed to be more intent on self-preservation than on showing any concern for others.

For the record, I have no intention of making public anything about what happened even though it has caused me much heartache. More heartache than you will ever know. I will be staying on in Italy until the end of the summer and will return home briefly before heading off on another contract. I'd really rather not be around for the foreseeable future.

I'll be in touch when I feel ready. And when that time comes, we will not dwell on the past but I doubt we will ever resume the closeness we once had.

I just hope, Diana, that the consequences of what you did don't come back to haunt you. Remember, we reap what we sow.

Julia

This was adult stuff and I had no idea what it all referred to but I clearly remember that my heart thumped in my chest, my throat constricted and I wished that I'd never read it.

Standing in my kitchen with Julia more than thirty years later, I could still recall the dread and anxiety that I'd felt, but now I had the opportunity to ask the author of the letter what it was about. My heart began to thump a little harder, just like it had way back, but I wanted to ask all the same. I wanted to ask and hear Julia laugh, to explain that it was all some silliness or to say it was such trivia that she couldn't even remember what it was all about.

Yet the words wouldn't come. The fear of what I might discover far outweighed my curiosity.

CHAPTER ELEVEN

Julia, 1976

I couldn't be certain how David would react to my news, but as I walked along the drive, past the side of the house and into the back garden, I wore the smile of a woman with a wonderful future ahead of her.

I could hear music. I had thought he wouldn't be back until later, but the sound seemed to be coming from the spare bedroom, so I imagined he must have finished early.

David had been at the house for a few days, since New Year's Eve when we'd all gone to Tony Markham's party two doors down. He'd explained to my parents how the heating in his flat had broken and in a rare show of beer-induced generosity, Dad suggested he sleep in the box room until the gas board had been over to fix the problem.

Before turning in on the first night, David had slipped his arms around my waist in the kitchen as I washed up the dinner plates. He gently kissed my ear and made a whispered suggestion that I wait a while after bedtime, and then make my way to his room. I giggled, not least because the breath on my neck tickled, but through nervousness; if caught, we were in big trouble and it wasn't worth taking the risk. In any case, once I had my suspicions confirmed in a few days, we would have to run the gauntlet of shock and accusations. Then my parents would finally relax and bask in the warm knowledge that they were to be grandparents.

I wasn't sure how Diana would react. She had been married to John for less than a year and I had imagined that she'd do her best to fall pregnant as quickly as possible. Knowing Di, she had probably drawn up charts and filled in diaries and was doing whatever she could to give herself the best chance of falling. Nothing was ever said, but I think all the women in the family were raising eyebrows at the lack of news. I hoped the fact that I was expecting wouldn't hurt her.

Now, a week later, as I opened the back door, I looked forward to surprising David.

Jean, my boss at the travel agency had picked up on my agitation and suggested I take the afternoon off.

'I don't know what's got into you today, Julia,' she'd said. 'But every letter you've typed has had a mistake in it and if I hadn't stepped in when you were making Mrs Wilson's booking she would be flying to Birmingham instead of Barbados!'

I'd blushed, the perfectionist in me feeling deep shame at such shoddy work.

'I'm so sorry Jean, I really don't know what to say. I'm not feeling quite right today. Shall I make us some tea? Perhaps that will straighten me out and I'll do a better job this afternoon.'

Jean lit another cigarette, waved her freckly hand in the air, and squinted her eyes closed as the smoke coiled its way towards her.

'I think you should go home, sweetheart,' she said with a slight chuckle that made her shoulders go up and down. 'There's not many customers coming through the door and I doubt things will pick up for another week or two.'

I started to protest but she shut me down, hands held in front of her face and cigarette now dangling from between her lips. 'No, Julia, you get off home now. Make the most of it. Once everybody's finished paying for Christmas, they'll all be rushing in to find the best deals for their summer hols. Then it'll be late nights and lots of hassle, so enjoy a bit of time off while you can.'

I thanked her and gathered my bag and coat and made my way down Gloucester Road to the tube. One hour and forty minutes later, there I was, standing in the kitchen listening to music that was coming from upstairs.

I stood perfectly still, savouring the last few moments of being the only person who knew of this little miracle that was growing inside me. I closed my eyes and blocked out the music, breathing slowly as I put my bag on the kitchen table and placed both hands over my heart. 'It will all be fine little one,' I said. 'Mummy has plans for us, for you, me and Daddy.' I started to sway from side to side, as if already rocking a baby. 'We'll travel and explore and have adventures and you'll speak lots of languages and we'll have an amazing life.'

I opened my eyes and heard the music change from *Bye Bye Baby* to The *Way We Were*. It was one of the cassette tapes I'd made.

I made my way upstairs and hesitated as I put my hand on the door handle, took a deep breath and straightened my back. I'd go in and tell him straight away. No point in messing around. I knew there would be shock at first and then he'd smile and though we would both be slightly scared of the future, it would be the cherry on top of our already rather delicious cake.

The music faded as the song came to its end and at that moment, I could hear the sound of moans and sighs. Male and female sounds. I couldn't stop myself opening the door to see what I was sure would be a logical explanation. It would be my silly mistake, hormones playing tricks on me, taunting me. In slow motion the door opened fully and David and Diana lay under the sheet, breathless, her head resting in the crook of his arm and both of them with their eyes shut.

I froze. Another song started to play but I couldn't have told you what it was. In the same instant, as if alerted by a greater force, they both opened their eyes.

I had to steady myself against the door frame as my heart beat so fiercely it rocked my torso to and fro. I didn't speak, just stared wide eyed at the carpet as a tornado of David's panic-stricken words spun around me, stinging as they glanced off my body. Then the sobbing began. Diana, wailing pitifully. I didn't look at either of them. I turned around and stumbled out. I held tightly to the banister as I made my way downstairs, ran through the kitchen to pick up my bag and out onto the street.

I got back to the agency at three thirty that afternoon. Jean was already closing up and her eyes widened when I tapped on the glass door.

'Blimey love, look at you! What's happened?'

Finally, my own tears spilled and as Jean opened her arms, the shock and trauma of what I had seen burrowed into a deep recess of my heart.

I never told Jean what had happened. She let me sleep on the sofa at her little mews flat for a few weeks and I'll always be grateful that she never pressured me to tell her anything. I told Mum and Dad that I was staying with her because Jean was having a few problems and needed some support. They never questioned that. David had already left, thanking them for their hospitality and fibbing that his heating was fixed. Diana, of course, was home with John and as far as my parents were concerned, all was well.

It was Jean who suggested that I look for work abroad.

'Whatever happened to you I can see it knocked you for six,' she said one night over a bowl of French Onion Soup. 'Sometimes, it's best to just get away, take your mind off things and have a bloody good time. Wish I'd done it when I was younger. You're so good at languages and I could help you find a position with a hotel on the continent, if you like. I don't want you to leave, you're great at your job, but I can tell this is not something you'll get over easily.'

So together, Jean and I contacted some of the hotels she'd been working with in France and Italy, and when the proprietor of a family run hotel in Tuscany offered me a job entitled 'Co-Ordinator,' without any explanation of what this would involve, I jumped at the chance and my ticket to Pisa was booked. Within two weeks, British Airways would be flying me away from the pain and anguish and my life would change.

I spent time packing and preparing, but not before I checked into a private clinic, booked for the week before I left. The baby I'd so wanted, the life I thought was mapped out was removed from me in a brief operation. I was given some painkillers and told to contact my GP if I was at all worried and given a leaflet about contraception. As if some pills and a leaflet would cure the cause of the real pain.

* * *

Mother was horrified when I announced I was hot footing it over to Tuscany.

Before I'd even finished my little spiel, I could see her rearranging her face into the judgemental scowl. She was comparing me to Diana. My sainted older sister would never do something so outrageous. She had towed the line, got a nice little secretarial job straight from school and then married John.

I tried to explain to Mum why I felt the need to live abroad for a while without revealing what actually drove me to flee.

'This country's a mess,' I announced. 'Unemployment's sky high and there will be no jobs for anyone soon.'

She'd rolled her eyes at this and said I was a presentable, intelligent girl who would be an asset to any business. Just like Diana was at Gates of Tanford.

'You could try writing to Alistair Gates,' she said. 'He's obviously very impressed with Diana and I'm sure he would offer you a post. Perhaps you could ask about the accounts department?'

Perhaps I could throw a bucket of frogs over me and bang my head against a brick wall. That would be equally appealing.

'Mum, you know I want to work in travel. You know I love languages. This job I've applied for is only for six months, it'll be a great experience and I'll get to speak Italian properly.'

She looked at me over the top of her glasses.

'Julia, you are nineteen years old. You are too young to be roaming around a foreign country on your own. Also, I understand that Italy is where the Mafia are, isn't it?'

'Yes, that's right Mother. But don't worry, if I wake up with a horse's head in my bed, I'll be sure to pack my bags and come straight home.' I shook my head. Did she have any idea how ridiculous she was?

Mum stood up and began gathering the cups and plates we'd put on the coffee table after our tea and biscuits.

'Well, I suppose that neither me nor your father will be able to stop you. You've always been headstrong.' Her downturned mouth told me all I needed to know about her thoughts on the matter. 'We will, of course, want you to write some postcards and telephone us occasionally, but that won't do much to ease the anxiety we'll be suffering.'

She spun around and marched into the kitchen, head held up so that she was looking down her nose.

I tried to ignore the knot in my chest. I knew this uncomfortable feeling was guilt; deliberately manufactured by Mother to try to bend me to her will. I knew it was unfair, I knew it was she who had the problem, not me. Yet however much I explained this to myself, I could never quite lose that feeling that I was a disappointment. It didn't matter how much I tried to quash it, her behaviour still triggered an acute anxiety and it crossed my mind, briefly, to tell her the real reasons I was going away for six months. Yet I wanted more than anything to put it all behind me. From now on, I would be focussed on my career. Any thoughts I'd had of a life with a man I could love, with my own family, had been obliterated. If people were prepared to behave the way my sister and David had, I would be better off alone.

* * *

I'd settled into my new role in Tuscany very well. The owners were very impressed with my work ethic, and although I'd always given my all to any task, my determination to keep my mind occupied had driven me on, so that I worked far more hours than my contract stated and focussed on making a success of the hotel. It was a fantastic learning curve for me as well as diverting my mind from the pain of the previous few months.

On my rare days off, I would either swim lengths in the pool or ride Chichi, the young horse that the owners, Angelo and Sophia owned. Chichi and I spent many hours gently exploring the area and he heard my story and felt my tears on his mane again and again.

I had just finished grooming him one day and was hauling his saddle back onto the rack when Sophia handed me a letter with an English stamp.

'Here, Julia, a letter from home. Your family I think, yes? You must miss them very much.'

I didn't reply. I just smiled and took the envelope.

Later that evening, after a dinner of pasta and tomato sauce, I went to my bedroom and opened the letter.

Dear Julia,

I hardly know how to begin this letter, and will hope and pray that you find enough forgiveness in your heart to read it through, and not tear it into pieces and consign it to the bin.

I have been so upset. I am an absolute wreck–John keeps commenting on it and I have had to make out that I have caught a virus, so that it explains my red eyes and the fact that I've hardly eaten a thing. It has also meant that I can spend most of the time in bed and not answer his questions.

I am so so so so sorry for what David and I did. I know you won't want to hear details but I do want to assure you that it only happened that once. When you came into the room, so did our senses and we both immediately realised what a terrible thing we had done. It was very selfish of us both. I love John very much as you know, and I am also well aware that David loves you.

It was lust Julia, pure and simple. One of those things. I know that you are much, much more attractive than me and so when David showed a little interest, I felt very flattered. When we found ourselves alone that day, a little harmless flirting got completely out of hand and I can assure you it was never meant to lead to the two of us sleeping together. Something took over– it was like being possessed – and I behaved completely out of character. I do think that David can be manipulative though, and I think that is something you should perhaps be wary of.

So, I am asking, as your sister who loves you, to please try to find a way to forgive me. I know it was a terrible shock for you and I don't know if you and David will continue your relationship but whatever you decide to do, I hope you and I can mend.

I don't really know what else to say. I have no idea how long you intend to remain in Italy but whenever you come back, I hope we can meet up and put this in the past.

When you feel ready, please write or telephone so that I know I can move forward without this horrible weight of guilt bearing down on me.

With my everlasting love,
Your sister,
Diana

PS. I understand that you might hate me and that there is a chance you may never wish to speak to me again. I wouldn't blame you, although I sincerely hope that is not the case. However, I would beg you not to breathe a word of this to anyone else. Especially John. This is not me simply trying to protect my marriage; I just don't think John deserves to be hurt because of this, as it really is none of his fault. I will do what I can to be the perfect wife to him from now on, but if he found out about my mistake, it would cut him deeply.

CHAPTER TWELVE

Maddy

There was supposed to be some thrill, some enjoyment in an illicit affair. But watching a man beat himself up on a daily basis plus living in a hovel and not having any proper contact with Max had not been part of my plan.

I wasn't sure how I'd got to this point. Amanda would no doubt raise her eyebrows at my confusion but I truly didn't know.

Things started moving along and the fun wagon I was towing behind me broke free, lost control and crashed.

My brief affair turned into two broken marriages. The intensity and passion of sex with someone other than Max wore off extremely quickly. And the lifestyle I'd enjoyed until then was a thing of the past.

It seemed that Max, too, was a thing of the past.

When Paul left Tanya—or when she threw him out—I had nearly stayed on at Amanda's. I only moved in with Paul thinking it would make Max jealous, make him beg me to return. I wondered if Paul was playing the same game and hoped it might make Tanya realise what she was losing so that she would ask him to return.

But Max had been resolute. He refused to speak to me. Amanda told me one day that she believed a line had been crossed and he would never take me back. That suggestion hit harder than anything. I'd a notion in mind that it would all be fine, that Max would realise boredom had driven me to the affair.

All Paul kept going on about was that one day he'd stop feeling guilty about Tanya and Ryan and it would all sort itself out because he and I were 'so in love' and we'd be happy together for the rest of our lives. I hadn't banked on him being quite so naive.

I took one last look at the note on the formica table, picked up my holdall and left the flat without a backward glance.

Paul,
We've had an amazing time together. You will always be very special to me.

But I think deep down we both know that this is never going to work long term.

I think you would feel much better if you went back to your family. I know it will be difficult to persuade Tanya but I'm sure she would rather have you around, and would rather do the right thing by your son, so eventually it will all work out. I will be going back to Max. Please don't try to contact me.

Good luck for the future, and I'm sorry it had to end like this. You can keep all the stuff I bought for the flat.

Maddy xx.

CHAPTER THIRTEEN

Amanda

'Oh, for heaven's sake!'

Julia looked up as I walked into the kitchen, mouthed 'Sorry' and was shaking her head at me as she listened to the person on the other end of her phone call.

I'd been shopping all morning, having decided I needed a new identity for my home. Out with Dan's old boring landscapes hanging on the wall, and in with fur throws, cushions, abstract art and masses and masses of scented candles. I'd put my bags on the kitchen table and smiled as I peered in at my purchases. Then I heard Julia begin speaking again.

'Well of course I don't condone violence. Punching somebody's lights out is not the right thing to do but you have to have a bit of compassion. As you say, it was out of character.'

Trust Julia to be back in the village for five minutes and get the local gossip before any of us did. She'd escaped to mine for some peace and quiet while I'd gone into town but that clearly hadn't worked.

'What? What's happening?' I asked in a stage whisper.

Julia held up a forefinger to stall me and interrupted the flow of chatter I could hear from the phone.

'Ok, Sarah. Sarah, I'm going to have to go now, someone is waiting for me,' she winked at me 'so we'll catch up later in the week. Yes, I promise. Speak soon lovely, yes bye, bye.'

'Well, that sounded juicy. What's that all about?'

'Not juicy no, just not good.' Julia frowned and shook her head. 'That Paul, the chap Maddy was messing around with, punched some man in the pub last night.'

'Really? Wow, he didn't sound like he was the sort to do something like that.'

'Apparently, Simon someone-or-other was commiserating with Paul over being dumped and tried to cheer him up by telling him that Maddy was a bit too free with her favours anyway and that he, Simon that is, had had sex with her in the back of her car a few years back.'

'What? That's not right, surely?' I sat up straight in my chair. 'I'm pretty sure if Maddy had had an affair before Paul she would have told me. I'm guessing it was Simon Finch. He's a bit of a ladies' man. I have to say, he does have charm but I still can't believe Maddy had an affair with him.'

'Not an affair,' said Julia, slightly exasperated. 'Just a one-off thing. After some fireworks party. Despite everything, you still want to see the best in her, don't you? Wake up Amanda. She manipulates everyone that girl, including you.'

She had a point. When Maddy had moved in with Paul, I told myself I'd not have much to do with her. I'd see her at Mum's or out and about, but I was going to detach myself.

But back she came to live with me again, getting in the way, having a giant Maddy pity party just because Max wouldn't take her back. It made me very uncomfortable, putting a roof over her head when actually all my sympathies lay with Max.

'Do you think Maddy knows?'

'If she doesn't yet, she'll soon hear about it from someone. You know what it's like around here. Sounds like Paul is in a bit of a state. Sarah said he's lost some of his gardening contracts since the whole affair became public knowledge and he has debts because of the flat they rented. Sarah said he was only in the pub last night because he'd borrowed money from his brother so he could go and drown his sorrows.'

'That probably explains him losing his rag, I guess. Just one thing after another.'

'Exactly. All because he met your sister and got a twitch in his trousers,' she said. 'And his wife is giving him such a hard time, making it difficult for him to see the baby. And she's divorcing him.'

I puffed out my cheeks.

'What a mess.'

'Yep,' said Julia. 'Another fine mess Maddy has got someone into.'

***

I lost count of the people, the books, the blogs, the 'personal growth' gurus who screamed at me every day to just move on.

As if I were simply a commuter on a train. *Move along the carriage now, there's a good girl. The buffet car is at the end and don't get off at the wrong stop will you, or you may find there are no more trains and you'll be stranded, alone, for eternity.*

I thought that within a few months I would surely be yesterday's news, but people hadn't forgotten. In fact, there were a few who still seemed to enjoy picking over the bones a bit too much. Most people had their own lives to get on with. They did their best, checking up on me, asking me over for dinner with a mix of other people, but it seemed to me as if everyone else was slicing through the water, while I was just bobbing around like a piece of flotsam, with no sense of purpose or direction.

Eve called.

'Hi gorgeous, what've you been up to?'

'Nothing much. Just trying to find some work.'

She asked what I was doing at the weekend. 'We're having a cheese and wine thing Saturday night,' she said. 'Yes, and I know, before you say it, that sounds a bit posh for us. But we've got about fifteen people coming so it should be a laugh, you know, a bit lively.'

'I think I'm free then.' Of course I was free Saturday night. I was free every Saturday night.

So I went along, heart sinking as I walked up the drive and rang the bell. It was the thought of being asked where my other half was. It had happened on each of the few occasions I'd braved a social function and I had started to feel quite militant about it. I wanted to lecture people on how rude it was to assume that a woman of a certain age couldn't possibly be single, or if she was, she shouldn't be allowed out.

I could hear Eve chattering away as I pushed open the latched front door. Her house was always slightly chaotic, with shoes and bags strewn around the hall. Too much stuff was crammed onto the old mahogany telephone table that had been inherited from some forgotten relative decades ago.

It was early autumn and there was a slight chill in the evenings. The lights in the kitchen looked welcoming and as usual Eve had scented candles everywhere but the aroma of the strong cheeses overpowered them tonight.

'Everyone, this is my lovely and bestest buddy, Amanda.'

All faces turned towards me but it wasn't daunting. They were all friendly, open faces who simply smiled, nodded and went back to their own conversations. For once, I didn't feel like an exhibit and was surprisingly relaxed.

'How's the job hunting going?' asked Eve as she poured a glass of wine.

'Oh, you know, a few irons in the fire but nothing yet.' I didn't want Eve fussing and trying to organise my life, didn't want to tell her that the tiny handful of applications had not even yielded a 'no thank you,' not a single response. I'd so wanted to have the possibility of some kind of work, if only because it would then put paid to Julia's idea that I go off the The Bahamas. She'd kept mentioning it and seemed to be getting more infuriated with me every time I tried to dodge the subject.

'Something'll come along love,' Eve said, handing over the glass before beckoning Marco over, who was the other side of the table talking to a tall, slender man.

'Hello, my lovely,' said Marco, giving me a hug and kissing my cheek.

'Hi Marco, how is the wonderful world of Collard Books?'

Marco had bought an old shop in the high street eight years ago with the redundancy package he'd got from his telecoms company. He loved books and announced that it would be not just be a bookshop, but they would sell coffee and cakes, and there would be squidgy sofas and local artists would have their works on the wall for people to buy.

Eve had told him in no uncertain terms that he was an absolute fool to even think of it.

'Don't be an arse. Nobody goes into bookshops anymore, not in this village anyway. Most of them probably can't bloody read!', she'd said, only half joking.

But Marco had been undeterred and spent hours and hours in the shop, getting it into shape. After six months, it became so popular that he took on casual staff and extended the shop out the back. He never said to Eve 'told you so' and she never apologised for doubting him. But it was one of the things about their relationship that I admired the most. They could disagree and roll their eyes at each other but still be the most loving, loyal couple.

'Collard books is very good, thank you for asking,' said Marco. 'Summer was quiet, it always is but we have a deal with some local schools for educational books so that's helped. In fact, it's all picking up so well I decided to get another full-time member of staff'

Out of the corner of her eye, I picked up on Eve nudging Marco's elbow. This obviously didn't register, so she very quietly said to him, 'Go on then,' He turned to look at her and as the penny dropped, suddenly said, 'Oh. Oh yes. Right.'

I held my breath. They were going to offer me a job, I thought. Marco would probably drive me mad because he can be a bit of an old woman, but yes, I could do this!

'So,' said Marco, clearing his throat. 'So obviously I needed someone with experience in the bookshop business and put an ad in the trade press. Had quite a few applicants but then finally found the right person. His name is Nigel. Come and meet him.'

For just a moment, I'd felt the breeze fill my sails. Now though, I was abruptly reminded of my actual driftwood status. But it gave me some clarity about my future.

Marco took me by the hand and led me over to the tall guy.

'Amanda, this is Nigel, Nigel, our lovely friend Amanda.'

Nigel smiled. He was a pleasant enough looking man, clean, well dressed and in good shape. I glanced at his left hand as I took a swig of wine and noticed that there was no wedding ring.

I knew at once what Eve and Marco were up to and as I looked around to speak, I realised Marco had already moved away to chat to someone else.

Nigel could make conversation so it wasn't completely awkward. But I sensed he was in on something that I had not been aware of, not been consulted about.

Whenever I mentioned one of my interests or places I'd visited, he'd say, 'me too!' with such obvious delight that he clearly took this as a sign that we were a great match.

And worryingly, I couldn't help but think how he actually ticked lots of boxes. He was intelligent, interesting, well-travelled and had quite a classically handsome face. So why did I so desperately want to wrap up this conversation and get away as fast as possible? However well suited we may have been on paper, it was also proof that there was another element to attraction, something that couldn't easily be defined. That sense of connection, of feeling you already knew each other, was blatantly absent.

As he gave a detailed account of his time spent in Sri Lanka helping underprivileged children, my mind drifted off.

After twenty minutes my mobile rang.

'My sister,' I said to Nigel. 'I really should take it.' Moving to the hall I instantly felt relief at being away from the situation. Passing Eve on the way through, I flashed my sternest look and under my breath, said, 'Thanks a bunch.'

'Too soon?' she asked, eyebrows raised, trying to look innocent.

Turning my back, I moved a pile of magazines off the bottom stair, sat down and answered the call.

'Maddy,' I said, laughing slightly. 'You're timing is perfect, well done, I was just…'

Then an awful sound came from the phone. A sound like an animal in torment.

'What on earth? Maddy, what's happened?'

'It's Paul,' she managed to say between sobs. 'Paul. He's dead. And it's all my fault.'

* * *

I had a couple of sleeping tablets left over from after Dan left, and when the hysteria stopped, I gave one to Maddy and ordered her to bed.

I'd arrived home to find her curled up in a chair, gasping between sobs, her face screwed up and wet with tears. She looked like a child. She kept repeating, 'He killed himself, he killed himself. My fault. He killed himself.'

I held her and rocked her back and forth and when she calmed down, I'd persuaded her to shower and have some hot chocolate. Now she sat at the other end of the sofa wrapped in an oversized towelling robe.

'I just can't—I can't believe he would, oh God.' She started gently sobbing again.

'Maybe we shouldn't talk about it tonight. Take the sleeping tablet. The best thing you can do is get some sleep.'

'No, not yet. I just need to tell someone. I need it all not locked inside.' She picked up her mug and blew across the surface of the steaming liquid. 'Karen Butterman phoned me. I didn't even know who she was at first but then I remembered she's Tanya's Mum. God knows where she got my number from.'

'So she was the one who told you about Paul? Did she say how…?'

'It was awful, so horrible.' Maddy took a long, juddery breath. 'She was shouting at me. At first, I thought she had just randomly called me to have a go about me having an affair with her son in law. She sounded so weird, I thought she was drunk. She was so abusive. I thought I could shout and swear when I lost it but she was just out of control.'

'Poor you. It must have been awful'.

'Then she starts telling me that Paul's body was…' She screwed her eyes shut and covered her mouth with her hand. She took a couple of moments to steady herself, then continued.

'His body was found in the woods. Empty bottle of whiskey by his side. Lots of blood.' She had to stop again.

It was unbelievable. It seemed shocking to think of someone being so rock bottom, feeling so hopeless, that they wouldn't even want to go on living.

'So of course,' Maddy said, taking a tissue out of her robe pocket 'It's completely my fault.'

'You know that's not true,' I said. 'He must have been very fragile. From what I hear, he was struggling financially and his wife was being incredibly difficult about him seeing the baby.' I looked down at my hands, not wanting to make eye contact with her. 'I think some people were winding him up too, and it sounds like he'd been drinking a lot lately. If he wasn't used to it…'

Maddy was lost in her own thoughts, her own processing of the shock she was feeling.

'But most of those things wouldn't have happened to him if he hadn't met me. He wasn't exactly loaded but before he took on the flat, he was okay. And Tanya being like that to him is because she's jealous. A woman scorned and all that. And on top of everything else, when I walked out he'd lost the love of his life.'

'Still, it wasn't your fault. It was his choice.'

'Everyone will blame me. Everyone. I know what they all think around here. Spoilt, selfish Maddy. Lovely kind sweet Tanya, nice man Paul, lovely little family unit, torn apart by that posh bitch. Maybe they're right.'

Maddy finished her hot chocolate and stood, rolling her head from side to side to relive the tension.

'I think I will have that sleeping pill now,' she said.

She went up to bed and I promised to let her sleep in the following morning. Of course, she needed to rest up having had such a terrible shock, but there was another reason for my being glad to have her ensconced in the spare room and away from me for a while.

I certainly didn't want her looking over my shoulder as I booked my flights and started listing all the things I would need to do before my trip to The Bahamas.

CHAPTER FOURTEEN

Maddy

The moment he walked into Amanda's kitchen, I knew, one hundred percent, that I would be sleeping in my own bed with Max next to me that night.

There's a connection between us so strong and no matter how much hell I've put him through, Max feels it as much as I do.

And for all my moaning, for all my acting like a spoilt brat, seeing his face and the gentleness in his eyes completely melted my heart. A sense of relief flooded through me and I relaxed for the first time since Paul's suicide. I know people think I don't deserve Max. Amanda and Julia definitely think he is an absolute saint ever to have put up with me. The thing is, they're probably right.

Amanda had shown him in and left us to it. I was sitting on the little two-seater sofa by the French doors and he came and sat next to me. It was all I could do to stop myself jumping onto his lap like some kind of small dog, desperately wanting to be stroked and reassured.

'I had to come and see you. I had to know how you're coping.'

'I'm so pleased you're here, Max.' I reached out a hand and, thank God, he took it in his own and squeezed it reassuringly. 'I can't find the words to explain how this has made me feel. The overwhelming sense of guilt, guilt for playing a part in someone ending their life. Guilty about you, about the pain I've caused.'

Max was staring down at our entwined hands. I didn't think he was going to say anything for a while. I understood that this was a defining moment in our lives. Whatever he said over the next few minutes would be key to my future. I held my breath.

'I've struggled so much with this,' he said. 'You know that what you did caused me such suffering, suffering I don't quite think you appreciate. You have a different outlook on life to me. You have this force field around you. I doubt you *feel* in quite the same way as the rest of us.'

I opened my mouth to suggest otherwise, but Max continued.

'I don't mean to be harsh. In some ways I envy you and I'm not blaming you for it. I'm well aware how much you were smothered as a child by Diana and still are in fact. But I need you to understand that I'm not as impervious to pain as you are. This whole affair really crucified me Madeleine.'

I too stared at our entwined hands. A lump formed in my throat. Max was in the driving seat of this conversation and I was just not used to being so helpless.

'I've thought a lot about this man and his family, the devastation this whole incident has caused. You mustn't blame yourself, you know. But you should learn something from it. You should learn that there can be dire consequences to your actions. But you didn't force him into having an affair with you and you didn't take his life away from him. Those were his decisions. It's incredibly sad. I can't stop thinking about what must have been going through his mind.'

'Max, it sort of is my fault. I'm partly responsible.' I had to blink. Tears were welling up and I didn't want them to fall, didn't want him to think this was an attempt at garnering his sympathy. 'And no, I didn't force him into anything. We all have free will. He made choices but unfortunately they were bad choices and the worst one of all was getting involved with me.'

We talked for hours, and Max even listened to my paltry excuses as to what had driven me to have an affair. I apologised again and again and I meant every word. Being bored, being tempted and wanting fun and excitement was absolutely no excuse for my behaviour. Max told me that our future was not guaranteed, that we would both need to work hard if we stood any chance of recovering.

'Go and get your stuff together,' he said. 'Let's go home.'

CHAPTER FIFTEEN

Amanda

I'd braced myself for a bad reaction from Mum and Maddy and I wasn't disappointed.

Knowing that the conversation might spiral out of control, I decided to reveal my plans to visit The Bahamas to them in a public place. Neither of them would get too animated in front of strangers. Mum's tendency to cast herself in the role of some kind of Lady Bountiful of the area would preclude any loud or aggressive behaviour. One should not display bad manners in front of the peasants.

I suggested we have a girls' shopping trip in Tanford as Maddy has been wanting to buy some new clothes from the autumn and winter ranges and Mum was after a new coat. After our shopping expedition, we planned to stop for lunch at The Brazen Lobster. We'd visit the little boutiques along the high street and then head down to the quayside restaurant for a couple of drinks and something to eat.

I was trying to figure out how to lever in the subject when as luck would have it, as we were all finishing our first glass of wine, Maddy began detailing how her friend Lucie was holidaying in Jamaica.

'I can't believe I haven't had a decent holiday since Max and I went to Greece in April,' she complained. 'Lucie's putting photos of herself on the beach every bloody day; it's driving me nuts. I have to tread very softly with Max at the moment, of course, but I quite fancy the Caribbean myself.'

'Poor thing,' said Mum to Maddy, followed by a little 'hmm' sound and a shake of the head.

We were interrupted by the arrival of our salads. I had been tempted by the battered cod and chips but since I'd decided to act on Julia's suggestion about going away, I'd thought that getting into shape had to be a priority and I'd already lost ten pounds. Just another four to go and I'd be down to my ideal, healthy weight.

When the waitress had moved away, Maddy continued.

'Obviously, the whole Paul affair has knocked me for six. I know Max is concerned about me, so I really hope he realises how badly I need to get away from here.'

'I'm sure he will take you away soon darling, you deserve a break.'

It never ceases to amaze me that despite Maddy's privileged life, Mum always has sympathy for her. Now she appeared desperately concerned that her darling girl hadn't dangled her delicate little tootsies into a hotel pool for a few months.

'Talking of holidays, I've decided to take a trip to the sun myself.' I looked across the table at them both, Mum sitting up straight to look at me as if I were a scientific specimen, Maddy stabbing a piece of chicken with her fork, one eyebrow raised. 'Yes, I think I need to get away, put a line under what's happened and take some time to relax and make decisions about my future.'

'Well, where are you going to go at this time of year to get some sun? Nowhere in Europe is going to be very warm now. So where? The Canaries?' Maddy popped the chicken into her mouth and looked at me with the challenge in her eyes that I knew of old. She wouldn't want or expect me to go anywhere too exotic, no locations that may be more exciting than a holiday she might take. And normally she would be right. For years now, Dan and I had arranged holidays so that they didn't coincide with term time. It was also easier with Sammy and Ben to stick to flights of only a few hours so we'd generally taken one foreign holiday a year, to France, Spain, Italy or Corfu.

'Actually, I am pretty much guaranteed sunshine.' I hesitated, knowing I was on the cusp of causing not only a sense of outrage, but for Mum at least, some real emotional pain. 'I've booked to go to The Bahamas.'

Time seemed to stop for a moment. They both looked at me as if I had spoken to them in a completely foreign language, as if I had said something so alien that they couldn't even try to decipher it.

I looked from one to the other but their faces didn't change. I could only imagine that they thought either that they had misheard me or perhaps that I was going to a hotel on one of the islands and would be staying there without any communication with the Saxbys.

I had no choice but to plough on.

'I'm going in ten days' time and I'm staying for a whole month.'

At this, Maddy put her knife and fork down and her expression darkened. Mum looked at me uncomprehendingly. Maddy looked like she had figured out that this was no quick break in an all-inclusive and that there could only be one reason, and one way, that I could go for so long.

'So are you saying what I think you're saying?' asked Maddy, pushing her plate away and folding her arms in front of her.

Mum swivelled her head to look at Maddy and then straight back to me and as the truth dawned on her, too. 'Amanda! Surely you're not suggesting that you would even consider going to visit the Saxbys are you?'

Maddy rolled her eyes. 'She's not considering it Mum. She's booked it. She's just done the most selfish, hurtful thing she possibly could.' She shook her head and gazed out of the window as if looking at me was making her sick.

'Oh Amanda,' Mum said, pushing her plate away too. 'Why on earth would you want to do that? I can understand that you want a little holiday but there are lots of places you could go. I can't fathom why you would want to stay so long with people you've never even met, quite apart from the hurt this is going to cause me and the disregard you seem to have for your father's memory.'

Maddy looked back at me and leaned across the table to drive her comments home. 'Yes, exactly, why do you want to do something so utterly heartless? If you want to be on an island, go to the Isle of bloody Wight or something.' She sat back in her chair and resumed her study of the street outside the window, where fallen leaves were blowing around in a mini whirlwind.

'Yes, there are lots of places you could go,' said Mum, brightening at the idea that I might be persuaded to play safe and have a package holiday for a week and be satisfied with that. 'Devon is lovely at any time of year, or if you did want it a little warmer, perhaps Portugal would be nice. In any case, how are you going to persuade the school to let you take Ben out for a whole month? It would be very disruptive to his education. Honestly, you really haven't thought this through.'

I too gave up on my salad, but I did take another sip of wine before continuing.

'I'm not taking Ben with me. He's staying here and Julia is going to move in and take care of him while I'm away.'

'Ha!' exclaimed Maddy. 'I should have bloody known Julia would be behind this. She persuaded you, did she? Told you to just go over there, meet that lot and to hell with what it might do to your real family. Well that just about sums her up doesn't it? She really is a selfish cow. I've never liked her. I wouldn't trust her as far as I could throw her. No wonder she never married. I mean what man would want to be stuck with *that*.'

'Julia didn't persuade me. It wasn't like that. She just pointed out that the opportunity was there and left me to make my own mind up.'

Maddy's verbal assault on Julia had bolstered me. It made me more determined not to be manipulated or tow-the-line just because either she or Mum had decided what I should do or where I should go. Enough was enough. This was uncomfortable and I was cringing inside but it had to be done. I had to stand my ground.

'We could talk for hours about the rights and wrongs of the other family and about things that happened years ago. It didn't even happen in our lifetimes, Maddy. Max will take you away on holiday, I'm sure, but I don't have the luxury of a husband who will whisk me off to somewhere wonderful. I know life has been difficult for you this year but the upshot is, nothing has really changed for you, has it?'

'Amanda, honestly! Maddy's life has been very badly affected by what's happened to her,' said Mum, in a breathy stage whisper. 'I don't know why you're trying to put your sister down. This discussion is about you and your behaviour.'

I saw the familiar smug look on Maddy's face, the satisfaction gained by having Mum pander to her.

'Look, I don't want to fall out with either of you over this. Yes, of course I'm staying with the Saxbys. I couldn't possibly afford to go for so long without that and frankly now that I've made the decision to go, I've realised how badly I need a proper break, not just a week or two in an anonymous hotel.'

The waitress nervously approached us. 'Everything OK?' She'd clearly seen three faces looking like thunder and three plates of food barely touched. The poor girl must have been waiting for a barrage of complaints.

'It's fine thanks, we're just not that hungry.' I smiled reassuringly at her. 'The salad was lovely though and the wine was very nice.' She looked relieved but cleared the plates and moved away from our table as quickly as she could.

'Amanda, I do understand that you need this and I don't want to fall out with you either. But I'm not going to pretend to be happy about it. My position regarding the other family hasn't changed so be under no illusion that what you are doing is hurtful and seems very disloyal not just to me, but to your father's memory.'

'Exactly,' said Maddy.

'And I'm unhappy that Julia suggested this to you, but not entirely surprised. She's never been one for family loyalty.' Strangely, Mum blushed when she said this. I wondered, not for the first time, what skeletons rattled when she thought of Julia and family. 'I don't think I really want to hear any more about it, unless, of course, you come to your senses and change your mind. But if you do insist on going, at least keep our family business private. Don't let them know what we do or what we have or anything.'

I smiled to myself at the thought of being interrogated by the Bahamian side of the family, at them being desperate to know what Maddy watches on television and how many cut glass decanters Mum had hidden in the sideboard.

'Don't worry, Mum, I won't. I just need to get some sunshine, some salt water and a complete change of scene. Everyone's been great. I'm lucky to have good friends, and family, of course. But I don't think my head will clear until I put some miles between myself and what's happened.'

Mum said nothing more. Maddy gave me a final withering look and said, 'We'll get the bill, shall we?' and that was the end of the conversation. It was stalemate as I expected, yet I felt euphoric that I'd managed to handle the conversation without once faltering, without allowing them to even begin to grind me down.

I was beginning to feel like the old me again.

* * *

The next few days were quite manic. Although I'd always booked and organised our family holidays in the past without any help, it was still a bit daunting to think I'd be flying alone, and that I'd be staying for four weeks with a whole bunch of people I'd never met before. There were a few moments when I lay awake at night stressing about it all and I did begin to wonder if I'd lost my mind.

Mostly though, the prospect was hugely exciting.

Despite Julia's insistence that she'd only met Robin Saxby briefly, she did seem to know a lot about the family and the business. Plus, she was almost gushing in her praise of Robin, insisting that she was absolutely positive that he would be the most charming, attentive host, and that his sister and his daughters all sounded 'divine' too.

Two days before my departure, Eve called round to help me pack.

'You sure you've got enough clothes?' she asked. I began to reassure her before I realised she was being sarcastic.

'I am going for a month, you know,' I laughed. 'I intend to spend as much time as I can on the beach so…' I reached over to one of the many piles of items on my bed and began to count the swimsuit and bikini pile '…six, seven, eight! Eight bikinis, a tankini and two full swimsuits. Then over there, we have four sundresses, three wraps, two pairs of flip flops, six pairs of shorts and ten T shirts. I haven't even got to bras and knickers yet. I'll sort the rest out later.'

Eve laughed and pulled me to her in a hug. 'This is the best thing you could have done you know, mate. I'm just so proud of you. When you first told me your idea, I'll be honest, I thought it would never happen, not once your Mum and your sister got their claws into you. And, let's face it, you're not always the most confident, dynamic sort are you?'

'Oh, thanks a bunch. Didn't realise I was quite so boring.' I made my comment sound lighthearted but it stung that Eve would think that of me. It was one thing to face up to your own shortcomings but to know that others saw them as clearly and your cover as *confident woman who knows what she wants and how to get it* had fallen flat, well that hurt.

Eventually, everything was done. My cases had been packed,

unpacked, rearranged several times, packed again and now had their padlocks on. Julia had surprised me with a beautiful soft leather shoulder bag, ideal for taking on the plane and now containing my phone, passport, printed tickets just-in-case, hand sanitiser, mints, a book, tissues and many other bits and pieces I'd decided I may need on both flights to the island.

I was ready. I felt like I was about to jump off a tall building, but I was ready.

CHAPTER SIXTEEN

Amanda

My flight from Heathrow seemed to go on forever and knowing I had to spend the night in an airport hotel before the next leg of the journey was so frustrating. I just wanted to be there.

There were only eleven other passengers on the little plane that I'd boarded in Miami to make the brief hop over to the island. The journey had been bumpy and the creaks and groans that came from the aircraft had me closing my eyes and gripping the armrests more than once. Yet by some miracle, we landed in one piece. In less than ten minutes, I was in the small airport building, through passport control and had already collected my luggage from the tarmac, where it had been unceremoniously dumped just moments after landing.

I was in The Bahamas. I could hardly believe it.

I saw, across the road, a lime green taxi just as Robin's email had described. The driver got out as soon as he saw me and ambled over, all six foot three of him. He thrust out a hand.

'I'm Thomas. You must be Amanda,' he said, shaking my hand vigorously, a wide and cheery smile spreading across his face.

No wonder he was smiling. This place had an aura about it. I could tell already. Even on the roadside of the airfield, there was calmness in the air and a heat that relaxed your very bones.

Thomas lifted my bags into the boot and we set off. Our windows were open so that I caught the scent of bougainvillea and the less appealing aroma of fish drying out on racks as we drove. Thomas had the radio on and told me it was his music, the music of the Islands. It was joyous. If I hadn't been sitting down, I would have danced.

In twenty minutes, we turned off the main road and onto a smaller but perfectly Tarmaced road that wound down to the water's edge. We passed under a huge metal arch which bore the words 'Saxby Marine'. Thomas dropped me off outside a suite of offices and I was greeted by a serene, smiling woman who welcomed me and led me through the modern building with its vast glass panels. We reached a light oak door with the words Robin Saxby engraved on it. I had arrived. It felt momentous. It felt like a beginning.

* * *

Robin Saxby was the sort of man who filled a room the

moment he walked through the door. He was tall and lean so it made him appear quite the giant.

There wasn't a booming voice though. If anything, Robin was quietly spoken, with a slight drawl to his words so that he sounded as if he'd just got out of bed.

He filled the room because he had that easy, self-assured manner that some men try to affect, but which so often brims over into arrogance. Not with Robin, though. Even if I hadn't known his background, I would have been able to tell instantly that this was a man of means who had spent his life assuming everything would go his way. And it probably had.

'Amanda, we are so pleased to have you with us. It's been way too long coming, but here you are.' He smiled generously and held his arms wide open as he approached me, giving me the sort of bear hug that would usually come from a very close friend. Yet it didn't feel as if he was crossing a line; it just made me even more certain that I'd done the right thing by making the trip.

'Thank you for having me here,' I said, sounding like a typical uptight English woman. 'I can't quite believe that I've waited so long to do this.'

Robin finally released me and gestured for me to sit back down on the huge leather sofa that was positioned to look through the wide glass doors and out to the ocean beyond.

Robin's elderly office assistant came into the room, concentrating on carrying a tray of iced tea which she placed on the table.

'Thank you, lovely lady,' Robin said to Emily with a smile

and a wink. Emily smiled back and walked out of the room with a little extra spring in her step.

'So,' said Robin, leaning back and taking a sip of tea. 'I hear there's been some trouble over in England. Julia says your schmuck of a husband has misbehaved. Must have been tough to handle. You did the right thing coming over here. You'll have a fabulous time and when you go back, he'll wish he'd kept it in his pants.'

I couldn't help a small giggle escaping, although I don't think he was trying to make me laugh. It was just his direct way of speaking that I wasn't used to but found so refreshing.

'Well, yes, it's not been a whole lot of fun to be honest but I'm trying to be positive and see it as a new opportunity. Just being here in the sunshine and feeling relaxed already is doing me the world of good.'

'This is the beginning of your new life,' said Robin with a big grin, sitting up and slapping his knee with his free hand. 'But tell me, Diana has a standing invitation to come over here. Every Christmas we send her a card and I've said I'll get my assistant to sort all the travel arrangements out and pay for everything but all I ever get back is a Christmas card with *Regards, Diana* on it. Why do you think that is?'

I felt myself tense up and straightened my back. 'I think it's out of respect to my father. It would have been very difficult when William ran off to the States with Christine. We know of course, it's not your fault, or Jane's or the children's of course, but…' I held my hand up subconsciously trying to halt any protest before a surprised looking Robin could say anything, '…you must see that there would have been some animosity from my father and those who love him towards William and his mistress.'

Robin placed his tea-cup back down onto the tray as I picked mine up and took my first sip. My heart was pounding slightly. I wasn't used to saying what was on my mind and it both terrified and exhilarated me. I wasn't quite sure where that came from.

'Oh, I see.' Robin sat upright with his hands together between his knees, nodding his head as if he'd heard it for the first time. He seemed surprised and I didn't want that to morph into anger.

'I'm so sorry Robin. I didn't mean to be rude. Really, there's no bad feeling from me and I think Mum only keeps you all at arms' length out of respect for Dad. And it's just because of when it happened. Let's face it, that sort of thing happens all the time now. I should know.'

I sneaked a glance at Robin and he looked puzzled rather than angry. He looked as though he was going to say something, but seemed to change his mind. Instead, he looked me in the eye and smiled.

'No need to apologise. Hey, why don't we go down to the marina? Cyndi and Rachel went over to Miami to pick up a yacht first thing and are due back any time now. I'd love you to meet them. They're great girls and I think you'll all hit it off extremely well.'

Normal service was resumed as Robin and I drove the

few minutes to the marina, this time in a beach buggy, which bumped along the track making us both laugh which seemed to egg him on to drive faster. It was such a relief. I had to say what I did but this whole speaking my mind business was not natural to me and I had a small knot of tension in the pit of my stomach.

Come to The Bahamas, get treated like a princess, welcomed with open arms and then insult them. Way to go Amanda.

* * *

Robin dropped me off, telling me that his daughter Rachel would arrive soon and that Thomas had taken my cases straight to her house. I was to stay with her, as her older sister Cyndi had just moved her boyfriend in, so Rachel had the most space. I was a little nervous, knowing that she was quite a bit younger than me and wondering if we'd get on. But meeting her was one of those times when you instantly click with someone. You don't need to get to know each other to understand that you will get on, that your values and your outlook on life are similar. That's how it was when I met Rachel Saxby. I knew we would be friends.

Her eyes sparkled as she took my hand.

'Welcome to The Bahamas, Amanda. I can't tell you how excited we all are to have a member of the British arm of the family over. It's taken so long to get one of you to come, but hey, you're here now.'

I couldn't stop smiling.

'My sister, Cyndi said she'll be along in a minute, so let's walk up and meet her on the way. She's just sorting out some problems with one of the moorings over on the East side of the marina. She runs that part of the business with our cousin, Brad.'

Rachel was a little bundle of energy, blonde and athletic with a beautiful smile and gentle eyes.

We walked along by the boatyard where repairs and servicing were carried out on the yachts that filled the harbour. They were all considerably bigger and more luxurious than the ones back home at Bernstone Point and the water was in complete contrast to what could be found in the mouth of the river Bern. The ocean was the most glorious shade of turquoise and the shimmer created as the sun speckled the surface of the water looked like a thousand diamonds.

'Thanks for letting me stay with you by the way,' I said. 'You're very brave!' Rachel looked at me and giggled.

'You know what, I've been so looking forward to it.' She linked an arm through mine. 'Everyone is going to want to spend time with you but we can have some great girlie trips out and really get to know each other.'

Her enthusiasm was so infectious. I'd wanted to get away and get my head straight but I hadn't envisaged being transported to such a different world, and meeting people whose outlook was so refreshing.

We left the boat yard area and began to make our way along the marina to meet up with Cyndi and Brad. All the people working around the marina, and the customers making their way to their yachts, laden down with supplies ready for their sailing trips, smiled as we passed. I was smiling so much my face was beginning to ache.

We eventually met Cyndi and Brad coming the other way. Cyndi was much taller than her little sister and had a classically beautiful face rather than the pretty, sweet appearance of Rachel. She was welcoming and friendly but already I knew I wouldn't be as likely to bond with her. Brad was an all-American boy, shaking my hand so vigorously I thought my shoulder would pop out of its socket.

After a brief chat, they both explained that they had to get back to the office to report on an issue with unpaid fees, so they left me with Rachel to make our way back to her house.

'I expect you'll want to freshen up and call home. You've done a lot of travelling the last couple of days and Dad says it might be better for us to stay in this evening so you can get an early night. And I can tell you about all the things we've got planned for you.' Rachel clapped her hands together as we reached the front of her modern villa. It was just a five minute walk from the marina.

I unpacked, had a shower and called Julia.

'Everything is absolutely fine darling. Ben's already gone to bed. It's eleven at night over here darling, you do know that, don't you?'

'Oh, yes, sorry. I did know but it's been so full on since I arrived that time's sort of run away with me.'

'So are you settling in? Have you met all the family yet?'

I told her I'd met Robin and his children and their cousin Brad.

'So, how is Robin? What did he have to say?'

'Oh, he's great. I really like him, he was so welcoming. I did put my foot in it a bit though, but he seemed not to worry. I just hope I didn't seem ungrateful.'

'Oh darling, whatever it was, I'm sure everything's fine. What did you say anyway?'

'It's just that he said something about Mum being embarrassed, about the whole family thing, and I sort of pointed out that our side of the family had nothing to be embarrassed about because after all, Ivy was the one married to William and he was the one who ran off and had an affair. I felt a bit bad after I said it. He'd been so nice, but I wanted to put the record straight. He just looked a bit confused, though. Anyway, he changed the subject after that, so hopefully there was no harm done.'

There were a few moments of silence from the other end of the line. I thought, perhaps, we'd been cut off.

'Julia?'

'I'm still here darling. But I think there is something you should know.'

* * *

I was absolutely right about Rachel.

We talked liked long lost best friends, opening up about

our lives and feeling the sort of comfortable closeness that usually takes years to develop. I went to sleep each night exhausted yet barely able to sleep with excitement.

Robin treated me to dinners out with various members of the family and Rachel and I went sailing in her twenty-eight foot yacht, *Little Miss Sunshine*.

'That's what Dad has always called me,' she said, her smile demonstrating exactly why she'd got the nickname.

I hadn't sailed for a good few years, but it soon came back to me and Rachel and I worked as a great team as we tacked along the shore line. The warm spray and the salty aroma made me smile and filled me with joy. I had no time to ponder the question of why on earth I'd allowed myself to become so inhibited by family, or by Dan, from doing the things that really made my heart sing.

I tried some stand-up paddle boarding too, but my balance was nowhere near as good as Rachel's. She taught Yoga in a studio at the marina and had no trouble at all. I fell into the water constantly, until hysterical laughter made me so weak that I could barely haul myself back on the board.

We sat by her pool one morning when she announced that she had a treat lined up.

'So hey, you know you said how there were things you wanted to do that Dan wouldn't? And you know you said one of those things was Scuba diving? Well, I've booked you on the Saxby Water Sport Centre Open Water Course. You can start tomorrow. That all right?'

I had to swallow back tears. I'd never felt so well looked after, so spoilt and so loved in a very, very long time. And now I had the chance to do something I had yearned to do for as long as I could remember.

Of course it was all right.

* * *

'Just remember to keep breathing. Slow and steady and never hold your breath.'

I was in the pool with Nick, my po-faced diving instructor. It was reassuring to know he took it all seriously but I had to wonder how much fun he'd be on an actual dive, looking at actual fish and stuff.

He showed me how to breathe through the regulator and we slowly descended into the water.

For the next twenty minutes we went through the basics of diving, so that I could feel comfortable with breathing underwater and understand what happens in the body when you descend. I couldn't help but feel it was a metaphor for how my life had been. Sink down into the depths and the very air you breathe will be crushed as the pressure increases. That sounded about right.

After the lesson Nick handed me some books to take away and study for the theory exam and suggested we go and get a drink and a bite to eat. I disappeared into the little wooden changing hut as Nick strode off toward the marina.

I couldn't believe I was finally going to learn to dive. I'd spent years feeling envious of friends who'd dived in the Caribbean and the Indian Ocean. Dan didn't want to learn to dive. Dan wasn't prepared to sit on shore or in a boat while I learnt, so I didn't do it.

I dried off, changed, then walked over to the little café to meet Nick and some of the other divers. I shook my head, giving myself a silent ticking off for all the things I'd never done, all the opportunities I'd passed on because of Dan.

The Wacky Wahoo Shack was a popular place, with little aluminium table and chair sets outside and a view over the smaller boats in the marina. There was always music playing and rum being consumed and lots of simple fish dishes being served. It was a favourite haunt of the yacht crews, the divers and the people who worked around the marina.

Nick was already sitting at a table flicking through a diving magazine. I still hadn't seen him smile. He looked up as I approached and said someone would be out to take my order soon.

On the table next to us was a much livelier bunch. A middle-aged man and a slightly younger woman who I took to be his wife were sharing a plate of chips and a shaggy haired Australian guy, with a surf dude look was talking animatedly about his morning dive, about the Manta rays that seemed to fly over his head. A young red head sat next to him, hanging on his every word and constantly flicking her hair back. She wore the tiniest blue bikini but I doubt the Australian had noticed; he was too enthralled by what he'd seen in the ocean that morning.

Nick looked up and followed the direction of my gaze.

'Oh, by the way, I'm sorry but I have to go to Miami tomorrow to source some new gear. The rest of your course is going to be led by Finn,' he said, nodding towards the Australian.

Finn stopped mid-sentence and looked over at me. He smiled and gave a brief nod and held my gaze long enough for me to feel embarrassed. He then had to turn his attention back to the redhead who was touching his arm and asking if 'those big fish were scary.' I liked the look of Finn. I suspected he'd be a whole lot more fun than Nick.

'Ah that's a shame, but never mind,' I said, trying to keep the relief out of my voice. 'As long as I get my course completed.'

I ordered myself the house speciality, a Wacky Wahoo n' Rice and stole another glance at Finn. He was looking at me again while the girl rambled on about being scared of sharks and would he protect her if they went diving and wow, wasn't he brave?

While she was mid-sentence he stood up, still smiling and walked over to where we sat.

'So Nick, this lady's the one you're handing over to me tomorrow is it? Finn Alexander,' he said, extending his hand.

'Yes, this is Amanda,' said Nick, not even looking up from his magazine. I shook Finn's hand.

'So, right, are you really called Finn? Or is that a joke?'

His smile dropped and he looked totally confused. He stood in front of me with his hands on his hips. 'What? What do you mean? I don't get it. Why would my name be a joke? What's odd about being called Finn?'

Now I really blushed. Yet again I'd managed to insult someone within minutes of meeting them. 'Oh, gosh I'm really sorry! No, you see I just meant, well, Finn it's like fin, isn't it?' I did a pathetic little wiggling movement with my hands to signify a fish. 'Like a fish? Fish have fins and I thought…'

Finn burst out laughing.

Oh no, why do I do this? I'm so slow sometimes. He put his hand on my shoulder, his warm and reassuring hand. He was still laughing as he spoke.

'You walked right into that one beautiful, right on in.' He hooked his foot around the nearest chair and dragged it over, thumping down onto the seat. 'I really am called Finn. It's on my birth certificate. I guess my Mother must have had a crystal ball. But don't worry you're not the first.' He chuckled some more and then sat back, legs apart and arms crossed in front of him. He wasn't especially big yet he somehow filled all the space in front of me. His eyes remained on me, a smile of amusement still on his lips.

'Well, Finn, it's good to know I'm not the first person you've met who's a complete dimwit.'

That set him off again. 'A *complete dimwit* eh?' He leant forward. 'That's so terribly British, what?' He was teasing me, imitating an upper-class British accent. I could see him close up now. It was difficult to guess his age. His face and body were very tanned and he had many laughter lines. His eyes twinkled. I don't think I'd ever seen a man with such twinkly eyes.

'I am terribly British,' I said, looking at him over the top of my sunglasses and giving him a wink.

'I'm Australian,' he replied.

'No kidding?' I raised an eyebrow. Two could play at this game.

Finn's smile spread wide again. 'I can see you're going to be a handful.' Then he added, in a quieter, cheeky voice, 'Hopefully.'

I didn't know how to respond to that, but I couldn't stop the smile spreading across my face. Luckily, one of the young waitresses appeared with my drink and Finn turned his attention to her, putting an arm around her waist and drawing her down for a kiss on the cheek.

'Hey Natalie, how are you today?' he asked.

That reminded me. It reminded me that men like that flirt with women all the time and I really shouldn't get carried away. Just because he called me beautiful. Just because his eyes twinkled and I was over the moon that he was going to take me diving for the rest of my course.

Natalie chatted to Finn about how it had been a busy morning and there were another three luxury yachts coming in later so the crews would probably all be down for a few drinks later that night.

I ran through scenarios in my head. Was she just a friend? Was she an ex who he was still on good terms with? (I bet Finn Alexander did that. I bet he kept in touch with all his exes.) Was she someone he had his eye on? Maybe he was madly in love with her?

I thought I needed to stop day dreaming.

Nick finished the last of his Cola and said goodbye, wished me well and headed off to the car park. By now, Natalie had gone to take some more orders from a couple of guys I recognised from the chandlery who had sat down with the red head, and Finn turned his attention back to me.

'So, you staying locally or are you in one of the bigger hotels from the other side of the island?'

'I'm just over there,' I said, pointing vaguely in the direction of Rachel's house. 'with family.'

'Ah, so you're a *Saxby*?'

'I am by birth, yes. But this is my first visit to the islands.'

'Wow, didn't realise that! What's kept you away all this time?' He looked genuinely surprised.

'It's a long story.'

Finn looked at his watch and jumped up suddenly.

'Oh heck, I've got a teaching session starting in ten minutes for the Nitrox course over at the classroom. I'd better get over there but I'm looking forward to seeing you tomorrow. Don't forget, eight-thirty outside the dive centre. Then you can tell me your long story about how you're related to the Saxbys.'

I smiled and looked away, not relishing the idea of getting into a discussion about family secrets and how my understanding of them had been wrong. Completely and utterly wrong.

* * *

Robin guided me into Maybelle's Brasserie for lunch. Everyone looked over at us and several people held their hands up in greeting.

'This'll get them talking,' Robin whispered into my ear. 'Everyone on this Island is desperate to see me get married again. Walking in here with a beautiful young woman on my arm will definitely give them something to get their teeth into.'

He seemed to find it very amusing.

We were shown to our table and Robin's eternally relaxed demeanour encouraged me to ask the question I'd been curious about since I arrived.

'So how come there isn't a current Mrs Saxby? I know Rachel has told me that you're still on very good terms with her Mum, but she also said she's moved on and remarried. What's stopped you?'

Robin thought for a moment, pulling a face as if no one had ever asked him this before. But I bet they had. He must be one of the most eligible bachelors anywhere.

'I guess I just haven't met someone who ticks all the boxes. Not someone who'd be able to commit to me anyway. Besides, as you know, I'm pretty busy with the Marina so I sure don't have any time to feel lonely.' The warm smile returned. 'Anyhow, keeping everyone guessing by taking women out every so often is much more fun.'

I couldn't imagine Robin would ever be short of a date. With that amount of charm, I supposed there must be women just praying for the phone to ring and to hear his drawl, and a casual invite to dinner.

We ordered our food and I decided to broach the subject that had been playing on my mind since my discussion with Julia. I'd been in The Bahamas a few days and I felt I'd got to know Robin well enough now to talk about the long distant past without feeling awkward. Besides, I owed him an apology.

'You remember when I first arrived on the Island, that very first day?'

Robin nodded. 'Well, I now know some family history that I wasn't aware of then. And I think I must have seemed very rude, and ungrateful.'

Robin smiled and nodded again, slowly. He seemed to know what was coming. 'I spoke to Julia the night I arrived and she put me straight. I wish she'd told me years ago to be honest but she said it wasn't her place. It seems that my Granny Ivy lied.'

The aroma of baked crab made us both stop and look over to the kitchen. Sure enough, the door swung open and Jayden, Thomas's son, gave us his wide smile and glided over with the tray of our lunch and our bottled water. Robin had a quick chat with him, laughing at how organised his Mum, Robin's

Vice President, Jasmine, was, and Jayden laughed that she was even worse at home.

When we were on our own again, Robin smiled and shook his head. 'Yeah, I was a little surprised. I kind of assumed Julia had told you, and Diana. But hey, don't worry. It's all ancient history and honestly, so long as you're here, that's all that matters. Absolutely no need to apologise.'

I took a sip of sparkling water, grateful for the chance to cool down in the midday heat, and relieved to have navigated my conversation with Robin without making it worse.

'So you start your Open Water course in a day or two, Rachel tells me?'

'Yes, and I can't wait. It's one of those things I've always wanted to do and it's so generous of you to pay for me.'

Robin waved his hand in the air as if swatting away a fly. I was not to worry about money. He owned Saxby Water Sport Centre, but I still found it overwhelming that someone I'd only just met could be so thoughtful.

'You're going to love it,' he said. 'Rachel tells me that Finn is now going to be taking the course. He is such a great instructor, easily the most enthusiastic member of the team. You'll fall in love with the underwater world. You will absolutely fall in love.'

CHAPTER SEVENTEEN

Julia 2010

We all knew about William Saxby. John had not talked much about his father but if he *was* mentioned, John's face would darken and he could no longer meet your eyes. He would walk away, often with Diana trotting loyally behind him.

I knew the story of course.

Then, twelve years ago, I walked into the bar of The Langham Hotel in London and found myself staring at a man who looked like a younger, handsomer version of William Saxby.

I had also caught the strangers eye too. His eyes locked onto mine and he hesitated for a few moments before getting up from his chair ignoring the man he was sitting with, and made his way over to me.

'Well, you have managed to light up the room on a dull day,' he said, extending a hand for me to shake. 'I'm Robin Saxby.'

I was mesmerised by his easy American charm as well as the realisation that he was my brother-in-law's half-brother.

'Julia,' I said, reaching out my hand to his. Instead of a formal hand-shake, he took my hand and kissed it, never letting his gaze fall from my face.

'Please, have a drink with me, will you?' My hand was still in his and I wondered how he would feel if he knew who my sister was. But I've always been intrigued by things I should probably stay out of.

'Thank you. I have time for one drink. I'm meeting someone here but I'm a little early. I have twenty minutes.'

'Then I'll have to make the most of that time and impress the hell out of you.' He glanced over his shoulder to the man waiting patiently at his table. 'Michael, I think we're done for today. I'll call you tomorrow and we'll spend some more time going through the figures.'

Without a word, the suited man gathered together his files, took his raincoat from the back of the chair, smiled and nodded politely as he made his way out of the bar.

'One of the accountants that takes care of my charitable works in Europe,' he said, leading me by the hand to the recently vacated chair.

One of the bar staff hovered nearby.

'Two glasses of champagne,' he said, and as the girl turned away, he raised his eyebrows at me and asked, 'That okay for you?'

A little laugh escaped me. This man clearly liked being in control and though I'd had my fill of such men— they held no truck with me any longer—there was something quite intriguing about this one.

We met for dinner that night and again the next night. He was staying in one of the hotel's exclusive club rooms, so after dinner on that second night we went upstairs to the club lounge, drank just a little more champagne and then without saying a word, he took my hand and we made our way to the lifts and up to his room, where he undressed me and took me to bed.

He was in his early sixties then, but there was nothing about the night I spent with him that didn't compare well with a much younger man.

We lay in exhausted, happy silence for a while afterwards. Then I rose, showered and came out of the bathroom to find Robin had made us both coffee and was standing at the window, looking out towards the BBC building opposite. We both stared ahead and without putting much thought into it, I said, very casually, 'I'm John Saxby's sister-in-law. Diana's sister.'

I expected a stunned silence or possibly some recriminations for not telling him sooner, but he replied immediately. 'Yeah, I know. I knew when I first saw you.'

I turned to look at him. His face was impassive, relaxed. He looked back at me.

'Seriously? How did you know?'

He laughed, gently. 'Don't you think I've wondered about the Brit side of the Saxbys? You all intrigue me. And there's this thing we have in America.' He smiled and the twinkle in his eye reached a new level. 'It's called the internet and you can find all sorts of things out on it.'

I nudged him with my arm and tutted but couldn't help smiling too.

There seemed to be nothing more to say about it. I'd built it up while I was showering, wondering if I should have said something to him before we'd got into bed. But now, I realised, the sex was going to happen anyway. And I was very glad it had.

We sat on the sofa, drinking our coffee. My legs were stretched out on his lap and he was gently stroking my legs. We spoke a little about many things: politics, travel, films we'd seen, restaurants we'd tried. He was such an easy man to speak with.

We finished our coffees and put the cups down on the table. We were gazing at each other in silence, just smiling, and he carried on stroking my lower leg. Then, he pushed my towelling robe aside and traced his hand up, to my thigh, then beyond and like before, no words were necessary and we both stood and slid off our robes and got back into bed, enjoying each other as much as we had done earlier.

When I left the hotel the next day, I had already decided that Robin Saxby was not a man I dared attempt to see again. There were a couple of reasons for this.

Diana would have a complete fit. John would probably explode and my relationship with them and the girls would be irreparably damaged. And I knew I couldn't start seeing him and keep it a secret.

Those two nights of flirting and the one night of blisteringly good sex, well that I could keep to myself. It would just be one of the things that, maybe forty years in the future, sitting in an old people's home I could recall and it would make me feel wonderful.

Also, he hadn't suggested that we ever meet again. Nor had I. We both knew it wouldn't work, not just because of the family connection. He lived in The Bahamas and led a full-on life. There would be no room for me. And there was no room in my life for him. I'd had male friends in the past, who I saw occasionally and it was uncomplicated. But I knew with Robin, it would become an obsession, something that would burrow into my brain and he'd distract me. I'd lose my head over him. And I knew it would be the same for him. We swapped numbers 'just in case,' but no promise was made from either of us to call the other.

My head was reeling. Not just from the impact he had made on me, but because of the details he had filled me in with about the family. He had been very open and forthright. He went into great detail about the business, and told me about his daughters, his sister and nephew.

Then came the shocker. The piece of the jigsaw that I never knew had been missing but made sense of everything. The knowledge I'd have to keep to myself, at least for now.

CHAPTER EIGHTEEN

Amanda

I joined Rachel's morning yoga classes. It was surprisingly addictive.

I'd never joined a gym or done fitness classes back home, and I only agreed to sign up with Rachel's class to be polite. Yet her teaching methods, geared towards helping divers, sailors, paddle-boarders or anyone spending time in the ocean, had me mesmerised from the first morning.

It must have been something about the fresh air and the sense that anything was possible, but an idea began to form in my head and the critical voice that would usually tell me I was not good enough and that it would never work, was strangely silent.

So for once I seized the opportunity and put my idea to Rachel, who was more enthusiastic than I could have imagined.

Rachel was a do-er. Within days, she had spoken to Robin

and we were having in depth discussions about how the *Saxby Health & Vitality* online tutorials could be produced.

'You know, I've always felt there was a market for this,' Rachel told me some days later. 'I couldn't quite put my finger on exactly what I needed to do but now you've come along and it's all happening. I always say there's a reason for people showing up in your life when they do. And this just proves it.'

We had ideas flowing from us like a river and we were excited about where our business idea might lead us.

'Talking of people showing up in your life, after you spoke to Dad the other day about your brother in law and the work he does with real estate in England, he decided to reach out to him. The Marina needs a new extension and we've been wanting to develop a marine conservation area too. Max has agreed to come out and work on the designs for the project. He arrives in a few days. How exciting is *that*?'

Maddy surely wouldn't like that. Although Max was definitely not treating her with kid gloves anymore, I was surprised that he'd agreed to come and work with the Saxbys. Surprised and thrilled that I would not be the only one in the family who dared to follow their own path.

What Mum and Maddy would make of all this, I could only guess. Selfishly, I knew that Max's involvement with the Marina business would put my little enterprise with Rachel well and truly in the shade. Mum and Maddy's frustrations would be diverted away form me for a change.

But for now, I tried to push all thoughts of home to one side. I knew Sammy would be back into the thick of her Uni course and her hectic social life in Southampton and that Ben was being well catered for by Julia, with occasional interference from Mum.

In any case, I had plenty to keep me occupied. The next day, I would be diving with Finn, and I couldn't wait. I had barely stopped thinking about it.

* * *

My day three qualifying dive was the best one. I ticked off so many species of marine life I never thought I'd get to see at such close quarters. When we climbed back onto the boat, Finn congratulated me and we hugged and took photos and then he asked Gary, the skipper, to take us back to shore.

'You did so well, beautiful,' Finn said. 'And to celebrate, I've booked us a little dinner tonight at The Coconut. I hope that's all right with you. Please don't say you're busy.'

I was surprised. The Coconut was transformed at night from the casual lunchtime eatery to a high class, haute cuisine restaurant. Robin had taken me there on my third night on the Island. There had been eight of us; Robin, myself, Jane and Bernard, her son Brad and his girlfriend Marie, and Rachel and Cyndi. Probably too big a crowd for such a romantic place. Couples sat at the other tables, all of them clearly in love. The twinkling fairy lights hanging under the canopy and the candles on each table reflected in the water made it so special. It was exclusive and I wondered if Finn took all his pupils to The Coconut to celebrate.

He told me he would call for me at seven, suggesting we stroll down to the restaurant and he'd book Thomas to take us home.

'What do I wear?' I asked Rachel when I got home. 'Help! Finn's taking me to The Coconut tonight and the only really classy dress I have with me I wore when we went out to dinner with your father and everyone.'

Rachel laughed.

'Yes, and I seem to remember that is now covered in seafood sauce.'

I rolled my eyes. I'd never got the hang of being elegant and well presented. No matter what I did or where I went, there was always smudged make up, unruly hair, a run in my tights or food down my front.

'Don't worry, I'll find you something.'

I was about to protest. Rachel must be at least one size smaller than me, probably more, but she ran upstairs and a few minutes later she called me up too.

'Right, we are going to make you look even more beautiful than you already are,' she said. Rachel is such a kind girl. I thought what a huge task she had ahead of her.

She told me to shower and wash my hair and that I should leave everything to her. I did as I was told and twenty minutes later, found myself sitting in a towelling robe on a stool in

Rachel's bedroom, with a mass of products spread about in front of the mirror.

'So, The Coconut. Just you and Finn.' She was grinning from ear to ear and looked at me in the mirror as she combed my hair. 'How very romantic.' She giggled and I couldn't help joining her.

'Oh *Rachel*, I'm sure he takes lots of people out for meals, stop being naughty!' She stopped playing with my hair and her eyes widened as she stared in the mirror at me.

'Not to The Coconut he doesn't! When I did my diving course he bought me a Cola at the Wacky Wahoo and then talked me into buying him a plate of conch fritters! No, I'm telling you, he's smitten. I knew it when you two got back from diving the other day. Natalie and I watched you from the other end of the pontoon and we could tell by the body language.'

I blushed. From the first moment I'd met Finn, I'd been swept along on a romantic ride but told myself it was just the surroundings, the fun of learning something new and doing something for myself and of course the fun of being flirted with by a younger, attractive man. Natalie, I'd discovered, was Nick's girlfriend and a good pal of Finn's. I told myself he was just a friendly sort of person, or perhaps just someone who couldn't resist flirting. I'd almost succeeded in telling myself that it was just a fun diversion and that I deserved it after the year I'd had. But when Finn had said he'd take me for dinner, I'd felt excitement and apprehension in equal measure.

'I think you're getting carried away,' I said.

'I always get this sort of thing right,' she said, her natural warmth lighting her eyes as she spoke. 'And I tell you, this is huge.' Then she giggled some more and started to sing, 'Finn and Amanda sitting in a tree, K- I- S- S- I- N- G'

I laughed loudly. 'Nothing will happen,' I insisted, smiling and chuckling.

This was how being single again should be, I told myself. Not the unrelenting tedium of being alone and having to get through each day. Being single should be laughing with a friend and taking chances.

Rachel was absolutely on a roll now. 'I bet, sometime before you go home, he'll take you in his arms, kiss you passionately, and you won't be able to resist and you'll flutter your eyelashes and he'll ask you if you want to '*do it*' and you'll be all proper and very British and you'll say no, I'm not going to '*do it*' but then you'll get carried away and you'll '*do it*' anyway, you'll go *all the way*.'

By now, we were both laughing so hard we were bent double and screeching and Rachel had collapsed backwards onto the bed. I realised I couldn't remember the last time I'd laughed so well and I promised myself that I would unleash this side of me and never spend so many years constrained, ever again.

When Finn arrived to take me out, I was in such high spirits that nothing could have spoilt my evening but seeing his reaction to me when I came to the door lifted me even higher.

'Jeez, you look amazing. Didn't think you could look any better than you do in a wet suit but here you are. I'm going to be the envy of every guy there tonight.'

Rachel had worked magic. She'd managed to put soft curls into my lank hair and used some of her lotions and potions in it so that it caught the light and looked healthier than it had done for years.

She'd done my make up for me and somehow made me look natural but with a touch of glamour. Then, she found a cream silk wrap dress which worked even though it was a probably a size smaller than me. She'd even lent me a beautiful gold necklace, bangles and earrings. They looked hugely expensive and I crossed my fingers that I wouldn't be clumsy and lose any of them.

We walked along the beach talking mostly about diving and Finn gave me ideas for dive sites around the world that he thought I should experience. Every so often, he would drop in a line like, 'Yeah, the Red Sea is great. Although obviously you should have me with you when you do that, it's one of my favourite places,' or 'Best I come diving with you in future, if you needed rescuing. I could do that and then I could give you the kiss of life even if you didn't need it.'

There was no arrogance about him. He said these things without the cocksure attitude that some men have. There was a nervous laugh when he spoke and it puzzled me that he was behaving as if I was the real catch, not the other way around.

The restaurant was as wonderful as it had been a few

nights previously. The food was to die for, the atmosphere was mesmerising and the company perfect. The conversation hadn't faltered and time had flown.

As arranged, Thomas arrived at ten to collect us and I wondered if Finn would now make some kind of move. I wondered if he would suggest diverting to his place for a nightcap or make some other thinly veiled attempt to get me on my own. But we sat rather chastely apart in the back of Thomas's car and when we arrived at Rachel's, Finn jumped out of the car and ran around to open the door for me.

'Thank you, Amanda,' he said. He kissed me gently on the cheek and looked into my eyes a fraction longer than necessary. 'It's been a great evening and I'm so grateful that you were prepared to put up with having a night out with a dull old Aussie like me.'

I didn't know what to say. This must be happening to someone else, surely?

Before he stepped back into the car, he reminded me that we were going to dive the old wreck tomorrow and then said, 'I have another dive lesson after that but how about you come over to my place and I'll cook for us tomorrow evening? It won't be a patch on tonight but I can rustle up something edible.'

'Of course, I'd love to,' I said, before kissing him briefly on the cheek again before heading into Rachel's enjoying the buzz that pumped through my veins and feeling my heart flutter for the first time in years.

* * *

I walked up the wooden steps to Finn's house. If you could call it that. It was like a very big, weatherboarded beach hut on stilts. Bleached by the sun's rays and pitted by years of being blasted by sand, it seemed to carry about it the same air of 'take me as you find me' that its resident exuded.

'Hi gorgeous.'

Finn opened the door before I reached the top step and paused while he looked me up and down. He smiled broadly.

'Wow. You look beautiful again. Scrub up quite well, don't you Amanda?'

'Oh charming, I'm sure,' I said, handing him the bottle of Sancerre that Robin had insisted I take from his wine cellar. Finn led me into the main room, the white boards continuing inside, cladding the walls, the ceiling and forming the floor. A faded rug sat in the middle of the room with two mismatched sofas either side.

'This looks good, but I already have a bottle chilling so let's get started on that first. I'll put this in the fridge for later.'

I wondered just how much alcohol Finn intended for us to drink tonight. A glass to two would relax me for what was, let's face it, my first 'date' for over twenty years. But I didn't want to lose all inhibitions. I wasn't going to throw caution to the wind. A few friends had said that I should go out and 'just get laid' or 'do what men do to us, use and abuse them then dump them and move on.''

But I never behaved like that when I was single the first time. So why would I do it now?

Although, as I watched Finn bustling around in his little kitchen, in his faded salmon pink shorts and ragged Tee shirt, looking so relaxed, I wondered if I should be ruling out a night of passion.

'There you go.' He handed me a glass of fizz. 'Bottoms up, as I believe you Brits say,' he gave me a cheeky smile and as we clinked glasses, his eyes drilled into mine. And yet, for all his swagger, there was a glimmer of nerves. A sense that maybe he was not quite sure of himself.

He sat next to me on the sofa, not so close that we touched but I could feel the warmth coming from his body. I had that glorious sensation of being completely alone with him for the first time and of my skin feeling hypersensitive, as if a single glance of his hand against my arm would be enough to melt me. It was inconceivable that he could not feel it too.

'So we have conch fritters to start, with a dip that I'd like to say I made myself but young Natalie whipped that up for me. Then chicken with rice and peas. Now that *is* my concoction. An old family recipe, with a few special extras in it and I can't tell you what they are. Old Granny Florence will come back and haunt me if I reveal her ingredients.'

'Sounds delicious. I'm loving the food out here so far. Love eating so much fish, so many fresh fruits and veg. Seriously I don't know what I'm going to do when I get home. The UK is so cold now, it'll be all stews and potatoes.'

Finn pulled a face.

'Don't be talking about going home just yet, gorgeous. I'm actually hoping we get an out of season hurricane sometime on the 24th that will ground all the planes. Then you'll have to stay here.'

I wasn't sure how to deal with this. Each compliment he paid me, balanced by his bantering, gave me a sensation that I hadn't experienced for so long. I felt my guard come up, heard my inner voice muttering about him *saying that to all the girls,* and even, *he's making fun of you.* Most important of all was the voice that said, *protect yourself.*

'Well, I guess that's quite a way off,' I replied, subtly pulling away from him, only a fraction, but enough to put a cooler space between us.

Maybe he felt it too, because he got up and wandered back over to the kitchen area, lowered the basket of fritters into the fryer and signalled to me to go and sit up at the small wooden table at the far end of the room.

He'd made such an effort. The table was neatly laid with a linen cloth and napkins, on which sat some highly polished cutlery. A small glass bowl filled with sand sat in the middle of the table with a gently flickering candle, even though it was still light outside. From the creases on the tablecloth, I would have said it had just been purchased or at least that it had only now been removed from its wrapper and was being used for the first time.

I looked up and out, beyond the open doors and billowing voiles, curious to see what view Finn had in his back yard. Most houses seemed to be arranged so that all the outside seating was set up for the best view of the ocean yet not Finn's house. But what a view it was. What a surprise.

He caught me gazing out. 'Go on out,' he said, waving the slotted spoon he held in the general direction of the doors. 'Take a look. I'm going to get these babies out of the oil now and we'd best wait a couple of minutes before we eat. Don't want to burn those luscious lips of yours, do we?' And there, again, that cheeky look with some shyness leaking through.

I stood at the top of the steps looking down a few feet into the little courtyard he'd created. It was a haven of peace. A cobbled area, with just enough space for a bistro table and two chairs, was surrounded by plants of all types, colours and shapes. Bougainvillea was placed to get the best of the sun, just dodging the shade cast by the flame trees on the other side. Aloe vera extended its long fingers towards the sky, with abundant fronds in various places around the courtyard. Cacti and succulents, hibiscus and frangipani were dotted here and there. There were about half a dozen metal poles, with hurricane lamps dangling from each. Although not yet lit, I could imagine how spectacular this area would look at night-time, with the glow of the candles and the scent of the flowers.

'Wow. Finn, you have a bit of paradise here don't you?'

I felt him come up behind me, close enough to sense that warmth again.

'I love it, you know.' I felt his breath on my ear. 'I spend so much time in the water, under the water, on the water. My heart definitely belongs to the ocean but it's also my work. This is my escape from that. My sanctuary. And I look after this little area. I'm always adding to it or taking something away or re-arranging it. I know it's not a huge space but I make it as welcoming as I can.'

Seeing what Finn had created somehow relaxed me, made me bring my guard down again. There was something nurturing about this space that made me question my assumptions about him. Made me wonder if maybe there was a sensitive soul beneath the outer shell.

We turned and went back inside. He even pulled my chair out for me, and brought two bowls of fritters to the table, and Natalie's dipping sauce.

We talked our way through dinner. The champagne flowed until the bottle was emptied and then Finn jumped up and opened my bottle of Sancerre. For a fleeting moment, I toyed with the idea of refusing any more alcohol but something made me feel as if I were on an inevitable path. There was no stopping. So I just smiled as he filled my wine glass. We carried on talking, finishing our meal but neither one of us wanted to move, as the subjects we discussed became more and more personal. Our upbringings were compared. I told him about Sammy and Ben and he described his unconventional childhood in Australia. I glanced outside and said aloud, 'Oh my God, it's actually dark!'

'Well spotted Sherlock,' he said, and after clearing away the plates, having point blank refused my offers of help, he suggested we go and sit in the courtyard.

He lit all the candles in the lamps and brought our drinks and a cushion out for me to put on the seat of my chair. It was warm and the air was still. I could hear the distant rhythm of the waves on the shore.

We sat in comfortable silence for a while, punctuated occasionally by the sound of a nearby tree-frog. After a few moments, Finn asked why I was on my own.

'So, what happened? Rachel Saxby said you'd been married for years then the idiot left you for some other girl. What a piece of shit. Bet he regrets it now but what about you? Are you hoping for some kind of reconciliation or are you done with him?'

So I told him my story. Just the facts. I didn't embellish anything and didn't touch on how Dan had treated me during our marriage, how he'd left me feeling like an empty shell. Other than Julia, Maddy and Eve, I wasn't prepared to admit to anyone yet that I'd been weak enough to allow that to continue for so many years. I just relayed the facts, in chronological order and without emotion, as I stared into the jungle of plants in the courtyard.

'So that's what happened. The big cliché. He ditched me for a younger model. Maybe he's having a midlife crisis or something, I don't know.' I shrugged my shoulders and realised that I truly didn't care what his excuse might be.

I looked up and glanced over at Finn. His face was as serious as I'd yet seen it. His eyes were soft but his expression was difficult to read.

'So I was right. He is an idiot. But the other part of that cliché, about a man ditching his other half for a younger woman is that he usually gets bored pretty quick and then realises what he's lost and begs wifey to take him back. And that's the bit I'm interested in. Would you take him back?'

'Take him back! Are you kidding me!' I surprised even myself with the ferocity I said this with. I let out a laugh. 'No. I've been stupid in the past but I'm not a complete fool.' I sensed that Finn may be about to interrogate me on what my marriage had been like. I'd had enough alcohol that it wouldn't have taken much questioning for me to say too much and worse, maybe let my emotions get the better of me. It was time to change the subject.

'So, what about you? Have you been married or lived with someone or is there just a girl in every dive centre?' I smiled as I asked but felt my stomach tighten while I waited for his response.

His face remained as serious as before. He looked down and brushed a piece of loose cotton off his shorts, took another swig of wine and now took his turn staring into the distance.

'Never been married. Nearly did, once. I lived with her—Anna—for about three years but that didn't work out. And yes, of course there have been a few women, although strictly speaking I'm not supposed to date clients but sometimes, you know, after the course is finished, they're not clients anymore and if they're still on the island...' He smiled briefly and shrugged his shoulders. 'Don't get me wrong, there have just been a few girls I've hooked up with like that and I don't string people along. I've never made any woman think it's more than just a little fun. If I think they want more, well, I just back off, you know.'

Silence.

Hearing how he operated, that his life seemed to be a series of empty encounters, felt like a heavy stone dropping inside me, from my throat right down to the pit of my stomach.

After a few moments, Finn turned to look at me, mouth open and panic on his face.

'Ah, shit Amanda,' he said urgently, reaching out to touch me on my arm. 'Hey, that's not what's going on here. I'm just being honest about how things *were*. I don't think of you that way. I'd never just want…ah, shit, I've really messed this up.'

He looked genuinely distraught but I couldn't fathom whether that was because he had feelings for me and was thinking about an actual relationship, or because he was looking forward to ending the evening with sex, and he'd just realised he'd blown his chances.

'You don't need to explain,' I said, as nonchalantly as I could. 'I don't go jumping into bed with near strangers, ever, so there is absolutely no chance of being mistaken for one of your quick conquests.' I smiled, raised my eyebrows and shook my head, looking him straight in the eyes. He still looked pained.

'Amanda, trust me, I truly don't see you like that. I invited you over because I really like you. A lot. You're great company and I want to get to know you better.' His hand was still on my arm. He brushed it down my forearm and took my hand. I quietly dammed him for the feeling I now had in my veins, the feeling that whispered to me to just go with it, just dive in and to hell with the consequences. He squeezed my hand and carried on speaking. 'Of course I've had some fun. Girls, well they come here or wherever I've worked on holiday. They do sometimes kinda offer it to you on a plate, if you know what I mean. And why not? Good for them I say, why shouldn't there be equality? But that's all it is, a bit of fun. Sometimes, you want something more substantial. More meaningful.'

We looked at each other and he entwined my fingers with his own. A thousand thoughts and questions passed between us and for once in my life, for once in my pathetic, humble life, I took the lead. Without once breaking my gaze, I stood up and moved a step closer to Finn. He watched me with a puzzled expression on his face. I sat down on his lap, leant in, closed my eyes and kissed him gently on the lips. Just a second later, I moved back and we gazed at each other, the slightest smile on each of our faces.

'Yep. That's it. Meaningful.' He said. He pulled me back to him and this time, he kissed me with enough passion that I could only be thankful that I was seated, because my knees would have given way.

We stopped and he put his hands each side of my face, staring at me as if I were a mythical creature. 'What is it about you?' he asked, slowly shaking his head, a frown creasing his forehead. 'I had this feeling that day we met at the Shack. It was almost like I knew you already. Like there was a connection. I remember having that Kimmy girl throwing herself at me but all I could see was you. It was like you were a magnet or something.' He spoke with conviction, as if it was important to him that I understood how serious and truthful he was being. Then he smiled and the cheeky guy returned. 'Plus, of course, I fancied the pants off you, couldn't wait to see you in a bikini and when you turned up for your first dive and I saw your figure properly, I had a hell of a job concentrating. I've only got to look at you and, well it can be embarrassing for a guy. Jeez, you're sitting on my lap, I think it's pretty obvious,' he said glancing down at his shorts with a slightly embarrassed laugh.

'Er, yes, I have noticed,' I replied with a giggle, feeling him against my thigh. 'But I did mean what I said earlier. I felt the urge to kiss you just now and honestly, it's so out of character for me. I'm not one of those girls you spoke about, that wants a holiday fling. I just, I don't know, wanted to kiss you.' I shrugged my shoulders. 'So I did.'

It felt liberating. Not just doing what I wanted but saying it too. Without feeling I should explain myself or worrying that he may have the wrong idea or be disappointed that I wasn't going to have sex with him. Not then, anyway.

'And I'm very pleased you kissed me. And I only want you to do what you want to do when you want to do it,' he said. Then the smile came back. 'Having said that, of course, anytime you want to get naked with me, don't be shy, will you?' he laughed, took his hands from my face and gave me a playful tickle around the waist. Then kissed me again before letting out a satisfied sigh. 'Shall we go back inside?' he asked. 'The sofa's more comfortable and if we are just doing the whole kissing thing tonight, I want to be snuggled up with my girl feeling nice and relaxed.'

And so, by the light of the candles, we half sat, half sprawled on the sofa, wrapped in each other's arms, kissing and talking like a pair of teenagers and I felt as light as a feather and as carefree as I have ever felt in my life.

CHAPTER NINETEEN

Amanda

It felt like a scene from a film. Meandering along the beach as the sun rose, holding my shoes in my hand so that I could feel the sand beneath my feet. I felt warm and cosseted. I could still smell Finn, in my hair, on my hands. I kept smiling. I kept taking deep breaths.

He'd kept insisting on walking me back but I needed this time. Needed to gather my thoughts and enjoy the moment. So I had been firm, told him not to be silly and that the walk along the beach to Rachel's was less than a mile and it would do me good. It also gave me time to think about what I was going to say to Rachel and whoever else was at the house, when she inevitably teased me about spending all night with Finn.

As I neared the Saxby estate, I saw someone jogging towards me, and recognised the blonde bouncy bob and the trim figure immediately. I knew Rachel liked making an early start but this was impressive even for her. After a couple of minutes, we drew level and she flicked her eyes up and seemed surprised to see me. She must have been in her own little world if she hadn't spotted me coming.

'Oh hey, Amanda, hi!' she jogged on the spot as she flashed her wide smile.

'Bit early for jogging, isn't it?' I asked, fending off the inevitable questions about what I'd been up to last night.

'I wasn't sleeping too well,' she said, blushing as she looked away from my face and turned to look at the sea. She stopped moving, took some breaths and then bent forward to stretch her back. She straightened up and stretched each arm up in turn. 'All good though.' She bit her lip and seemed distracted. I wondered if she was having second thoughts about the business we'd discussed. She turned back to me and it seemed as if she had suddenly realised what time of day it was and where I was coming from. 'Amanda!' she said, the excitement clear in her voice. 'So...the date with Finn. I'm guessing *that* went pretty well?' The big, beautiful smile was back. She stared stretching her hamstrings and waited expectantly.

'It did go very well, thank you,' I said, a grin spreading across my face. 'And no, before you try to find some way of subtly asking me, we didn't.'

'You didn't what?' Rachel tried to sound innocent but couldn't help raising her eyebrows.

I laughed. 'We didn't *do it*. We didn't go *all the way*.' We both started laughing like naughty schoolgirls. I thought again how much I wished Rachel were my sister. She was much younger than me but I already felt protective of her. She was like no-one else in my life, Why I didn't have more of these gentle, kind and loving people around me back home? I loved Maddy in my own way but she was a complete mystery to me. I loved Eve to bits and knew we'd be friends forever, but she was such a cynic about everything, whereas the whole positive vibe I was breathing in here in The Bahamas was intoxicating. I needed more of it in my life.

'Come on, let's get back to the house,' she said. 'I won't challenge you to a race so you carry on at your own pace. I'll get back and make us a smoothie. Then you can tell me all about it.' She spun around and was off, barely leaving a footprint in the sand as she skipped away.

In the time it had taken me to walk home she had got in, jumped in the shower, and was standing in her robe blitzing fruit, yogurt and coconut milk in the blender. We took our smoothies and sat at the breakfast bar.

'Right. Spill.' Rachel looked sideways at me and took a long swig from her glass.

'Not much to tell really. He cooked me dinner. We talked. We got on really well. He's easy company, you know? And what sort of surprised me is, he's a real gentleman.'

'You were surprised by that?' Rachel tilted her head to one side. It seemed it had never occurred to her that he wouldn't be. 'I've always thought he was definitely one of the good guys. I wouldn't have let my new bestie go on a date with him if I didn't.' She gave me a playful nudge in the ribs. 'Anyway, go on. Let's get to the juicy bit.'

I told her how we had eventually kissed although I felt shyer of telling Rachel than when I was actually doing it with Finn. I told he how we'd spent the next hours kissing and talking some more and it had gone no further. I told her I liked him but I was realistic. I told her it was all very sweet and I kind of believed that he wasn't just after a quick fumble. But I would go home to England and he would be here in The Bahamas. He'd continue to be pursued by sexy young things in bikinis made out of two bits of string and that would be that.

When I had finished, she fell silent for a few moments, considering what I'd said.

'You know, I don't think that's necessarily the case.'

'It seems to be his modus operandi, Rachel. And let's face it, he's a guy. He might be truthfully interested in me but I'm well aware that when I've gone home, there will be women in the picture and he's not likely to keep himself for me is he, like some kind of Jane Austen novel. I can't imagine him saying, 'Away with you, hussy' as he peels a half-naked blonde off his body.'

We both chuckled but truthfully, I was too wounded. Dan had made a fool of me and I couldn't risk it happening again.

'He behaved himself when he was with Anna, though,' said Rachel.

'Are you sure? He mentioned her. Said he lived with her for a few years but it didn't work out. He only mentioned her in passing so it wasn't clear how significant she was.'

Rachel finished her smoothie. I handed her my empty glass and she rinsed them under the tap before putting them in the dishwasher. I watched her expression. She bit her lip.

'Maybe it's not my place to tell you,' she said. 'But it was pretty serious with Anna.' She stood up and stared into the middle distance, recalling a different time. 'No, it was very serious. And I'm as sure as I can be that he was completely loyal. Then she went and broke his heart.'

My phone rang. It was Maddy.

'You answer that,' said Rachel. 'I need to go and get changed anyway. I've got a class up at the hotel in an hour. Maybe see you there?' She backed out of the kitchen door and turned to skip up the stairs before I could ask anything. I'd hoped she was about to tell me more about Anna and her relationship with Finn, but now the moment was gone. I reluctantly pressed the green button on my phone to speak to Maddy. .

'Yep?'

'Hi Amanda, it's me.'

'I know. Your name flashed up on the screen.'

'Oh well *you* sound in a good mood. Not.'

'Yeah, alright, sorry. I was just in mid-conversation with Rachel, that's all.'

'Which one's Rachel? The sister or one of the daughters? Oh well, never mind, who cares anyway. I was just wondering if you'd spoken to Max since he's been there? I tried calling him a few times but he never picks up. Has he said if he's missing me or anything or talked to anyone about me?' she asked.

'I haven't really spoken to him, only for about two minutes yesterday morning to ask how his flight was. I think he was due to spend most of yesterday in meetings with Robin and I don't know what's happening today. I doubt he'd have mentioned you anyway.' The next sentence popped into my head and I knew I shouldn't speak it but I did. It just popped out of my mouth like an egg from a chicken. 'I mean, why would he? He's hardly going to say, "O*h by the way, you all must meet my lovely wife who shags other men and breaks up families but even so, I took her back,*" now is he?'

Silence. Unsurprising. I assumed it was a gap into which she expected me to pour my heartfelt apology and tell her I didn't mean it. It was an uncomfortable silence and I felt guilty but it was true, it was an accurate reflection of the facts. It struck me that maybe, if Maddy heard the truth more often in her life she might just be a better person for it.

'There was no need for that.' Maddy spoke with a flat voice. 'However, I've just realised that you are quite a few hours behind us, so I'll put that down to having woken you too early. Maybe I'll call again in a day or two. Say hi to Max for me when you see him. Tell him I love him.'

The phone went dead. There was no pleasure to be had from making Maddy feel bad yet neither was there my usual default of beating myself up for someone else's reaction.

However, I would go and find Max as soon as I'd showered and changed, and see if I could glean how he felt about his marriage. It was clear that Maddy was uneasy about the way he'd been since she'd moved back in but I somehow doubted anything would ever change. Max was too loyal, and maybe too wary of change to do anything about his situation.

Some things never change. Including me, once again doing Maddy's bidding.

* * *

I walked into the bar at The Coconut and saw Max sitting at one of the tables by the water's edge. He looked deep in thought and I felt a little guilty that I might be about to spoil his one chance of being carefree, by questioning him about my sister.

'Hey Max,' I called.

He looked over and rose from his seat, giving me a hug as I got to his table.

'How was your morning? Did you have a good meeting with Robin?' I asked.

Max sat back down again, taking a sip of his diet coke and removing his cap to wipe sweat away from his forehead.

'Yes, very good thanks. He's a very interesting chap. I think we can do some good work together. He's very open to suggestions and wants to plough a lot of his wealth back into society. I liked his air-conditioned office too. This is a bit hot for me but I see you've acclimatised!'

Max did look a little uncomfortable. He'd always loved his skiing and his mountaineering so I don't think this heat agreed with him. He also looked troubled and I hadn't even mentioned Maddy yet.

The barman interrupted us and I gave him my order.

'So, what do you think of the family?' I asked quietly.

'You know what, they are all so nice. I feel it's such a shame there has been this big division, a big hole in the Atlantic that our British lot seemed to want William and Robin and everyone to fall into. It's such a shame for Diana, especially now that your Dad's not here. She has this whole other family willing to welcome her but she won't go there. And neither of course will Madeleine.' I saw the quick roll of his eyes.

'No, well, I guess you have to understand Mum's loyalty to Dad.'

'Oh, I do, absolutely,' he said. 'Although I suspect Maddy jumped on that bandwagon not through loyalty but from sheer jealousy.'

'Well, there could be some truth in that,' I conceded.

I knew he was right. Despite what she says, Maddy wouldn't have been too worried about hurting either of our parents. But she liked to be the queen bee. So she never told anyone at home that she was related to the people that own Saxby Marine. Just incase they might be more interested in that than in hearing about what an amazing person Maddy was.

As Max had mentioned her name, it seemed the ideal time to discuss the state of play with their marriage.

'So how have things been since Maddy moved back in? I know it must take a bit of adjustment, but do you think you'll get everything back on an even keel again?'

Max pulled his lips into a lopsided frown and fanned his

face with a menu. He was looking out towards the harbour and took a moment to think before replying.

'There is a lot of adjustment,' he said. 'I can't help but be cautious. We'll see what happens, I guess.'

He sounded vague, non-committal. From what Maddy had said, they hadn't fallen back into step yet and it was probably unreasonable to expect Max to revert to his accommodating, caring self. He was definitely wary.

I wanted to say more. I wanted to ask if he still loved her, if he felt it would all work out. But I hadn't expected him to be quite so dismissive when talking about her.

The waiter came over.

'One strawberry daiquiri,' he said, placing the pink concoction on the table in front of me.

Max didn't look up. He continued gazing out to the harbour, still fanning his face, deep in thought.

I decided to circle back around to talking about our hosts.

'So, you've met Robin, obviously. What about the rest of them, met anyone else?'

Max turned his body back towards me and leant forward, putting the menu back on the table.

'Yes, yes, they're all nice. Jane was lovely. Brad is like some kind of action man.'

'Yes, he is,' I smiled, 'and what about the girls? Did you meet Cyndi and Rachel yet?'

'Um, yes, I have.'

Max folded his arms across his chest.

'Oh, of course, you went out for dinner with the whole

clan last night, didn't you? So what do you think of Rachel?' I asked. I was as sure as I could be that she would be a great business partner but still, it would be nice to get an unbiased person's view of her.

'Why?' He frowned. 'She's fine, I suppose.'

'I don't know if she mentioned it, but the two of us are looking into setting up a business together. With my background in marketing and Rachel's knowledge of Yoga and Pilates and nutrition, we think we can put together a good health and lifestyle company on-line. So did she say anything?'

Max was still staring out to the water.

'Yes, she did mention it. Not the details, but I told her you're reliable and that it seemed like a good idea. But that was all. It wasn't a long conversation.'

I wasn't finding it easy to talk about either Maddy or the family here. Max seemed closed off and was giving nothing away. I could almost—not quite, but almost—understand Maddy's frustration with him.

I changed the subject and we talked about the project he was working on. The new office extension for the marina and an additional small building devoted to marine conservation. Max finally relaxed once he was on safe ground but I wondered what the future would hold for him. He clearly wasn't too happy with Maddy and was a fish out of water over here. What, or who, would prise him out of his shell was yet to be discovered.

* * *

I haven't felt this way for a long time.

Finn is here, in my head, all the time. He fills the air around me, he courses through my veins and stomps around inside my head. He burns my skin and has made the wiring in my brain short circuit. I don't know if I should take this as a sign that what we have is a once in a lifetime thing or if it's a warning that such intensity never lasts.

It reminded me of holiday crushes I'd had as a girl. Especially the flotilla holiday when we sailed around the Greek Islands when I was sixteen and I met Jim, the boy from Manchester. I convinced myself that he and I had a connection so strong it couldn't be broken by the miles between us. It all seemed so real and intense when I arrived home and he never called me and never wrote to me, the reality took a long time to sink in. I learned a lesson from it though.

When Dan left, the thought of another man seeing me naked was impossible to imagine. If it were ever to happen, it would be excruciating, an ordeal to be endured. I'd pushed it to the back of my mind. Feeling so in tune with a new man, unashamed and uninhibited, was a complete shock.

On my last night in The Bahamas, celebrating with the family and Finn and some of the other divers and staff at the marina was going to be a bittersweet experience.

The barbecue was in full flow when Rachel and I arrived. Music blared from the speakers Finn had set up outside his house and the aroma of wahoo and sizzling tuna steaks filled the air. Everyone who worked at the marina was there, some were dancing about, kicking sand up while others sat cross legged on raffia mats, tucking into food and swigging their rum punches.

Finn saw us approaching and waved a spatula in the air, beckoning us over.

'Hey, beautiful.'

I walked over to him and he kissed me on the lips. I blushed and looked away, noticing a few people smile and raise eyebrows at each other. It was our first public display of affection.

'Hey fugly-mugly,' he said to Rachel. She laughed, playfully slapping him. They were like brother and sister, full of teasing and banter. They'd known each other a good few years now and had the sort of affectionate relationship that only people who truly aren't attracted to one another can have.

'You'd better help yourselves to some grub girls, half this greedy lot have started coming back for seconds already and I don't want you to miss out. Drinks are over there, Robin's in charge of the bar but he keeps getting distracted and chatting up all the women.'

Rachel rolled her eyes and gave a lop-sided smile.

'Typical Dad. I'll go and get us a drink. Amanda, what are you having?'

I gave her my order of home-made lemonade and watched her go off to get our drinks and to try to encourage her father to stop flirting.

Finn had taken a plate from the pile and was heaping

coleslaw and potato salad next to the enormous tuna steak he'd whisked off the barbecue.

'Here you go gorgeous. Get that down you.'

I took the plate and tucked in, aware as I stood with Finn that the eyes of some of the party were still on us.

'So. Tomorrow then.' Finn couldn't look me in the eyes. We ate in silence for a few moments before I tried to lift the mood.

'Yes, well, all good things come to an end.'

'I hate the sound of that word. End. Your holiday may be coming to an end but I'm kinda hoping we're not. Or have I been reading it all wrong? Last night was…well I hope you feel the same. I hope you understand how I feel?'

Going to bed with Finn had not been a premeditated act. I'd gone over to his the night before expecting we'd maybe go to the shack for dinner and that I'd leave it there. Up until then, we'd been like a couple of nervous teenagers, wanting to take things further but both of us, not just me, holding something back. Playing safe.

Then last night, desire took over and the coy, funny little romance of Finn and Amanda transformed into something deeper, something that burned away the sugar-coated sweetness we'd been hiding behind. Everything else faded. The agonies of betrayal and divorce and all the stress became irrelevant. I was shocked by the power of it and again the camera lens twisted into focus. Everything became sharp and defined.

* * *

Leaving extra early for the airport had been a stroke of luck. Robin had laughed when I said I wanted to allow plenty of time. 'You haven't got miles to drive and you've seen our airport, Amanda. It's not exactly Heathrow.' But as it turned out, just before we turned onto the main airport road, I had a sudden hot flush as I scrambled to remember putting my passport in my bag.

'Wait! Hold on please, Thomas, I just want to check something.'

He stopped the car by the side of the road as I unloaded my bag. Phone, make up, bottle of water, book, purse, inhaler, hairbrush, disintegrating bits of tissue, hair slide. But no passport. I was feeling nauseous now and my heart thumped. I'd been so distracted by thoughts of Finn and where our relationship may or may not go. I began to feel useless, not in control and felt tears prick my eyes. I rewound a little tape in my head and watched myself folding my clothes and filling my case. I left a half empty bottle of shampoo and some body lotion in Rachel's bathroom as it didn't seem worth bringing them home. Then, I saw my passport on the bedside table, under the lamp. I'd picked up my suitcase, grabbed my handbag from the bed and headed downstairs for a final hug with Rachel. We'd had a few tears and I promised to call her once I was home. Then Thomas had tooted the horn and we were loading up the car.

'I'm so sorry, I'm such an idiot. I'm pretty sure I've left my passport upstairs at Rachel's. We'll have to go back.'

'No problem.' Thomas was such a laid back, easy going sort of man.

I'd grown really fond of him and he was just the sort of person you needed around you when panic set in. 'We got plenty of time, don't you worry. I'd say it just means deep down, you don't want to leave the Island.' He looked at me in his rearview mirror. A smile spread across his face.

'You may well have a point,' I said as he smoothly turned the car around and we headed back to Rachel's.

The day was already warming up and I knew that Rachel would almost certainly be around the back, doing a few laps of the pool before heading to her office. I needed to be in and out quickly, so I walked briskly along the side of the house, feeling slightly embarrassed that I'd have to explain why I'd come back and then we'd have to go through our whole 'goodbye' thing again.

That's when I saw them. Standing at the other end of the pool, near the steps down to the beach, kissing and stroking each other's faces, completely in their own bubble.

The curves of Rachel's body fitted like a puzzle piece against his body. They were so engrossed with each other, neither of them noticed me. I quietly let myself in the back door, raced upstairs to get my passport and let myself out the front door.

I couldn't face them. I needed to get my head around this. I didn't want to embarrass Rachel.

Or Max, for that matter.

CHAPTER TWENTY

Amanda

I spent the entire flight back from Miami recalling every moment of my trip. Letting it all sink in.

When I'd first allowed Julia to persuade me to go and visit the other Saxby family in The Bahamas, I'd never imagined that so much could happen, that my life would be turned on its head for the second time inside six months. The only difference was this time it was an entirely pleasurable, uplifting change.

Back at home, I went straight to bed and slept for hours before heading over to Mum's to pick Ben up. I didn't stay long. I just wanted to see my boy again and get him home.

'So. Did you enjoy yourself?' Mum sounded frosty. She preferred to act as though I'd just been on holiday somewhere or other. I knew she would never ask me any details, or how I got on with the family. She still found the whole thing difficult and I understood why but I could no longer allow other people's prejudices, other people's sensitivities to play a part in my own decisions.

'It was fine, Mum, very good.'

'Well, you've got a nice tan dear,' she said, avoiding eye contact. 'Ben's been here for the weekend while Julia had some business to attend to in London. He's been wonderful company.'

On cue, my wonderful son came barrelling downstairs, threw his arms out wide and gave me a huge smile.

'Mum! Yaye! Did you have a good time? When you phoned and said you were diving, I so wished I was there too. I'd love to do that, do you think you could take me out there one day?'

I drew back from him and glanced up at Mum. I could see distress in her eyes, thinking another one of her family might be seduced into the lifestyle of The Bahamas.

'Come on, let's get you home. I'll tell you all about it and show you my photos. I think your nan deserves a break now, don't you?'

Ben thanked Mum for looking after him and she softened a little at that. I realised that this would probably be the only conversation I'd have with her about my trip. She would try to blot it out, but how she would react when I announced I was going out there again was something I didn't want to think about just yet. And I still had a heavy conversation to have with Rachel. I'd decided on the flight that I would own up to having seen her with Max. It might, of course, have been a fling and God knows Max deserved one. But if it was anything more serious it was going to cause huge waves within the family. From the few seconds I saw of Rachel and Max together, my instinct told me it wasn't just a casual encounter. It looked like there was more to it than that.

Ben and I sat together on the sofa as I uploaded all the photographs from my phone onto my laptop, skipping through a few of me and Finn that I didn't want Ben to see. Not yet anyway.

I knew he'd be keen on the diving and was asking what the course was like. I smiled to myself when I told him how good it was.

'I'm so glad I did it. The sensation of being in a whole new landscape and seeing life that I always thought I'd only ever see on a television screen, honestly Ben, it's something else. I'll probably arrange to go out again before too long, maybe to do my advanced course and see some more amazing sights.'

He was open mouthed as he looked through the pictures on the screen. Bedazzled by the scenery and the photos of the Coconut Bar and the marina but especially impressed when I showed him the few uploaded photos that Finn had sent me of the underwater scenes.

'Oh Mum, can you go when I'm on school holidays? Can I come with you? I've just *so* got to start diving.'

'We'll see.'

I had to get my head around exactly what my relationship with Finn might become.

I'd been up and down constantly. One minute thinking how silly I was being, that it would all fizzle out very quickly despite his promises and how I needed to protect myself, keep a little back. Next, I'd be thinking that I really needed to be a more positive person, to trust what Finn had told me. That it wouldn't be easy but why shouldn't we try to make a go of things?

I fixed us something to eat, chucked the first of several loads into the washing machine and took myself upstairs. It was just after nine o'clock in the evening which meant it would be the afternoon over in The Bahamas. Time to call Rachel.

She answered the phone with a squeal of delight. 'Amanda! You got home okay? I *so, so, so* wish you were still out here. It was like having a new big sister. I actually think poor Cyndi is a little jealous. We all miss you so much already.'

'I miss you guys too, Rach. How is everybody?'

I heard that cheeky little tone in her voice. 'By everybody, do you especially mean Finn?'

I laughed. I loved her directness. It reminded me a little of Aunt Julia, yet Rachel framed it quite differently.

'*No*, not just Finn, I mean all of you. But yes, especially Finn,' I laughed.

'Well, let me see, hmmm, apart from pining and shuffling around like a lost puppy, I guess Finn is okay. But we are all missing you, honestly. Dad keeps saying that he wishes you would all come out. You, your mom, and your Aunt Julia.'

I noticed she didn't mention Maddy.

'Your Dad is great,' I said. 'I don't know anyone else with his level of drive and charm. He's a bit of a one off.'

'He sure is,' said Rachel.

'So,' I began, trying to put the right words together. 'You've told me you are all good, but how is Max getting on? He flies home the day after tomorrow, I think, doesn't he?'

There was a tiny pause and if I hadn't been expecting it, I wouldn't have noticed it, but it was there.

'Um, yes, I think so. Yeah, I think he's busy with Dad working on this new extension.' There was something about how she spoke that sounded a little too deliberately casual. There was nothing for it. I was just going to have to come out with it.

'Look, Rachel, I've got something to confess to and I don't want to make you feel bad or embarrass you or anything. I just kind of need to know the situation because I have to be prepared if any trouble comes this way.'

'Right.' She spoke very softly, almost in a whisper.

'I had to come back to yours after I left for the airport, because I'd left my passport upstairs. When I came around the back to the pool, I saw you. You and Max.'

'Oh.' She sounded as if her mouth was being covered by her hand and I could imagine her eyes closing and the feeling she must have in the pit of her stomach. She knew all about Maddy's affair, about how furious I had been and how I didn't have much patience for her. But Rachel knew the importance of family loyalty and she must have thought I'd stand by my sister. And I should have, but blind loyalty sometimes goes out of the window when you see how someone treats other people.

'Rachel, look, the last thing I want to do is fall out with you. Max has been treated like dirt by my sister. I don't think he owes her anything. But I have to know, was it all just a flirty moment that went too far or are the two of you in deeper? Because if it was just one of those things, I'll forget I ever saw anything, but if you are getting involved with each other, inevitably Maddy may find out. And believe me, she will go off like a hydrogen bomb.'

Rachel took a deep breath. I could feel her embarrassment but I couldn't un-see what I'd witnessed by the pool. I needed her to be truthful with me.

'Amanda, I can only really speak for myself. As soon as I saw Max, I thought, huh, what a crazy fool Maddy must have been. He's so sweet and shy and nothing like most of the guys I meet. They're usually over-confident, you know. Max was the opposite. Typical of me to meet someone I really would like to get to know, but he's not only married, he's married to a relative. So, I put the whole thing out of my mind. But then, that night you went to dinner with Finn, I was supposed to be having dinner at Maybelle's Brasserie with Dad, Max and Cyndi, but Cyndi wasn't feeling so good and Dad ended up having a conference call with someone in California, so it was just me and Max.'

'So that night—that was when I saw you running on the beach the next morning wasn't it?'

She didn't answer but now it made sense. That's why she was distracted, why she seemed uneasy.

'I've never talked to anyone like that the first time I met

them. It was all so obvious. We sat across the table from each other and talked and talked and only broke eye contact when a waiter came over. Max ended up telling me about him and Maddy, although I knew most of it from you. He kept saying that he didn't normally speak like that to anyone, and I don't think he was lying. He seemed sort of shocked that all these thoughts and feelings were coming to the surface.'

Rachel went quiet for a moment. I could tell she was recalling the evening, seeing it all in her mind's eye, just the way that I kept replaying every moment with Finn.

'Then he walked me back to mine. I just didn't want him to stop talking to me. I was melting at the sight of him but even at that stage, I didn't think anything would happen. I just thought, poor guy, he needs to get this all out in the open so he feels better. So when we got back to the house, I invited him in to see the place. You hadn't got home and I wondered how your evening was going. I made us both a coffee and we sat out by the pool. He told me about the guy Maddy had her affair with, the one who committed suicide. He said he'd taken her back because everything was a mess, but then he found his love for her had died with that poor man. He said that anyone who could create such a horrific situation and then just think about themselves was unworthy of love.'

We were both quiet now. The weight of all this had worn Max down, that had always been clear, but I hadn't seen how much. I hadn't been allowed to see it because I'm Maddy's sister and because, despite the few moments that Max and I had connected when we'd both been cheated on and felt wretched, he'd never wanted to open up to me like that. And I could see what a perfect match Max and Rachel might be. Both hardworking, both able to see the best in everyone and both with a desire to love that they had trapped inside, looking for someone to share it with.

'Ah, Rachel.' I too spoke in a near whisper now, understanding how this had come about. 'I'm guessing that you spent the night together?'

'Not like that!' she said, sounding somewhat horrified. 'I wouldn't do that. I wanted to though. Also, I didn't know if you would come home. But, well, how should I put this… we spent several hours that night in the same way as you and Finn did. Since then we've met up whenever our schedules allowed. Mostly, just to talk. But yes, there have been a few moments when we've not been able to resist each other. As you saw. So I don't know if I can answer your question honestly, Amanda. It all seems a bit surreal. And I guess I completely empathise with your situation with Finn. Not knowing what will happen next. But please believe me Amanda, I'm desperately uncomfortable with all of this. Max is married. I don't do affairs. It's a bit of a mess to be honest. I'm so, so sorry. I feel so guilty, I shouldn't have…' she broke off as a sob escaped her and I wished I could be there to comfort her. Instead I calmly told her that I too felt guilty, guilty that I felt no pity or sympathy towards my sister. That I thought a great deal of Max and that if I could choose the ideal partner for him, then I was speaking to her right now. But I had to finish with a warning.

'I get that you don't know what will happen next,' I said. 'But please, just be prepared for that bomb to explode if Maddy finds out. You'll need to be strong. She may be four thousand miles away but trust me, the whole world gets to know when Maddy's angry.'

* * *

Finn called me daily. Still two months after my visit, he was doing his best to prove everything he'd said about his being serious about us. The only time he sounded frustrated was when he asked me when I thought I'd be going to The Bahamas again, and I simply couldn't give him an answer.

Christmas Day had been difficult. Sammy and Ben were subdued. It was all so different for them without their father there. Then, they spent Boxing Day with Dan and Penny. It was the worst I'd felt since we first split up in June. I couldn't help but imagine them all together, couldn't help but wonder if they were enjoying the time spent with their father and his girlfriend more than they had the day before, when it was just their boring Mum. I sent a text to Finn saying I was feeling a little down and he called immediately, spending over an hour on the phone saying all the right things. Then he called again at midnight, to check that I was alright. Speaking to him on that day was the only thing that kept me sane.

'I've been looking on Ben's school website,' he told me during one of his calls.

'Really? Are you a stalker now?' I'd joked.

He ignored my remark. 'He gets a school holiday in May. Why don't you bring him over? I've already sounded Rachel out about it and she says you can both stay with her. I can teach him to dive and then we can spend a bit of time on our own too. What do you say?'

It was lovely to hear that he wanted to meet Ben. It would have been so much easier to persuade me to come over on my own, but he knew how I felt about my children. Still, I felt it was probably a step too far too soon.

So we had continued speaking on the phone, texting and getting to know each other more. He'd sent me photographs of him as a youngster in Australia, his unmistakable eyes and cheeky grin in almost every shot, with magnificent scenery in the background. He told me about his hippy parents, how they had travelled a lot and he'd not had much formal schooling. He opened up about how this had left him feeling that something was missing, although it had made him the person he was. He'd had more adventure by the age of eighteen than most people see in a lifetime. But he'd never had a sense of permanence, and he craved that now.

One Wednesday evening, we were chatting on the phone as usual. I mentioned that he sounded tired and he answered that he was, but was he looking forward to a great evening.

I was just about to ask him what was happening when the doorbell rang.

'Oh hell, there's someone at the door. Hold on a minute, keep talking, I'll just answer this and get rid of them.'

'Yeah, whoever it is tell them you're busy. I'm missing you so much and all I get of you is a voice at the end of the line.'

'Don't worry,' I replied as I uncurled my legs from under me and made my way to the front door. 'This'd better not be my sister coming over to make a big drama,' I said as I turned the door handle.

A suitcase had been left on the door step. 'What the hell?' I said and then realised someone was standing just out of vision at the side of the porch. Then I saw the scruffy deck shoes, and heard the laugh, and Finn yelled 'surprise!' and he took me in his arms and I screamed and held on to him as if he might disappear into thin air.

'I don't believe it! I can't believe you're here!' I said through the happy tears. We pulled apart and stared at each other. My hands were shaking.

'I'm here—I couldn't stay away! I was going insane so I got Nick to take over my courses for the next few weeks, found a cheap flight and got on it.'

I dragged him inside leaving the door open and his suitcase still outside in the late January drizzle. I realised I still had my phone in my hand, still connected to Finn. We looked at each other and giggled like schoolchildren who had just got away with some naughty manoeuvre.

Then we kissed. Like two people finding an oasis in the desert, who hadn't realised how thirsty they'd become.

Finn had come to me. Finn had shown how serious he was and proven to me that I could rely on him, and that his feelings for me were at least as strong as mine for him. I could let myself relax. I could give myself permission to feel.

He heaved his case inside and we shut out the dreary night.

'I still can't believe this is real,' I said, hands up to my face.

'Well, it is. You couldn't come to me, and I get that, but I couldn't go on any longer without being with you. So here I am.'

We went into the kitchen and I put the kettle on, still smiling and shaking my head.

'So, do I get to stay here tonight? Or should I be looking for a hotel to go to? I know what I'd prefer but I don't want to make Ben uncomfortable.' Finn leant back against a kitchen unit, arms folded and looking serious now.

Ben was at an orchestra rehearsal with the school. This first meeting with the man who his Mum was seeing was always going to be tricky, for me at least. But it would be awkward then or six months later.

'It's fine,' I said. 'Of course you're staying here. Besides, Ben is going to love you. That's the problem, you're probably tired after your flight and Ben is going to bombard you with questions about diving and fish, and coral. Although he's not back for another three hours.'

The moment I'd said this, Finn's eyebrows raised and he stepped towards me, slipping his hands around my waist.

'In that case, maybe I need to go to bed and get some rest

before I meet him, eh?' He kissed my neck. It felt like I had been drugged. My breathing deepened and I stroked the side of Finn's face.

'Lead the way gorgeous.'

The weeks that followed went far too quickly.

As I expected, Finn and Ben bonded straight away and I was impressed by how Finn's passion lit Ben's eyes up and naturally, at every opportunity Ben told me how I must take him out to the island and listed all the amazing things he and Finn were planning to do and see.

We spent a lot of time just talking together and didn't venture out much. We did walk down to the riverside one afternoon. I wanted him to see the area where I grew up, but I couldn't completely relax. I wasn't ready for Finn to meet my family yet, or even Eve, who knew all about him.

Max popped over for coffee one night and I felt a deeper level of betrayal but continued a dialogue in my head, that Max deserved some joy in his life. I knew he wanted to speak more openly with Finn now that he had the chance, so after an hour or so, I feigned tiredness and took myself off to bed, leaving them to it.

Later, Finn slipped in beside me and said, 'I tell you, those two are so full on.'

I rolled towards him, looking at his face in the shaft of moonlight that sliced through the window.

'Like us you mean?' I smiled. Finn smiled too and kissed my forehead.

'Maybe. It all seems very intense—and I know we are too—but we also have depth. Do you agree? I hope it's not just me that sees all this,' he said, pulling back a little to see my face properly.

'It's not just you. I see us as—this is going to sound so corny—I see us a calm ocean. Deep and vast, but without huge crashing waves stirring things up.'

Finn smiled again. 'Clever you, that's such a good way of putting it.'

He cuddled me to him and I closed my eyes, taking in his scent.

'Max and Rachel though, they might be like that, but I see them as more like the rapids. Fast moving water that's exhilarating but eventually chucks you over a waterfall. Rachel's a sweet girl. I think she'd want the little house and the picket fence and all that. She's moving *towards* Max. But I sense from Max that he's found someone kind and loving in Rachel, but all he's really doing is moving *away* from Maddy. That's the difference.'

I mulled this over. Max wouldn't deliberately hurt anyone, and in lots of ways he and Rachel would make a great couple. But I knew how cautious he usually was and his relationship with Rachel had been full speed ahead. I thought about how Finn and I had got to know each other, and that despite my concerns we were moving forward. I asked myself if this was love? It's a question I'd been toying with for weeks. I'd been so focussed on being wary, protecting myself that I'd not allowed it to be a real possibility. But the last days had changed everything. This was scarily like the L word, but neither of us were prepared to give voice to it quite yet.

'I will say, this is all very out of character for Max,' I said finally. 'He likes to have everything planned out down to the last detail. That's one of the things that I know used to drive Maddy crazy. He's far from Mr Spontaneous.'

I wasn't entirely sure Finn had heard me. His breathing had slowed and I felt his arms relax. Very quietly, I said his name, but got only a murmured 'mmm?' in response.

We spent two days in London, celebrating Valentine's day. I asked Julia to come over and stay with Ben. Finn was his usual charming self but seemed to have met his match in Julia.

'Wow, she's one classy woman! You want to watch it, Amanda,' he teased, 'you know I like older women, maybe I should be looking at one with a few more miles on the clock than you, eh?' He said, nudging my arm.

'Oi,' I replied in my unique ladylike way. 'You're with me remember? Or maybe I should do the same thing and go and spend some time with Robin and his friends. How many millions did he say he had?' I pulled a puzzled face and tilted my head, staring off into the distance.

We were like this most of the time now. Teasing, playing, having fun. I enjoyed showing Finn around London and was relieved when he didn't want to do all the touristy things. I'd spent so much time with Sammy and Ben over the years doing Tussauds, the London Eye, the Tower of London and hundreds of other things that I was well and truly over it now.

Luckily for me, Finn seemed more interested in finding little side streets, quirky shops but mostly stopping in independent coffee houses and restaurants. People watching was his favourite pastime and we had plenty to intrigue us.

We stayed in a hotel with a view of the Thames, had our Valentine's dinner in a small but romantic restaurant and went to bed early. We merged together in our own universe, and drifted off quickly to a very contented sleep. My eyes were closed, my breathing heavy and I was almost gone, but not before I heard Finn whisper, 'I love you, Amanda Saxby.'

We got back to Bernstone Point on the lunchtime of his last full day. I knew we had lots to discuss. We'd already touched on the subject of when I was next going out to The Bahamas, but he needed something more concrete before he left. Like actual dates.

I made us a sandwich and pot of tea, and we sat opposite each other, tucking into our lunch and each studying our phones, me to work out the dates on the school holiday calendar and Finn looking at flights. We were getting somewhere when we were interrupted by the doorbell.

I couldn't turn Maddy away. When I opened the door, my heart sank. I hadn't wanted her or Mum to know anything about Finn. There would be a never ending barrage of questions, and unspoken accusations of disloyalty. Not only had I 'disobeyed orders' and gone to visit the other Saxby family, but there was now a link to those people sitting in my lounge. Any hopes they had of this being a one-off never to be repeated visit would now be thrown into question.

I introduced Maddy to Finn, barely keeping the reluctance out of my voice. I tried to say something along the lines of us being good friends as he was the person who taught me to dive, but I knew that was futile.

Maddy shook his hand and eyed him, not smiling and I could see her taking his appearance and demeanour in, ready to report back to Mum. What I also saw was her subtle change of posture. Her weight transferred to one leg, shoulders went back and her torso extended. She tilted her head to one side and brushed her hair behind her ear as she looked him up and down. Not everyone would pick up on it, but to me, it was a classic Maddy posture of making herself look desirable. The human equivalent of a mare on heat, announcing her sexual availability.

Finn and Maddy exchanged pleasantries, both as uncomfortable as the other. Finn stood up to shake her hand and she sat down on the sofa, next to the area he had just vacated.

'I um, I just need to make this call then,' said Finn, giving me a quick wink before disappearing out to the kitchen with his phone.

'Well, well, well,' said Maddy, stretching her arms along the back of the sofa. 'Cute little beach bum guy. Has he been here all the time? Did you bring him back in your luggage?'

'Oh, he's just been here for a couple of days. He's off again tomorrow.' I tried to sound as casual as possible.

Maddy's crooked grin and the way she turned to look at me with a slow and exaggerated blink of her eyes showed me how well that bit of deception had worked.

'I've come over to have a chat with you about Max but you obviously have your hands full. Is he really leaving tomorrow?'

'Yes, he is.' I was deflated. I wished I could deceive with as much success as some of the people around me.

'Looks like I've scared him off.' She looked over to the kitchen door. 'So he's your diving instructor? I could make all sorts of jokes about *going down together*, but I'll resist. Still, don't blame you, he's quite fit.' I shook my head and looked away. Any other woman who was trying to save her marriage and was concerned about how her husband was feeling, wouldn't have noticed another man.

Maddy stood up to leave, giving me a last self-satisfied smile before she turned to the door.

'So, after lover boy goes home, and assuming you can still walk after your last night with him, give me a call and I'll come over and we can talk about Max.'

She let herself out. As the door clicked behind her, I muttered under my breath, 'You mean, we can talk about Maddy.'

As he heard the front door close, Finn came back in from the kitchen.

'So, that was my sister. What did you think?'

Finn puffed out his cheeks and raised his eyebrows. 'Didn't really want to stay and chat to her. Recognise the type and I guess given half a chance she'd have asked a lot of questions. And not just about us, about Max too, which would have been a bit tricky.'

'Ha! You'd have found it tricky? Welcome to my world. I dread to think about what's going to happen when this all comes out.'

CHAPTER TWENTY-ONE

Julia, 1994

Amanda's eighteenth fell on the best of autumn days. The first few leaves had fallen to create a mottled pattern on the lawn. The air was crisp but not yet truly cold and the sun shone in a vivid blue sky. Diana had insisted that friends and family mix to celebrate before the birthday girl headed out to the bright lights, for dinner and clubbing.

I had seen the look on Amanda's face when Diana had suggested this. The poor girl had been mortified.

'I think we should have a little tea party,' Diana said, eyes sparkling. I could see her mind racing as she played the whole scenario out with herself at the centre. 'I know you'll be out with your friends later but I think they should all come here and have some cake with your family. Family is important and I think your celebrations should start with us. And Julia is home just to see you on your eighteenth so it would be rude not to have her there.'

'Hey, whoa, don't involve me! Seriously, I'm here for a few weeks. As long as we get some time together that's fine,' I said. Diana glanced at me with some disdain and looked back at Amanda.

'Well, I don't know, Mum. Everyone usually goes round Trina's house to get ready when we're all going out. She's the one with the big bedroom so we spend a couple of hours in there, doing our hair and stuff.'

I'd smiled at that. No doubt, they would be having some cider too to get in the mood and probably talking about which lad they'd want to get off with.

'They can all do that here,' said Diana, gesturing to the room in general with her hand. 'Then we can all be together.' A frown creased her forehead and her mouth set itself into a puckered little round. 'I'll be so disappointed if you don't agree,' she said. She clasped her hands together and looked intently at Amanda.

I willed her to say *no Mum, I don't want my life dictated by how you think it should be*, but of course I knew she wouldn't. The fiesty girl I'd first got to know a few years ago was being gradually suppressed. The plans she'd had, her dreams of working on yachts and travelling, her *can do, will do* attitude had become was like a fire without oxygen, slowly dying. But she couldn't see it.

And so here we were, Diana and I making sandwiches and cutting up cake. I'd tried to reason that as they were all going out for dinner, it seemed pointless to be laying out enough food to feed an army but that objection was dismissed.

John came home from work at about four. He'd left early on Diana's insistence, to help put up happy birthday banners and balloons. I cringed inside for Amanda. The room was looking like a party for a ten-year-old, and the next few hours would be excruciating for the poor girl.

People started to arrive. Amanda's friends, all looking bored to tears, and then Diana's elderly next door neighbours, Esther and Ron, went and to collect Granny Ivy. The three elderly people sat on the sofa, coats still on, looking as uncomfortable as the teenagers.

Maddy was a few weeks short of thirteen. She had been in and out since she'd arrived home from school but not offered, or been asked, to help. Unless you include helping herself to crisps and lemonade.

Amanda was expected to take plates of food to her gran and the two neighbours and then take drinks orders.

'Look at your friends,' her mother had whispered to her. Some of them have empty glasses! You're not being an attentive hostess. Chop chop!' She'd clapped her hands together and Amanda had dutifully gone off to collect and refill glasses. The poor girl looked as crestfallen as it was possible, and the chasm between her and her friends grew larger before my eyes. They were all sitting together, laughing and whispering and no doubt quietly making fun of everyone else, as young girls do.

Maddy sidled up to where I stood, leaning against the sideboard at the far end of the room. She too looked towards where Amanda was trying to get back into the groove with her friends and then she said, 'Aunt Julia, I've got a secret. I know something and I think maybe I should tell someone about it.' She spoke not as a person with a worry, not as someone who needed guidance or comfort. Her words were spiked, triumphant. She had some information she knew would cause trouble and she was giving me a peek, a pre-warning.

'Well, Madeleine, we all have secrets. But once you tell someone then it no longer is. So, you have to ask yourself, would spilling the beans on what you know be the right thing? Might it help someone? Or will it simply create a drama? And could anyone be hurt?'

We both still looked ahead. Maddy said nothing for a few moments.

'Sometimes Aunt Julia, I think that even if someone gets hurt, it's the right thing to do. But let me think about it. I'm just trying to make sure that certain people don't lie to certain other people.'

I stole a look at her. Her chin was up, arms folded and she looked very pleased with herself. She looked across at me, smiled and then made her way out of the room. I would have to keep an eye on her. She may have been just a child but she was already developing a devious streak. I'd seen that sort of thing before. It shone like a beacon to me.

Another hour passed and things were beginning to wind down ready for the night ahead. Amanda had managed to join her girlfriends and had noticeably relaxed. Their make-up bags were on their laps and lipgloss was being shared around, mirrors held up to faces that admired themselves from left and right to make sure they looked their best. I was just thinking how charming it was to see, when Maddy strutted back into the room, apparently hiding something behind her back.

'Daddy, Mummy,' she said in a voice louder than her usual speaking voice. A few of the girls looked up, but soon looked away again, more interested in their preparations.

'I found this in the bin in Amanda's room, and I wondered what it was. Do you know what it is?'

She took her hands from behind her back in one swift movement, and held aloft a used pregnancy test.

Everyone fell silent and looked at the tableaux before them. Diana and John, stooping slightly, smiles still on their faces, and the little girl, holding the stick in her hand like the Statue of Liberty.

I closed my eyes and held a hand up to my face. I heard one of Amanda's friends quietly say, 'Oh shit,' and watched as John innocently took the proffered item from Maddy's hand. Still smiling, he said no, he didn't know what it was. Was it some kind of pen? Someone tried to stifle a giggle. I looked up. Amanda sat, scrunched between her pals, unable to speak or move, her crimson face distorted. My heart lurched.

Diana's face morphed into an expression of realisation and horror as she snatched the offending article from her husband's hand and ran from the room. John, who was by now also beginning to understand the significance of what he had seen, followed her.

Maddy beamed. I stared at her. She showed no remorse. She was revelling in her achievement. If she was this sly as a child, what would she be like as an adult? The thought of what was to come saddened and horrified me.

Poor Amanda. She sobbed from such a deep place, it must have felt as if she was turning inside out. I walked over to the sofa, leant down and pulled her up and into my arms. I was about to lead her into the kitchen when John reappeared. His face was contorted with rage. He visibly shook and tears filled his eyes.

'How could you? How could you, you stupid girl! Do you want to be left with a baby, to bring up on your own? Because don't think you're going to offload onto me and your mother, who incidentally is crying her eyes out upstairs. Who is this, this idiot who you've been a slut with?' Spittle flew from his mouth.

'Dad, it was negative though, I'm not pregnant. I was just a bit sick and I thought…' She trailed off and moved away from me, towards her father, desperate for him to calm down and to be her loving Dad again.

'But you thought you *could* have been. You stupid girl.'

'John, I know you're upset but I really think you're overreacting.' I moved forward trying to speak as calmly as I could, not wanting to add fuel to the fire. 'She is over the age of consent and women mature earlier these days, they have a different outlook on life.'

He regarded me with utter disdain. I was furious with him, furious that he could humiliate his daughter this way. But I knew his own private demons were squeezing all the compassion and understanding from him. It wasn't his fault. But I had to protect Amanda.

'*You?*' He bellowed. 'The one person in the family who doesn't give a hoot for anyone else, who did as you wanted from day one, leaving your sister and your poor Mum while you went gallivanting around the world. Too bloody selfish to have a family of your own. Don't talk to me about morals. Don't talk to me about being a parent.'

I slapped him. Not particularly hard and not because I cared too much what he thought of me. But he had touched a nerve, this man who hardly knew me. I slapped him because his hostility seemed to be increasing and he needed to be stopped in his tracks.

We stared at each other. The room fell into complete silence. He was breathing heavily and after a moment, took a step back.

'Please leave my house now,' he said quietly. He turned and went back upstairs to comfort his wife.

Amanda ran back to me and I hugged her, whispering that it would all be alright, everyone would calm down and things would soon return to normal. But I was lying. I knew that even though life would carry on, this day would forever scar her like a cattle brand. It would destroy her self-worth.

Twenty minutes later, I had ushered the other girls out, suggested to Maddy that she make herself scarce and placated Ivy who understood only that there had been a scene but, thank goodness, had no idea what about.

I made Amanda a cup of tea and suggested she go off to bed and try to sleep.

'Speak to your parents in the morning,' I said. 'They're a different generation my darling, they can't help it.'

Between sniffs Amanda said, 'But so are you, Aunt Julia. And you understand.'

I reached across the kitchen table and squeezed her hand.

'I'd better get going. I don't think your Dad will be pleased to see me still here. I'll just nip upstairs and get my things from the spare room and let myself out. Try to sleep tonight. And you can always talk to me about anything, you know. I'll write to you when I'm away next and let you know where I'll be, so you can call me or write back.'

She nodded, mascara smudged down her face and looking more childlike than she had for a long time.

CHAPTER TWENTY-TWO

Amanda

Dan stood at my door one Saturday morning, looking slightly untidy and with an air of an elderly dog that had lost its way home and was looking for attention.

We'd spoken as little as possible in the months since he'd left. Just necessary talks about money, the house and mostly about Sammy and Ben. They had been business like, frosty conversations which neither of us had enjoyed.

'I hope you don't mind me turning up like this?'

Actually, I did mind. It was an interference in my life which was no longer entwined with his. I don't think he'd have been too chuffed if I'd turned up on his doorstep and disturbed his cosy Saturday with Lady Penelope.

'Want to come in?' I stood aside and gestured for him walk through into the lounge. His eyes glanced around, no doubt taking in the changes I'd made and the wholly new identity my home now had. *My* home.

He sat on the large leather sofa and I wondered if he was remembering the fun we'd had on there in the early days, the kids safely in bed, and the two of us finishing up a bottle of wine and playing around.

'So, how are you? How are the kids?'

'All good thanks.' Keep it short and sweet Amanda. Don't be drawn on anything.

I sat opposite him, the coffee table in between us like a bouncer in a club, ready to separate two warring factions.

'Ah good, right, good to hear. So, what have you been up to? What's happening on the work front? Steve and Suzie were over for dinner the other night and said you've been setting something up with one of the girls from Saxby Marine. Is that right?'

Damn Steve and Suzie. They'd been so full of how much they would support me when they found out about Dan. Suzie even said, 'We're on your side honey,' although I'd never asked them to take sides. Yet they were having cosy dinner parties with Dan and Penny.

'Yes, we're doing a bit of work together. Early days though, you know, just something I'm trying out.'

'Ah. Good.'

More silence. What did he want? Where was this leading?

'So, how are you?' I asked. 'Business going well I take it?' How bizarre that we sounded like two near strangers making small talk in a queue.

He rambled on about work going into more detail about individual projects than he had ever done when we were together. As ten minutes drifted into fifteen, I began to wonder at the fact that this was a whole chunk of time I would never get back, that I wasn't remotely interested and that there surely had to be some other purpose to this visit. Eventually, his story dribbled to and end and he sat forward.

'The thing is Amanda,' he said, 'I seem to be spending vast amounts of time thinking about you lately. I'm getting completely lost in the memories I have of us, of how good things were. And I'm getting lost in the haze of wondering why on earth I did what I did. I miss the kids so much and I miss you too. I miss *us*'

How could I respond? What on earth had brought this on? I felt neither torn nor angry that he was now having second thoughts. My initial amusement was swiftly followed by complete distrust. What was he up to?

I tried not to sound too unkind.

'Well, perhaps Dan, you should have thought of all this before you had an affair. That was the time to remember what we had, to think of the kids and how much you'd miss us.' I took a breath and looked away from him, shaking my head, my eyebrows slightly raised. 'I don't know why you've chosen now to say all this, but, well, it's all a bit futile isn't it?'

I looked back at his face, saw he was chewing his lip, staring at the coffee table, trying to piece his next sentence together. I felt a wee bit sorry for him.

'Is it? Is it futile? The Decree Absolute hasn't gone through yet. We are actually still married. I know we'd really need to sit down and thrash a lot of stuff out. I know I would have a lot of work to do to make up for what I put you through but, but we could. You and I, Amanda and Dan. We were such a team. Everyone thought so.'

I sat back in my chair. I could barely believe what I was hearing. At no point since he'd left had he given any indication that he still had feelings for me. I had assumed that everything between him and little miss perfect was going well.

'Yep, they did. *I* thought we were a great team.' I looked him in the eyes and leant forward myself. 'But clearly I was deluding myself. What I believed we were—I'd got that so wrong. I'd definitely got you all wrong. The man I *thought* I was married to would never have had an affair. Even if things had been difficult, if we'd been having troubles, he would have talked to me, not just gone off with some other random woman.'

'I know! I know!' he said, sitting up straight as if having a revelation. 'That's exactly my point! I wonder why on earth I did what I did because it wasn't truly *me*. I think stress at work had got to me,' he held up a hand to forestall any argument, 'which is no excuse, but I wasn't thinking clearly. You know, in a funny sort of way, my little breakdown, whatever it was, could be the best thing that's happened to us.' He smiled.

My mind raced as I tried to fathom what he was doing. Had he heard about me and Finn? Was it a case of *I don't want you but I don't want anyone else to have you either?*

I wondered whether to confront him with a few home truths. Wondered if I should let him know that my friends only thought we were *AmanDan,* that fabulous team, because I kept quiet about what my life was really like? Should I tell him that I'd made the amazing discovery that other happy couples weren't like us? They didn't have one partner manipulating the other, sulking when things didn't go their way and slyly using guilt to get what they wanted.

Should I tell him that I knew about his flirtations? That although I had no hard evidence, I'd gleaned enough over the last few months to be fairly certain that Penny was not the first woman he'd slept with. She was just the first he'd left me for.

I would love to have seen his face. To watch him squirm. But something told me to hold my tongue. I just sent a silent prayer of thanks that this hadn't happened in the first few weeks after he'd left, because I probably would have taken him back. Not for me, but to give the kids stability, to slide back into the safety of my little box labelled 'wifey, good Mum, Dan's Mrs, all round good egg.'

'Dan.' I was slowly shaking my head. 'You know that's not going to happen. It's gone way too far. Nothing has changed. You can't *un*-cheat on me. You can never erase the pain that the kids went through. This can't be fixed and it's not one of your work projects that you can just throw money at and it all magically resolves itself.'

He sat back and let out a long sigh and stared at the door as if he was willing himself to be on the other side of it.

'I can't fix those things, I know. But I can make up for them. I can make sure the future is better for us all. What do you say?'

'There's really only one thing I can say to that Dan.

Whatever you tried to do to redeem yourself, to give us the best possible life, the one thing that won't change is me. And you see, I don't *want* you back.'

After he left, I lit some scented candles. His aftershave had lingered and I wanted rid of it. The peony aroma and the soft glow of the candlelight lifted my spirits. I was shocked and wondered if he thought I was now mulling over what he'd said. In a way this was true, but not to consider his proposal. I thought about *why* he'd said it, what his motives were.

As the evening drew in, I poured myself a glass of wine, laid along the sofa listening to some background Cafe del Mar, surrounded by my candles and I smiled to myself. How far I'd come. How well I recognised that nothing with a person like Dan was what it seemed. Nothing came from the heart. Everything had an ulterior motive. And in time, I would discover what that motive was.

* * *

'You are going to love this,' said Eve, eyes shining as she stood at my door on a chilly late February morning.

'And hello to you too,' I said, and stood aside to allow her in.

Her oversized coat was covered in cat hairs and smelt of bonfire. Her wild hair was particularly scruffy and her face, as always, was more interesting than attractive. But to me, Eve has always been beautiful. So full of life, so fiercely loyal and unapologetic when standing up for what she thinks is right.

She flopped down onto the sofa and beamed at me. This was my cue.

'So. You obviously have some salacious gossip you need to pass on. Let's be having it then.'

'Well, this morning I bumped into George Bearman, Dan's ex accountant from the business,' she said.

'What do you mean *ex accountant*? George has worked for Dan since, well, pretty much forever.'

'Not anymore.' Eve slipped her coat from her shoulders. 'Any chance of a cuppa?' She raised her eyebrows and couldn't stop grinning.

I went off to make us tea, wondering what could have caused George to leave and why Eve was clearly so pleased about the whole thing.

I brought two mugs into the living room and found Eve flicking through the local paper.

'So, come on then, what's the big news?'

'Well, like I said, I bumped into to George. He'd come into the bookshop while I was helping Marco change some of the displays around. So, I say to him, has he got a day off or whatever, and he says, no, he doesn't work for—and I quote—"that complete arse" anymore! Well, you can imagine, I was beside myself.' She folded the paper up and chucked it on the floor by her feet.

'That does surprise me. George was always so loyal. Did he say why he left?'

Eve chuckled.

'Of course he did. I wasn't going to let him out of the shop before getting the full low down on what had occurred. Made him a coffee, sat him on the sofa, looked all concerned about him, I did.' Eve was enjoying the fact that she had been such an ace investigator and still had the big reveal up her sleeve.

I tucked my legs up underneath me and took a sip of tea. I wished she'd just get on with it.

'So I asked what happened, made him think I was more worried about him, you know, have you got another job lined up, all that stuff, and he says he's quite happy having a few months off but wasn't prepared to stay another day.' Eve sipped her tea now, pausing for effect. 'After what happened.'

'Oh, for goodness sake, get to the point. This is like an exceptionally slow episode of Poirot.'

'It turns out,' she said, putting her cup down on the coffee table, 'that things have gone seriously downhill for Dan. He's lost two big clients in the last month. He'd been refusing to pay suppliers and that caused arguments between the two of them because there were some small companies not getting paid. But that wasn't what made George walk.' She leant forward. 'Dan asked him to commit fraud. I didn't get all the details but according to George, it wasn't just a bit of creative accountancy, it was downright dodgy! So he tried to talk Dan out of it, and said he wasn't prepared to do anything that was basically illegal, and Dan went nuts!'

'What the hell? How bad have things got? Has the company really run into trouble?'

'It's bad,' said Eve, looking serious now. 'And I have to say, while I kind of think, good, that's Karma, I hope Dan loses the whole bloody lot and looks a complete bell end in the process, it's a worry for all the staff and the suppliers and what not. And from what George said, it looks like the whole thing is on the point of collapse.'

We both fell silent. Whatever Dan had done to me, to have the company he'd worked so hard to build, disintegrate around him gave me no pleasure. There were fourteen staff working for him and little local companies that had bent over backwards in the past, fulfilling urgent orders and cutting their own profits back to retain the business.

Eve and I chatted for another half an hour, wondering if it was really as bad as George had said, and mulling over how things could change so much within just a few months.

'Just think,' said Eve. 'Six months ago Dan was married to you, had a really successful business and we all thought he was OK. Bit of a tool, but generally OK. Now, he's lost you because his brain is in his pants, lost the respect of the kids and all of your friends because we now know what a nasty piece of work he really is. And on top of all that, it looks like he's going to lose his business *and* he's going to have to fork out half of what he's got in a divorce settlement.'

Eve's final sentence flashed at me like huge neon letters in the air.

Of course.

Eve hugged me goodbye, with the usual 'You know where we are, don't hesitate,' spoken into my ear before she released me, twirled around and saw herself out of the front door.

Of course.

I was under no pressure to sell the house. Both the kids were still in full-time education and I knew I'd have a reasonable case to insist the family home was kept together until they were both working. In Ben's case, that would probably not be for at least five years. He would also be expected to pay some sort of maintenance towards their keep and I knew he'd want to do that. Not because he is a delightfully loving father but because he would hate to think of people saying he was failing his children. His act, his carefully constructed persona had to be upheld.

Of course.

My instincts yesterday had been right. There was an ulterior motive in asking me to take him back, and the motive was not to lose half his wealth.

* * *

People kept saying I needed to rebuild trust and that was something I had to work on for my relationship with Finn to survive. But it was one thing trying to trust someone new and quite another trusting someone who had already let me down.

I questioned myself, questioned if I was being too cynical in my immediate assumption that Dan had mislead me over the state of his relationship with Penny. But sometimes, it's worth trusting instincts—that pull in the pit of your stomach that says, *this is wrong, things are not what they seem.*

Going to see her also gave me a twisting feeling in my stomach. To know I'd be face to face with her. I wasn't entirely confident that I could conduct myself in the way I would want to. But I had to do it.

I checked the drive to see if Dan's car was there, and when I was sure he was out, I rang her bell and took a deep breath.

Penny opened the door and the smile on her face faltered. She quickly recovered giving me a thin-lipped, nervous smile.

'Hello. Hello Amanda.' She seemed to hold her breath and looked like she was bracing herself, unsure of what my intentions were.

Even though I was the one intruding on her territory, I felt as if my space was being invaded. Being up close to her was suffocating and strangely intriguing. All these months had passed and here we were, in this pause, this moment.

'Penny.' I smiled as naturally as I could and spoke gently.

'I wondered if we could have a chat. Nothing awful, I just want…well I just want a little closure, I suppose. Could I come in or would you like to go down to the cafe?'

She licked her lips and swallowed. I imagine her mind was racing through all the possible scenarios, all the reasons why I could have chosen to come and see her now. I wasn't exactly in control of the situation, not knowing for sure what I was going to say, but it must have been pretty uncomfortable for her.

'Well, um, by all means, come in.' She stood aside and let me in.

I walked down the short hall straight into her lounge. It

smelt of air freshener and furniture polish and was clean and tidy and entirely devoid of personality.

'Would you like a tea or coffee?' she asked, hovering by the kitchen door.

'No thanks, just had one. Mind if I sit?' I didn't wait for her reply and sat on the chair at right angles to the sofa where she now sat herself, on the edge of her seat, hands loosely clasped together in her lap. I couldn't help feeling a little enjoyment from seeing her so unnerved.

'Don't worry, Penny. I'm not here to cause trouble, not here to thrash anything out with you. I guess, well, the children see you when they visit their father and they are the most important people in this situation.'

'Oh, absolutely, couldn't agree more,' said Penny sitting even straighter like a puppy wanting a pat on the head.

'So, now everything has settled and we've all moved on, I thought it would be a good idea for you and I to meet, so that when we all have to go to an event like Sammy's graduation, no-one will feel awkward.'

Penny smiled and nodded and seemed to relax, as if this had been bothering her too. I watched her closely. If things were as bad as Dan had implied, although she might not admit it, her body language might give something away and a slip in her words might betray her worries.

'You know, I absolutely agree. I respect that you come first as their mother but thought it a shame that I might have to miss out on events in the future, like you say, Sammy's graduation, twenty-first birthday parties, weddings or christenings and so on. And I do think you have lovely children, Amanda.' She was on a roll now. Almost gushing.

'I'm perfectly fine with you being there,' I said, as casually as I could muster, smiling and shrugging my shoulders. Like it was nothing to me either way. 'I mean, you and Dan are a couple now, you're building a future together and I've certainly accepted that and the children have. Everyone else will just have to get on with it.'

Penny nodded and smiled and I saw nothing to suggest that I had hit a nerve. The strange thing was, although it was uncomfortable for me, sitting there, I didn't hate her. She probably could have become a friend once upon a time if our paths had crossed more than briefly. There was something honest about her, about her eyes. That's what made me sure that as far as Penny was concerned, all was well with her and Dan. I was right. He had other reasons for trying to get me back.

'Well, I know both me and Dan would love for you to meet someone special. I'm sure you will, you know. I was on my own for four years before Dan—well, I'm just trying to say sometimes something good is worth waiting for.' She was trying so hard. She actually sounded sincere and I couldn't help smiling to myself as I looked away from her face and studied the vase of flowers on the coffee table. It was good to know they knew nothing about Finn. It made me feel warm inside, made me think it would taint our relationship if his existence, his importance to me, was common knowledge.

'Oh well, life is good anyway,' I said. 'And it clearly is for you two? Got any holiday plans this year?'

Penny beamed.

'Life is very, very good thanks. And yes, actually, I'm taking Dan off to a lush hotel in the Cotswolds for a bit of pampering for a couple of nights. We've also started to look at an all-inclusive in St. Lucia so that would be nice.' She blushed slightly, perhaps realising this might be conceived as crowing over her love affair with the man who was, ultimately, still married to me.

'Ah, lovely,' I said, feeling slightly odd that I was congratulating her on this. Especially with what I now knew. That Dan was willing to dump her to keep hold of any money he would have to split with me. I actually felt sorry for her.

CHAPTER TWENTY-THREE

Julia, 1998

I hate weddings.

It's not just the ridiculous waste of time and energy that goes into that one, stressful day. It's the fakery of it, the false smiles, the people pretending to be someone they are not.

I made absolutely sure my niece was not aware of this, of course. I did my expected share of pretending too, allowing myself to be caught up in conversations about colour schemes and flowers and cake. My enthusiasm knew no bounds.

You would have thought.

And when the day dawned, I have to admit, Amanda did look quite beautiful. For once, Amanda would be the centre of attention and all eyes would be on her. I silently urged her to lap it up, while she had the chance.

The flowers decorating the church and the marquee in John and Diana's garden were exquisite and the sun shone brightly. As I walked the few minutes from their house to the church,

I watched the other guests. Mostly, the women looked like walking versions of the little netted bags of sugared almonds that were at the wedding breakfast place settings. Pastel pinks and blues, box jackets and skirts, with high heels that made walking on the gravel drive to the church entrance quite challenging. Fascinators were stuck to the women's heads, as if a flock of kamikaze birds had suddenly gone on the attack and spiralled out of control, crash landing into their hair.

Most of the men wore shiny suits that matched their shiny faces. Dan and his posse of ushers stood around outside the church, occasionally stopping to greet guests but mostly sharing a cigarette. Not much ushering was going on.

As instructed by Diana, I waited by the little plastic wishing well just inside the churchyard, with the *Help us buy a new roof!* poster, and a money box sitting inside the well, secured with a thick chain and padlock.

Most of the guests had made their way inside. The best man anxiously insisted that Dan and the ushers move inside the church and take their places. As they disappeared from view, Diana came trotting down the road, looking a little red faced and puffing. She stopped as she drew level with me and caught her breath.

'Is everything alright?' she asked me.

'I guess so. If you mean, is the groom here, then yes. How is Amanda?'

'Oh, she's fine, she's fine.' Diana gave a dismissive wave of her hand. 'She has her dress on and it does suit her, she looks very nice and Madeleine is in her bridesmaid dress and looks adorable. I think John is quite nervous about his speech, not his sort of thing is it, public speaking?'

'Oh, he'll be okay. Give him a couple of glasses of champagne and he'll be well away. So, no last-minute doubts then? Bride definitely going through with it, is she?'

Diana straightened her back, pulling her neck back as if trying to get a better look at me.

'Of course she's going through with it. What a ridiculous thing to say!'

I realised then of course, that at no point since the engagement would Diana have spoken to Amanda, offered her the *get out of jail free* card that would have allowed her to open up, voice any doubts, question her mother about what a lifetime of commitment to one person entails. Diana's entire focus would have been on this day, about her displaying her expertise as the perfect hostess.

'Sorry Diana,' I said, reaching out to squeeze her shoulder. 'I just meant did she have any last-minute nerves, that's all.'

'Oh, just the usual, worried about everything being perfect, everyone having enough to eat, that sort of thing.'

No, you silly woman, I thought. *That's you. Those are your worries.*

We turned to make our way into the church. We chatted about how lucky we all were that the weather was so lovely, about how cousin Ian had made it over from France and hadn't Sue lost a lot of weight since they were over last time. Inside, I was kicking myself for not having found time to visit and have a heart to heart with Amanda myself before the wedding.

She might be perfectly happy. She probably was. Only, I'd met the groom once or twice and I could already see that he was a strong, forceful character. Amanda was a little too easy going, too obliging. I'd hoped that over the years she would toughen up a bit and the girl with ambition might re-surface. But I knew how it felt to be so worn down that you saw no point in making yourself heard.

After the ceremony, came the endless posing for photographs. I managed to detach myself from the group and made my way back to the house where the caterers were busily running about, giving a final polish to champagne glasses and putting finishing touches to the canapés.

I escaped to the spare bedroom and slipped off my shoes, lying down on the bed, secure in the knowledge that there would now be another round of photographs and of course the bizarre 'receiving line,' a spectacle not far removed from a police line-up, but with the suspects shaking hands and hearing the same platitudes from every person who congratulated them. I took the opportunity to close my eyes for a few moments.

It must have been half an hour or so later when I heard footsteps climbing the stairs in a hurry. I sat up quickly, just incase anyone came in the room, so that I could make out I was just about to reapply my lipstick. Another set of heavier footsteps followed, then I heard Amanda say something about just wanting a moment to sort her hair out, and maybe ditch the veil. Then Dan spoke.

'Hurry up then.' He sounded grumpy, insistent. 'I want to get a drink and I think we should go and get one together. Christ, that bloody photographer took his time, didn't he?'

I had some sympathy with Dan. I've seen it so often. A couple having their day taken over by all the peripheral services that they were made to feel were absolutely necessary. Why more people don't just sneak off to a registry office to quickly and simply tie the knot is a mystery to me.

'I know, it did take a while, but this is our one special day. I want to make sure we have memories of this that we can show our children and grandchildren and great grandchildren!' she laughed.

'And why can't your bloody mother keep her mouth shut? She went on and on about how hard she'd worked on all this and making remarks about the cost of it all. Jesus, she really needs to show a bit of respect towards *me*. She might as well have stood in the middle of the churchyard and shouted "My new son in law can't afford everything but I can so cheers, it's all on us."' I held my breath. This time, I could hear the spite in his words. I could imagine Amanda's dream day being tarnished. I felt guilty for eavesdropping and worse because I couldn't do anything. Again, he did have a point. But Diana and John *had* paid for everything and there was no way Dan and Amanda could have afforded such a lavish reception.

I could hear the rustling of material and guessed that Amanda was standing up and moving towards her new husband to try to placate him.

'She doesn't mean it like that,' she said. 'She just gets carried away. Please don't be upset Dan, please let's go down and enjoy the day.' She spoke with desperation.

Then he said, in a resigned voice,

'Stupid bloody cow, your mother.'

I let out a small gasp but I don't think they heard me.

Amanda sounded even more desperate.

'Please Dan, please don't! She's my Mum and she drives me nuts sometimes but she's only doing her best.' Her voice was reed thin from trying not to cry.

A short silence followed.

'Right, well I'm going downstairs now. Don't be ages. If I'm on my own and they start asking where the bride is, it's just embarrassing.'

I heard Dan leave the room and descend the stairs.

I wanted to go after him. Not to tell him he was wrong about my sister, although he was wrong. She's more misguided than evil. I wanted to tear him off a strip for spoiling his new wife's day, for thinking he could speak to her like that on this of all days. For thinking it was ok to make her feel this way.

Of course, I didn't. I sat on the bed, wondering what to do. Then I heard a sniff from Amanda's old room. I pretended I was just coming up the stairs, cleared my throat and called out her name.

'I'm in here, Aunt Julia.'

'Hello darling, how are you feeling?' I took her hands in mine and smiled. 'You really do look absolutely beautiful. Dan must be a very proud man today.'

She smiled shyly. 'Thanks Aunt Julia. Thought I'd just take the veil off before we go and eat. Can you help me sort my hair out? I'd better be quick.'

So together we detached all the various combs and clips that attached the veil and I followed her instructions to get her curls back in the right position.

'You must be so excited, starting your new journey. I expect life will be very full, what with being Dan's wife, having so many friends and a career. What thrilling times lie ahead.'

Amanda had been working for a mental health charity, organising events and fundraisers and heading the marketing team. She loved her job and had already been promoted twice. The future looked bright for her.

'Yes, I expect it will be busy.' Her answer was guarded, unsure. 'Obviously we'll want to start a family fairly soon, so that will have an impact on our social life and of course my job.'

Alarm bells rang. Again, I regretted not having spoken to Amanda long before today.

'Oh, of course, a baby will have all your attention for a while, but I'm sure the charity will work around you while you're on maternity leave. You're obviously very highly thought of so they'll do all they can to keep you happy. You've always said they're very family focussed so I don't see it being a problem.'

Amanda was quiet for a moment or two while I finished fiddling with her hair and picked up a can of Elnett .

'Actually Julia, Dan and I have decided that once I'm

pregnant, I'll give up working. He thinks—well we both think—Mums should be at home until the children have grown up and can look after themselves.'

My heart sank. Our eyes locked in the mirror on her dressing table. In that brief moment, I could see sadness and despair. It was heartbreaking and I felt utterly helpless. I stood back, looked away and then shook my can of hairspray and drowned us both in the mist.

'I'd better get back down to the reception now,' she said, regaining her composure and smiling at me again. 'Thanks for helping me with my hair, Aunt Julia.'

She gave me a quick kiss on the cheek, turned and swished her way downstairs, leaving me utterly bereft and fearful for her future.

CHAPTER TWENTY-FOUR

Maddy

I knew it would take a while for Max to re-adjust to our set-up. I was quite prepared to be patient, because I had to face the fact that this had been my doing and I was lucky Max had taken me back so quickly. Paul's suicide really was a tragedy, and of course I'd rather it hadn't happened, but I suppose the only good thing that came out of it was that Max realised how futile us being apart was.

He's such a stickler for doing the right thing. He told me the other day that he'd given a cheque for five thousand pounds to Paul's wife. It was brave of him to go and see her. He didn't go into too much detail but he did say that she was angry at him to start with, but that he explained that the money wasn't a crass attempt to make up for her husband not being there. He told her it was just to help her take care of her child and that he would rather no one knew about it. Although I have let it slip to a few people that we are helping her out financially.

But the weeks ticked on and it still felt like he was a thousand miles away from me.

Then he went to The Bahamas and came back with a brick wall around him.

'I've booked a weekend away in the Cotswolds,' I told him one evening over dinner. 'Just you and me, in a spa hotel, in two weeks' time.' I smiled at him across the table, but he didn't return my smile.

'Right. So, the usual then. You've booked it, I'm paying for it.'

That really hurt. When we married, he'd been perfectly happy for me not to work. He said he had no problem being the wage earner. I could spend what I liked.

'Max! You know I have to do that! It's the thought that counts. I want us to spend some time together.' I realised I was pouting and even if it was justified, it wasn't going to help me persuade him that I'd done a good thing. I reached out my hand and placed it on top of his. 'Please, Max. I think after everything we've been through, we need this. And our sex life has been pretty sparse since we got back together. Actually, it's been non-existent since you got back from The Bahamas.'

He snatched his hand from underneath mine and looked away. I withdrew my hand and took a gulp of wine. 'I know. I get it. It's been difficult in the bedroom because Paul has kind of been like a ghostly presence. But it's been five months now since I was with him. I don't think about him, you know.'

Max stared at me. A look of contempt on his face. 'Well you damn well should think about him. You should think about him every day of the rest for your life.'

'I don't *mean* like that,' I said. 'I don't think about him when you and I are having sex. I never have.'

Max sat back in his chair, looking at me like a stranger. He took a breath and shook his head.

'Maddy, I appreciate what you are trying to do. But,' he shrugged his shoulders, 'maybe not yet, eh? I'm pretty busy at work especially having to do this project at Saxby Marine. Best cancel the trip to the Cotswolds. Maybe another time.' He stood, folded his serviette neatly and placed it next to his plate of half-eaten dinner.

'I'm just going up to my study. Got a lot of work to do tonight. I need to phone someone at Saxby, so I'll probably go and sleep in the spare room, rather than wake you up when I come to bed. Night, Maddy.'

I sat at the table, utterly deflated. The reality was, rather than a slow defrosting of our relationship, new ice crystals were forming, freezing Max into an untouchable figure. I couldn't understand it. Time was supposed to heal. The third person in our marriage didn't even exist anymore and I thought I'd proven to Max that I've learnt my lesson. And I had, I was sure.

I cleared away the dinner things, watched some rubbish on television and then decided to get an early night. I went upstairs, and as I passed the closed door of the study, I could hear Max speaking to someone. It was ten minutes to ten. He must be talking to one of the people on the Saxby Marine project.

I pressed my ear to the door. I couldn't hear what he was saying, the sound was too muffled. But the tone of his voice was odd. Softer, more chatty than I would have thought from a business call. Then I heard him laughing.

I moved away, had a shower and used some favourite body lotion. Then put on a satin robe. I thought it might be worth another try. He would be off the phone by now and maybe if I went into his study I could warm things up a bit. But as I went to go in, I could hear he was still talking. I went to bed, on my own. I lay awake for hours, pondering the question that was in my head; who was he speaking to in such gentle, intimate tones?

It shamed me to think I was 'the type' to play away. But Max just wasn't. Yet I knew that if any one of my friends had said their husband was making late night telephone calls, had gone off sex and was generally withdrawn, I'd tell her not to be an idiot and that the truth was staring her in the face. I even wondered if he was having some kind of platonic relationship with another woman.

When I woke up the next morning, Max hadn't joined me in our bed. He must have slept, as he'd threatened to, in the spare room.

I couldn't let this go on. A marriage that has grown so cold and distant is worse than being alone, and I would be no good at either. I had to tackle Max about it.

A week later, I got my chance.

It was Valentine's day. He always liked to go to a particular restaurant, Da Vinci's, just the two of us. So I booked a table as usual and even asked them to make him a small heart-shaped cake and to put a bottle of champagne on ice. I was so paranoid about him being cross that he was paying for it, that I sold some stuff on-line—a couple of old ski jackets I didn't wear any more and a designer handbag that I'd never used. I bought them all before I'd even met Max, so this meal was going to be entirely on me, and I'd make sure he knew.

He'd actually slept in our bed the night before, so that morning, I tried waking him up in a way that I thought he wouldn't be able to resist. I was wrong.

'Er, Maddy, I don't think so,' he said, manoeuvring himself away from me. He jumped out of bed, naked, and the sight of him proved to me that everything was in perfect working order. This was not a mechanical problem of some kind. This was him not wanting *me*.

'Max, please.' I was kneeling on the bed, entirely uncovered and wanting him so badly. More than I had ever wanted Paul. It wasn't excitement I craved at that moment. It was love. 'I so want to show you how good we are together.' I reached out and took his hand. 'It's more than sex. It's us connecting again, it's about finding our way back to each other.' I felt tears welling up. I looked down Max's body and saw that the desire I'd ignited earlier, the desire that had apparently revolted him and made him pull away from me, had now gone.

'I'm sorry Maddy.' He sounded truthful and resigned. He let go of my hand and sat down on the bed, his back to me. 'I know this situation can't go on. I know we should be connected and neither of us are happy at the moment. But I can't find my way back to you. I'm not sure I know who you are. I'm not even sure I know myself.'

Tears streamed down my face now. I didn't know what to do next.

Max got up and went into his bathroom and when he returned he dressed in silence. I was still kneeling on the bed, wiping tears away with my hand, rooted to the spot. Max put his watch on and turned to leave the room. Then turned back to me and squeezed my shoulder rather like one would a casual acquaintance who has just had some bad news.

'Don't cry, Maddy. I know I've been difficult to live with lately, but I don't mean to hurt you.' He sighed. 'Bit of a mess isn't it? Look I have to go to work now, let's go out for our dinner tonight as planned and maybe we'll sit down and have a frank discussion at the weekend, okay?'

I nodded. I was uncomfortable with his wording. I would rather have had a 'talk' or a 'chat' or even 'thrashed a few things out,' but 'frank discussion' sounded more like a meeting in which I would be made redundant.

We had our dinner and he tried to be nice. He did seem to appreciate the efforts I'd made with the cake and the champagne. When I insisted on paying, and he pulled a face, I told him that I'd got the money together myself. I was very careful to say that in a gentle way, to insist that I wanted to do that. He said it was very thoughtful of me and thanked me for a lovely evening.

It was all very nice. We talked about lots of things, both carefully avoiding any subjects which could eventually lead us into a dark place. We even laughed, remembering some of the other Valentine nights we'd spent at Da Vinci's, about the time the waiter spilt soup all over Max and the time a man on another table proposed to his girlfriend. They had both been drunk and he couldn't speak properly. He went down on one knee and promptly fell over.

When Max and I got home, I didn't even bother trying to initiate anything, even though he did sleep in the bed with me.

As we lay there in the dark, I touched my finger to his lips.

'I do love you, Max.'

A pause.

He kissed my finger, and said, 'Thanks again for a lovely evening, Maddy. It really was thoughtful of you. It was nice for us to be together without silences or arguing. Night-night.'

And I knew that was the best I could hope for. No affirmation of his love for me, just a little encouragement that we can be in each other's company without it being awful and that we don't hate each other. A scrap thrown from the table.

The next day, I went over to see Amanda. She had been so busy lately, starting a business with the girl from The Bahamas. She was making no effort to see me or Mum, and I wanted to go and have a heart to heart with her about Max. I knew our *frank discussion* was looming and I wanted to get someone else's take on it all. Amanda may once have been a bit useless on the relationship front, but she had really started pulling herself together since Dan had left her. She had a new energy, a confidence about her and it made her glow. I admired her for that.

'Oh. Maddy. Hello.' Her voice was flat when she opened the door. Talk about not exactly being excited to see me. I went into the lounge and there on the sofa, was a tanned and rather sexy guy.

'This is Finn. He was my diving instructor in The Bahamas. He's over for a few days.'

Amanda always was a nightmare at subtlety. But apparently, she was now also a bit of a dark horse. I looked the guy up and down and was quite impressed with her for hooking up with someone like that. He was probably just what she needed. I shook hands with the guy, Finn, and he made his excuses and went off to the kitchen on the pretext of making a call.

I couldn't help teasing Amanda. But bless her, she told me he was leaving the next day so I thought it would be a sisterly thing to leave them alone. I just had a quick chat with her and came home, quite excited to tell Max.

'Hey, you'll never guess who I've just met,' I said as I pulled off my jacket and threw my car keys onto the kitchen worktop. Max looked up from the book he was reading. 'I just went over to Amanda's and met her Aussie diving instructor, er, Fenn. No, hang on, Finn. She kept that quiet!' I marched up to put the kettle on, excited to find out from Max if he'd met this guy when he was over there, and if so, what he thought of him. Max closed his book and put it down, folding his arms and looking, I thought, quite intrigued.

'So, did you speak to Finn? What did he say?' Max asked. I took two cups out of the cupboard and went to the fridge for the milk, looking over my shoulder at him.

'So, you know him then?' I smiled. 'Didn't really talk to him. I think Amanda was a bit embarrassed to be honest. She kept that quiet didn't she, saucy little minx!' I laughed and carried on making the tea. 'Good for her, though. So, what's your take on him, Max? Is this serious or is she just getting her leg over?'

Max licked his lips. I got the feeling that he knew about this already, and it just made me feel the vast space between us even more acutely. The secrets between us were multiplying just when I was trying to blast them out of existence.

'Finn is a good guy,' he said, staring at the kettle as if it was going to inspire him as to what to say next. 'Er, yep, good diving instructor by all accounts. Don't really know how serious it is but I can't see it being casual. He's flown all the way over here and I guess Ben must have met him.'

I poured the water into the cups and considered what effect it could have on us all if Amanda was serious.

'This'll be disruptive to her life but she's already said she'll need to be going over there on business a few times a year so I guess she'll work around that. Not sure how Mum is going to feel about it all though.' I shook my head as I handed Max his tea. 'I mean, that's where Julia can be a bit of a cow. She persuaded Amanda to go, knowing how Mum feels about The Bahamian Saxbys.' I noticed Max straighten up. I didn't want him to think I was having a go at him. 'I mean, I know you're now doing this project over there but you're not a blood relative and what you're doing is purely business There's no personal relationship so that's different.'

Max put his untouched cup of tea down onto the coffee table. The air became suddenly dense, as if a thunderstorm was brewing.

'Maddy, sit down a minute. There's something you need to know.'

CHAPTER TWENTY-FIVE

Amanda

'You absolute *BITCH!* Don't you dare go anywhere. I'll be over in five minutes.'

Maddy slammed the phone down. I felt like my insides were shaking and I wasn't entirely convinced I wouldn't need to make a run for the bathroom. Finn had borrowed my car and gone into Tanford to buy a new case for his return journey, but he'd only just left and I knew he'd be at least a couple of hours. I'd have to endure this on my own.

I hadn't been expecting it, not yet. When we'd seen Max for coffee, he'd said he was working up to telling Maddy about Rachel but I thought we were talking about the future. Not pretty much immediately. Then I got the call and Maddy sounded like a raging bull at the other end of the line. She screamed at me about being a vicious cow who had no concept of loyalty. It sounded a bit rich, coming from her. But still, I couldn't disagree entirely. This whole situation had me tied up in knots from the very beginning.

She rang the doorbell, about five times in succession and then I heard her rap her knuckles on the door so hard it must have hurt her. I took a deep breath and opened the door.

'I don't know how you can talk to me about loyalty and morals and look down your nose about the way I've behaved in the past when you've done this to me, your own sister.'

She had started ranting almost before I'd got the door open. The words came out of her in a torrent as she brushed past me into the lounge and then spun around, her hands thrust into her coat pocket. Her eyes were bulging and her face pink.

I closed the door, although the air outside had seemed less chilly than the atmosphere indoors.

'Maddy, I really do understand how upset you are and believe me, I hate to see it,' I said. 'But I only found out about it for sure myself quite recently.'

'You should have told me. You should have told me straight away and I sincerely hope you've told that little American slut that you'll have nothing to do with her anymore.' Maddy half turned away, eyes going everywhere as she roughly combed a hand through her hair. I'd never seen her so agitated.

'I think we'd better sit down.'

Maddy wrestled her coat off and threw it with some force over the arm of the sofa. She sat down with arms and legs folded, breathing heavily and shaking her head.

'You know what bothers me most?' She leant forward. 'None of this would have happened if you hadn't gone running off to The Bahamas. You're so bloody selfish, Amanda. You knew how much it would hurt Mum, for one thing. Don't go thinking it's a storm in a teacup because it isn't to her.'

'I didn't think that, I just felt...'

'You've stirred up a hornets' nest, that's what you've done.' She looked away from me and leant back into the sofa. 'You and Julia, you're both to blame. She should have known better than to encourage you but you are a grown woman. And as for Julia, she's been pushing the American Saxbys on us for years now. God knows why. Just because she met one of them in a hotel and spoke to him for five minutes, she now thinks she's the family conduit between us and the States.'

I was still standing by the door and felt like gravity had suddenly taken on a greater force. I made my way to the kitchen and Maddy stood and followed me without saying a word. She sat on one of the stools and dropped her head into her folded arms on the breakfast bar. She was shaking her head.

'The truth is Maddy, this would have happened with someone, somewhere. I know it seems particularly distressing that it's with a Saxby, but the way things were with you and Max, it was going to happen anyway.'

'But it didn't happen with someone, somewhere did it?' Her voice was muffled as she spoke into the sleeves of her jumper, not even lifting her head.

I pulled out another stool and sat next to her. I tried to reach out to stroke her back but the instant she felt my touch, she shrugged me away. Then I heard a sob.

'I know I've messed up.' She was weeping now. I could

hear the thickness of her throat and the pain of her tears in her strangulated voice. 'I know what everyone thinks of me. But this is killing me. I've seen a photograph of her online. She even looks a bit like I did when I was her age.'

I could have argued with this. They may both be slim and have blonde hair, and they were both pretty. But Maddy had always had a shrew-like look to her face. Sexy yes, but self-satisfied. Rachel was innocent looking, open and sweet, rather than sexy.

'I just needed more time to show Max that I could change, that I could put things right for us. And I would have done.' She lifted her head, wiping her nose on her sleeve as she did. Her face was blotchy, streaked with tears and despair. 'And now I probably won't be able to do that, all because of you.' She spoke calmly now, resigned. So much emotion had broken her and she sat, swaying slightly like a drunk person. She sniffed, let out a deep sign and looked at me. 'So, what about you and golden tits then? The American bitch? Have you broken off contact and told her you won't work with her?'

Maddy's eyes held a challenge.

It was my turn to sigh.

'I haven't, no. And the business is still going ahead.'

Maddy let out a pained 'ahhh' sound and looked away from me again.

'Look, I know it won't be easy and I'll make absolutely sure not to speak to you about Rachel or to her about you for that matter. And if things had been different, if I thought you and Max were fine and it was going to work out, I might have acted differently. But the harsh fact is, I think you're fooling yourself if you thought he was ever going to settle down with you again. You said yourself, even before he met Rachel, that he was distant and that things weren't right between you.'

Maddy tilted her head back and studied the ceiling. She looked like she did when we were children and we were both being told off (usually for one of her misdemeanours, although we always shared the blame) but tears were still forming in the corners of her eyes.

'Doing what you did with Paul, and everything that happened after that was a big ask. To expect him to just shrug it off and carry on as before. I know Max can be a bit, well, dry sometimes, but he's not made of stone.'

We sat in silence for some minutes, Maddy rubbing a thumb along the edge of the breakfast bar. She seemed to be examining her nail but was deep in thought. I was about to ask if she wanted a drink when she got up from the stool.

'I don't know if you and I can recover from this either, Amanda. I know I told you after Dan left to try putting your own needs first for once, but I didn't mean you should stomp all over everyone else's.'

And those were the last words my sister spoke to me before she collected her coat and shut the door behind her.

CHAPTER TWENTY-SIX

Maddy

I tried, I really did. The frustration of playing a waiting game, hoping everything would all go away, took its toll on me. It drained me.

But still I tried. I didn't hassle Max about his affair I smiled sweetly when he came in. I sacked the girl from the cleaning company although I suspected I'd re-hire her in a few months, once things had settled down. I cleaned, cooked and ironed, wanting him to believe he was truly cared for, that I was contributing. I even tried seducing him after a couple of glasses of wine but he rejected me. So I gritted my teeth and told myself to just give it more time.

It was a Tuesday morning when Max went off to see a client and I saw the 'Rachel phone' had been left on his bedside cabinet.

I'd found his secret cell phone in a sports bag in the bottom of his wardrobe a few days before. I knew there would be one somewhere and it only took twenty minutes of searching to uncover it. Max wasn't very good at deceit. Once I'd satisfied myself that it wasn't in his study, I looked in his wardrobe, checking his jacket pockets first before opening his sports bag. And there it was.

I had a knot in my throat when I held the phone in my hand and started trying a few possible PIN numbers. I looked out of the bedroom window to check he was still busy cleaning his car and on about my fifteenth attempt, when I tried the date he'd first flown out to The Bahamas, the phone became accessible.

The only contact on it was Rachel and there were no messages. He must have deleted them all. Yet I still felt sick, just seeing her name on the screen, just feeling my imagination go into overdrive. The pain was indescribable. But I would have to keep quiet about it. It wasn't as if I didn't know he was having an affair. But I hadn't given up on us yet. Far from it.

The day he left it on the bedside cabinet, I knelt on the floor next to the bed and I scrolled back. There were some messages that he'd not deleted. Stupid, childish little notes.

Rachel S
Love you so much baby, you make my heart sing xxxxxxxxx

Max
Rachel, you are the best thing that ever happened to me. I can't wait for us to be together. I'll call you tonight xxxx

Something inside me darkened. It wasn't as if I was unaware of this pathetic little fling. I figured they probably talked on the phone when Max was in his car but this was in my face and my anger had to vent. All the times I had contained my feelings and dampened my fury, all that repression became ignited inside me, resurfacing into a burning rage that I had no control over.

I called Max on his main phone. I didn't plan what I was going to say but the moment he answered I spewed out every vile, hateful thought that had been festering in my head for the last few weeks. I don't remember exactly what I said but I know my language was foul and my vitriol towards Rachel was unbridled. It was violent, disgusting and the burning in my chest was the only thing that made me stop.

Almost a whole minute of silence followed. I had no idea if Max hated me, pitied me or if he was laughing or crying. Eventually he spoke.

'Maddy, I really didn't need any further persuasion. My mind was pretty much made up but you've now confirmed that leaving you and being with Rachel full time is absolutely the right thing to do, but sooner rather than later. In fact, I'm going to come home right now and pack some things and get the hell out of your circus.'

The line went dead before I could reply.

I felt like my head was inside a big bass drum. The house was silent yet I felt an echo, a pressure in my head as if the loudest noise was about to burst my eardrums. As if a bomb had gone off.

There were no tears. I could barely blink. Kneeling on the floor my phone was in my hand but my eyes focussed on the blank space in front of me.

I'd always been so sure of myself, so sure of Max. Even when I'd seen the texts, found out what was happening with Rachel, I still somehow thought that it would all burn itself out. She was not me. She may be sweet and cute and new and shiny, straight from the 'fluffy-bunny' catalogue of girlfriends, but she would never be me and I was what Max wanted. I was what he needed even if that was a curse to him.

Tears came. They filled my eyes so that I could only see a blur and a huge sob escaped as I curled forward and let out a howl.

I sobbed and whined and banged the carpet with my fist a few times before pulling myself together and sitting upright.

This wouldn't do. I wasn't a quitter.

I made my way into my dressing room, swiftly looking through the rails and selecting a dress I knew Max loved. He'd bought it for me the year before last; poppy-red silk, a shift dress that skimmed the best bits of my body. Each time I wore it, he would grin and pull me to him, his hands on my waist and the kiss that followed was always full of intent, full of 'Max and Maddy.' It allowed no room for thoughts or fantasies of others. That was the Max who could make me weak at the knees, the Max I loved to see peer out from his mask of seriousness, but who seldom did. I wondered if that Max was the one Rachel Saxby was now enjoying. The thought turned my stomach.

After showering, I dried my hair, fixed my make-up and then slipped that magical dress over my head. Max's car pulled into the drive. This was it. This was far, far more painful than him finding out about me and Paul, more delicate than our reconciliation after Paul died. It was my last chance.

He walked straight up to the bedroom, passed me without a glance or a word and opened his wardrobe. At the bottom, under his sports bag, was a larger case which he now removed and threw, opened, onto the bed.

'Are we going to talk? Can we just sit down, take a moment and try to work our way through?'

'Bit late for that, don't you think?' he said, grabbing a fistful of hangars at once, the shirts that draped from them twisting this way and that. They would crease. My efforts at ironing them had been in vain. He swung them into the case, hangers and all.

'Max.' I took his arm, stopping him from going back to the wardrobe. Once, I could have engineered this. I could have looked annoyed, told him he was being unreasonable and affected the air of someone who had the upper hand. In the past, this would have worked. He would have stopped in his tracks, fearful of losing me, and we would have talked and he would have been on the back foot. But not today. Today, he didn't care.

He pulled away from me and opened his cupboard, took out a stack of jeans and trousers and laid them out like random roof tiles over the pile of shirts.

'This really is it, Maddy.' Finally, he stood straight, put

his hands on his hips and stared at me. As cold as an empty church, his eyes no longer had any glimmer of compassion. My heart folded in on itself, my face turned to the floor and I shut my eyes.

'There's obviously a lot we have to sort out, but all in good time. I'm going to a hotel tonight but I've booked my ticket to go out to the marina again on Saturday so I might be back before then to grab some more stuff. If I get time, I'll go and see a solicitor before then too, get the ball rolling.'

I opened my eyes and looked up again. He was moving back to his cupboard, pulling out more items to throw in his case, disinterested in my reaction. I no longer seemed to feature in his life in any way. I was simply a problem to be dealt with.

'Max, I just want to see if we can—'

'Don't bother' he cut in. 'There really is nothing you can say, no amount of tears or histrionics that will make one iota of difference. Not a damn thing.'

He said the last with a little smile. A victorious tilt of the head.

I couldn't stand there and watch this any longer. There were things I wanted to say but they were stuck in my throat and I couldn't speak them any more than I could swallow them back down. I heard the words 'All Is Lost' so clearly in my head that I thought for a moment that Max had spoken them. Tears formed and rolled silently down my cheeks but they weren't for effect. I turned and walked away from the man I should have loved better and made my way downstairs, where I sat quietly, eventually hearing his footsteps, hearing the front door open and close and the sound of the wheels of his suitcase rumbling against the gravel of the drive.

Then he was gone.

I had done this. I had let this happen. No longer vibrant, sexy, enchanting Maddy, I was nothing. All my life, my confidence and my chutzpah had been garnered from having a man adore me, from Max and Paul over the last decade and from the boyfriends and admirers before them. I was just an empty vessel, a champagne glass with no bubbles, no allure, no power.

I had been dispensed with. I was finished.

CHAPTER TWENTY-SEVEN

Julia, 2012

Diana rarely spoke about her marriage to John. At least, not in an honest way.

In all their years together, she had never criticised any aspect of him, never even rolled her eyes or had an innocent moan. Not to me, anyway. I imagine I would be the last person she would confide in. But it was unnatural.

So I was surprised when she called and asked for advice. I was in Paris at the time, looking at apartments for a wealthy client to rent for a few months.

'I'm so worried about John,' she said, almost whispering down the phone line as if someone might be listening. 'I know all about the pain he's going through from when I lost Mum. I found it very difficult to even carry on functioning for a good few months.'

She spoke as if she were an only child, the only one who had felt the sting of grief, who'd experienced the strange emptiness that follows the death of a parent. Her relationship with Mum was so much better than mine but it didn't mean I was unaffected.

'He seems so angry all the time. He was quiet at first but when he went to clear out Ivy's flat, it seemed that he couldn't cope. I was with him. I went through all Ivy's dresses and her jewellery. He did the paperwork and when we left on the second day, he became distant. If I spoke to him about Ivy, he closed down and got cross if I pursued it.' She paused, and I could hear the quiver in her voice. 'That's how it's been ever since. That was four months ago and he won't open up to me, won't even discuss how he feels. There's this anger simmering just below the surface. We just go through the motions of everyday life and there's this dark cloud above us that I can't mention. If anything, it's getting worse. I sometimes wake up in the night and he's not beside me. He doesn't sleep very well and looks older. I don't know what to do.'

I'd not spoken to John much after the debacle at Amanda's eighteenth all those years ago. I hardly felt I knew him before and even at the best of times, we would run out of conversation very quickly. He may as well have been from another planet. Yet I knew, or at least suspected, what had happened to bring about such a dramatic change. I tried to soothe Diana, telling her that grief is a funny thing, no two people react in the same way and so on, although I knew she was still upset when we finished the call.

That's when I rang Robin Saxby.

At The Langham, he'd given me his card 'in case of

emergency,' he'd said. I never intended to use it and this wasn't exactly an emergency. But still.

'Julia, my lovely Julia, it's so good to hear from you. How are you? Is everything okay?'

Hearing his voice took me back to that night nearly three years before. Even though I sat in a hotel room over four thousand miles from him, I felt myself blush slightly at the memory.

'Hello Robin. I'm well, thank you. And it's very good to speak to you.'

We spent a few minutes catching up and I could hear the smile playing on his lips as he spoke. I didn't doubt he could tell that I was smiling too.

'I have a rather unusual request actually Robin. I'm not even sure this is going to be the right thing, so I'd value your thoughts.'

'Now I'm intrigued,' he said. 'I suppose it's too much to hope that this request might involve you getting on a plane and coming over to see me?'

I closed my eyes to steady myself. I felt a heat in the very pit of my stomach that threatened to turn into words that I shouldn't say. It threatened to tell Robin I'd be on the next flight and to hell with work commitments or promises I'd made to myself.

I took a deep breath.

'I don't know if you are aware, but Ivy died a few months back.'

'Yes, the solicitor got in touch. Dad paid Ivy a pension so it was a formality that they let us know. He did react when we told him. I'm sure it all weighs heavily on his conscience you know.' His voice was sad and serious. 'It must have been a very sad time for your sister and John. I wish I could reach out to him, I mean, he's my half-brother. But I totally get what you told me when we met.'

Of course, Robin wouldn't have contacted John. I'd made it very clear that any approaches would not be welcome and that I doubted, after all this time, that hearing the truth of what happened back in 1948 would ease the pain. It would probably increase it tenfold. And I suspected that was exactly what had happened.

'Thing is Robin, I don't know for sure but I believe that when John was sorting through his mother's things, he found some papers that confirmed that William and Ivy were never married. And if I'm right, he may also have discovered that what he called 'the other family,' all of you Americans, were actually William's proper family and Christine was his wife. He most likely worked out that it was Ivy who had the affair with a married man. John is a very traditional sort. It would have been very shocking for him to discover he was born out of wedlock.

'Ah, I see. And so you're not completely sure of this, Julia?'

'No, not completely,' I said. 'But Diana is so worried that she can barely mention Ivy's name. John isn't in a good place and I can only imagine, with the way Di described him changing suddenly after they'd been to Ivy's flat, that he's made the discovery.'

We were both silent for a few moments, thinking through the consequences of telling the truth or keeping silent. Both seemed equally likely to cause disruption.

'Do you think I should write to Diana? Just privately to her, so that she knows what has caused John to change.'

'That's exactly what I was thinking. He obviously doesn't want to tell her. He's quite an old-fashioned guy. It's been hard enough for him thinking his father left his mother for a mistress. If he's found out Ivy was a fling on a trip to Europe…well, that would have devastated him. He'll never get over that.'

'You could tell Diana. You're her sister, probably the best person to tell her.'

'Robin, you know I can't do that. I've mentioned meeting you but have always said it was very brief, a quick hello and exchange of contact details. It would seem very odd that I have knowledge of her husband's background.'

'Yeah, I know. I kind of knew you'd keep our weekend of passion between ourselves. Just as I have. Still, those memories eh?'

I felt myself blushing again and bit my lip.

I glanced at my watch. It was six thirty in the evening and I had a table booked for myself and Danielle, my counterpart in Paris, for seven. I needed to change and have a shower but I didn't want my conversation with Robin to end. I hadn't realised it would affect me this much. It would be lunchtime in The Bahamas. I imagined myself sitting by the ocean, with him, chatting easily as we had done in London.

'Look, I have to go now,' I said. 'I've got a table booked for dinner and I need to get ready. Let's think about the best way forward and I'll call you again tomorrow, same sort of time. Let me think everything through. Please don't contact Diana without running it past me. Would that be alright?'

I heard a sigh of resignation from the other end of the phone.

'Yes, of course it's alright. You can call me anytime you want.' He sounded a little flat. 'So who is the lucky guy you're having dinner with tonight?'

I almost rushed to reassure, to tell him it was just a female business associate. But I knew a little artifice never hurt.

'Oh, no one special,' I said. 'Tomorrow then?'

I never did get to call Robin the next evening. Instead, I received a call at six that morning from Max. He told me that John had suffered a heart attack late the previous night and had passed away an hour or so before. The girls were distraught and Diana was in deep shock.

I packed my things and took the next flight home.

CHAPTER TWENTY-EIGHT

Amanda

'Don't worry, I'll be fine,' Finn told me during his daily phone call. He had that slightly exasperated edge to his voice that I recognised from Sammy and Ben. The way they spoke when I was fussing too much, to let me know they were perfectly capable and I should stop flapping.

'I'm sorry, can't help myself. I'm a Mum. It's a natural thing to worry about people I care for when they do crazy things.'

'I've been diving with sharks tons of times. Never had a problem and they rarely attack divers anyway, so stop worrying. I'm not crazy. Only crazy about you.'

He'd mentioned oh so casually that he was going on a dive, way out to one of the other islands. It would be an all-day thing and Max was going along for the ride, although sensibly, in my opinion, he would not be going into the water.

Rachel was over at mine on the day of the dive. She

had arrived in England three days earlier, after I'd made us appointments with the bank and solicitors and various other people who we needed on board to launch our business. She had been upset that it meant she wouldn't be at home while Max was at Saxby Marine, but they'd be reunited within a few days.

We'd gone through the logo suggestions the designer had come up with and had finally agreed on simple turquoise blue wave design that we thought would work well on screen and printed onto paper or clothing. It was starting to get quite exciting now.

We had lunch at home. I'd gone out the day before to stock up on bread and sandwich fillings, some soup and a selection of vegetables. Rachel had said she'd cook some fresh fish I'd bought for the evening meal and having tried her healthy food out in The Bahamas, I was looking forward to tasting it.

'Sorry Rachel, we'll have to stay in all day,' I told her. There's too much risk of bumping into Maddy. I'm still hoping she doesn't drive past. I told her I'd be out all day to put her off the idea of dropping by, not that that's likely. She's pretty much disowned me.'

'It's fine. I understand. I know it's hard for you, working with me under the circumstances. I do have a lot of sympathy with her. She must be feeling awful and that gives me no pleasure at all, but I think Max had already had enough and when we met, and it's just been all consuming. Soul mates who have searched for each other and finally met. Nothing could have stopped it happening.' She smiled at me, an innocent smile, of someone to whom something uncontrollable had happened. As if neither she nor Max had any influence over it.

'Even so, I think you have to be prepared for some rough times ahead. My sister is not the sort to calmly accept being left behind.'

'Oh, I know,' said Rachel. 'I'll just have to withstand whatever comes my way. For Max.'

I was worried about the intensity of their relationship. It was all so quick. That didn't necessarily mean they weren't absolutely right for each other, but it just struck me that they were behaving like fourteen-year-olds. I could remember myself at that age, thinking that the only possible man for me was Tom Cruise because I'd watched Risky Business about a hundred times. I thought all we had to do was meet, and he'd realise we were destined to be together.

'Just be careful though, Rachel,' I said, trying not to sound too negative. 'It's early days for you and Max and he's been through quite a tough time. I know you are very into each other and that's great, but try to give him some space too, eh?'

Rachel simply shrugged her shoulders and said, 'Sure.' She carried on eating her tomato soup. Her mind was clearly made up. She and Max were locked together now and that was that.

We finished eating and she helped me clear away the dirty plates.

'Anyway, Amanda, you get what it's like. Look at you and Finn! I tell you, when you're not together it's like he's running on fifty percent battery. I mean, he still has the energy and the passion for diving and all that, but something is kind of on hold. What do you think is going to happen with you guys?' She closed the dishwasher and gazed at me.

'I'm not sure. We'll work something out long term but there are so many obstacles in the way. Like four thousand or so miles, like me having two children, like my family being over here—there's all sorts standing in our way, to be honest.'

'But something so good is worth working at. Love will find a way, Amanda, for both of us.'

We went back to work but I still had a strange feeling in the pit of my stomach. I was sure Rachel stood a serious chance of being disappointed. It was great to see Max so relaxed and shrugging off that serious persona, but it was fundamentally who he was. It must have been so refreshing for him to feel so adored and although I felt Rachel was definitely a step up from Maddy, I wasn't convinced it was the right thing for either of them. He needed someone kinder for sure, but I was certain Rachel's verve and zest for life, her pure energy would start to grate on him, eventually. But I had to bite my tongue. I had learnt the hard way that sometimes, things just happen.

By the time we'd put our laptops away, sent a few emails to various suppliers and set up some social media accounts, we were pretty happy with what we had so far. *Saxby Health and Vitality* was coming alive before our eyes. I could never have done anything like this before. Dan would not have been any support at all and living with him had eroded what little confidence I had. I wouldn't have even tried.

'I'm really happy with how this is all looking,' said Rachel. 'I think tomorrow, we'll just go through the scripting for the videos again, but we're nearly there.' She clasped her hands together and smiled broadly, making an 'eeeew!' sound and hugging me. 'Why don't you pour us a couple of glasses of wine and I'll get to work on the sea bass?'

Rachel bounced around the kitchen, finding pans and knives and chopping boards, while I poured our wine and selected some music. She asked me again about Finn.

'So, is he the one?' she asked, gently lowering the sea bass into the frying pan to sizzle.

'You know, I may be a bit too cynical now to think of things that way. I thought Dan was the one once. That's the thing, no one gets married thinking that it'll do for now, with an expectation that maybe, sometime, you'll go your separate ways.'

I was sitting on the little two-seater by the French doors, my legs curled under me. I thought about what I'd just said and about how quickly life can pick you up in a whirlwind, twist and turn and put you down somewhere completely unexpected.

'I mean think about it. Nine months ago, I was still with Dan, sleepwalking my way through life, and not expecting much from him or from myself. I hadn't a clue that there might be a man out there who would treat me the way Finn does. I thought it didn't exist. I'd not even contemplated going to The Bahamas, not known the truth about the family and definitely, *definitely* never been anywhere close to launching my own business.'

'*Our* own business,' Rachel turned around from her position at the hob and smiled at me, spatula held aloft in her right hand.

'Absolutely! *Our* business, and I'm so glad I've got the chance to do this with you. So I can say that Finn could be the one now, at this moment. But I was royally let down not so long ago, so I'm not putting all my eggs in one basket.'

Rachel soon had dinner served up and just after we'd eaten, Julia called.

'Hello darling,' she said, 'how is the business set-up going? I'm absolutely beyond excited for you.'

I told Julia what we'd achieved. It was good to have someone to talk to about it. Naturally, Mum didn't want to speak to me about anything connected with the Saxbys, especially Rachel. She was barely speaking to me at all. Eve was so busy with the shop and by her own admission, was a bit of a technophobe and had never got involved in the business side of Collard Books. She was happy to serve in the shop and gossip and re-arrange the shelves and the furniture, but whenever Marco spoke about the finer points of running a business, she would do an exaggerated yawn.

'So, will I get to meet Rachel?' Asked Julia.

'Come over tomorrow,' I suggested. 'We've got a bit of work to do in the morning but we should be finished by lunchtime. And we're kind of stuck indoors, for obvious reasons.'

'Hmmm, yes, all a bit tricky isn't it? I tell you what, why don't I come over about two? And tell Rachel I'll bring some photo albums to embarrass you with. I have a few pictures of you as a child and of me and your Mum.' Then she lowered her voice, 'Of course, I'll take out any of Maddy. But I really can't wait to meet Robin's daughter.'

'Okay, well come whenever you like. I'm sure Rachel would like to meet you too. Then she can go and tell the rest of the family about you. How many years ago did you say you met Robin?'

Julia sounded slightly flustered and embarrassed as she tried to recall exactly when it was. 'Oh, gosh, must be nine or ten years ago something like that. Just bumped into him in a hotel. Just to say hello.'

Poor Julia. She must have been made to feel guilty by Mum for just daring to speak to an American Saxby for a minute or two.

I told Julia we'd look forward to seeing her and ended the call. Just a few seconds later, my phone rang again but it was a number I didn't recognise. I expected it was going to be a sales call and was preparing my best offish voice to end the call quickly. Then I heard an American accent.

'Brad! Hi! Lovely to hear from you!'

Rachel made a little 'whoop' sound on hearing her cousin's name and came and stood as close to me as she could, straining to hear the conversation.

'Amanda, are you on your own? Or is Rachel with you?'

Brad's voice was trembling. I felt my throat constrict. Rachel looked sideways at me. 'Yes, she's here,' I said. She took my hand and I put the call onto speaker phone.

'I'm so, so sorry to tell you,' Brad was struggling to speak now, the weight of his words catching as he spoke. 'Today, out by Cat Island—I'm so sorry, there's been an accident.

CHAPTER TWENTY-NINE

Amanda

Somehow, I managed to call Julia and asked her to come straight over. I didn't say why but she would have known from how I spoke that something terrible had happened.

I felt strangely guilty. I experienced the most horrible mixture of emotions. I watched Rachel, curled into a ball in the two-seater, silently crying, her face not visible.

No one was entirely sure why Max had collapsed and died on the boat. Gary, the skipper was apparently just watching the water after Finn and Brad descended and Max had stood up to fetch a drink from the cool box. He turned and asked Gary if he could get him anything, and then fell, as if he'd had his legs cut from under him.

Gary radioed a mayday and asked for a medivac. Then he started revving the boat engine to alert Finn and Brad that something was up and they made an emergency ascent. Finn started trying to resuscitate Max and carried on until the seaplane arrived. But it was too late. Finn was beside himself with grief, sobbing along with Brad and Gary as Max's body was stretchered into the plane.

Julia arrived, taking stock of my tear-stained face and hugging me without even noticing the figure curled up on the sofa.

'Darling, tell me what's happened,' she said, trying to manoeuvre me onto the stool by the breakfast bar.

It was difficult to speak. My mouth was dry and my jaw felt as if it was wired half shut. I told her about Brad's call. Then I nodded toward where Rachel lay. Julia said nothing, but her eyes were filled with tears. She walked into the lounge and I heard the creaky lid of the blanket box opening. She returned and put one blanket over Rachel and draped another around my shoulders. Only then did I notice how violently I was shivering.

We sat in silence. I could see Rachel's body heaving beneath the blanket but no sound came out. My head hung down.

After a while, Julia made three cups of tea. They all remained untouched. Eventually, she took Rachel firmly by the shoulders and held her tight as she walked her up the stairs and into the spare room. Rachel's eyes were so red and puffy that I doubted she could see anything through them.

After a few minutes, Julia came back down. She went into the lounge and came back with two brandies. We sipped them and the warmth seemed to release the tears that were held behind my eyes.

'I can't believe it. It feels like a nightmare. We'll never see Max again.' I took another sip of brandy as Julia wiped a few tears away with a tissue.

'I take it Maddy doesn't know yet?'

I felt a renewed level of nausea. I had of course thought that Maddy needed to know but somehow it hadn't crossed my mind that it would be a job for one of us to do. I rolled the various relationships Maddy had with each of us round my mind.

'I think we need to tell Mum and she'll have to tell Maddy,' I told Julia. 'Let's face it, she's never got on well with you and I'm the devil incarnate at the moment.' I nodded to myself. 'Yes, we have to tell Mum.'

Thankfully, Julia volunteered for that task and after checking that I was going to be alright, she set off to go and see Mum and deliver the awful news. 'I'll come by in the morning,' she said, giving me one last hug.

* * *

The group that came through arrivals at the airport were like waxwork dummies of the people I had last seen.

Finn smiled when he saw me but there was so much unspoken pain between us that it would be unseemly to rush into each other's arms and make a fuss.

'I've missed you so much,' he whispered as he embraced me. 'I've never felt so alone as I have since we lost Max.'

I couldn't speak. I looked over his shoulder at Robin

and Brad, trying to be practical, replacing passports into backpacks and steering the wayward trolley. Everyone still looked shell-shocked.

I pulled away from Finn and greeted Robin and Brad with a feeble smile and a brief hug. We said very little as we made our way out to the car park and loaded up. They looked exhausted as well as broken and while Finn got into the seat next to me, the other two men slipped into the back, both folding their arms and closing their eyes. I expected they would feign sleep rather than have to discuss the whole terrible episode again.

Finn explained that Max's body was going to be collected the next day and brought home. The funeral was going to take place three days later. We were dreading it.

I dropped Robin and Brad off at the Excelsior in Tanford and then Finn and I went home. We spoke little. Finn unpacked and showered and then we went to bed, holding each other, both lost in thought until exhaustion led us into a fitful sleep.

The following days were spent in a bit of a fog. I had to spend time over at Mums. Max's father and mother had flown back from their home in Portugal and I realised I'd not seen them since Maddy's wedding. I knew Max hadn't been particularly close to them and although they were obviously upset, they seemed to be in their own little bubble, grateful for me and Mum for organising the funeral and wake.

The day itself passed in a bit of a blur. I'd tested the water but it was decided that Robin and Brad shouldn't attend the funeral itself. They would come along to the grave a few days later. When I'd nervously told them we'd thought it best they stay away, Robin had put his hand over mine. 'That's perfectly understandable. But I needed to be here, on British soil, while Max was laid to rest.'

Rachel stayed at my house. She was barely functioning and deeply distressed that she had been advised to stay away from the funeral. She took the news that Max had died of a brain aneurism badly; it had seemed too unfair that something so instant, so random could have snatched away their chance of happiness. I was worried about her, but Robin suggested that perhaps it was better for her to let it all out now, to face her grief and not to bury her feelings away.

Finn could just about get away with attending. He wasn't a Saxby and I made sure that Mum and Maddy, and Max's parents all knew how hard Finn had tried to try save his life.

The Church was packed and people had to stand outside. It was a bright spring day, but cold. Those who stood in the churchyard among the daffodils rubbed gloved hands together and shuffled their feet around to keep warm.

Eve and Marco had slipped into the pew behind me, clutching their Orders of Service. I turned and gave Eve a weak smile. She immediately welled up with tears.

'Don't, oh don't' she said, shaking her head. 'I'm trying to keep it together here. You know how I cry my eyes out at the slightest thing. This is going to send me over the edge.' Marco nodded agreement.

I could hear car doors slamming outside and a few minutes

later, a hush fell over the congregation as the coffin containing Max's body filled the doorway. The pallbearers made their way down the aisle, followed by Max's parents, Maddy and Mum. *Adaggio for Strings* began playing and that was enough to reduce most people to choking tears.

The vicar spoke kindly words about Max. She had obviously spent some time in the company of Mum and Maddy, as her next words made me turn and raise an eyebrow at Eve, who was mouthing 'What the hell?'

'...Max was a keen skier and it was while enjoying this pastime that he met Madeleine, fell in love, and married her some two years later.

When people pass away, it is often a great comfort to recall the happiness of a life well lived and the love of the people around them. With Madeleine, Max found that deep and abiding love. They were a devoted couple and Max often spoke of his gratitude towards Maddy, for showing him the levels of kindness, loyalty and love that most people can only dream of.'

One or two people cleared their throats at this point. I felt grateful that the Americans weren't around to hear it. Even Finn pulled a face at me and I knew he was struggling to keep his composure.

After the service, we filed out to the churchyard and stood around the grave as the last tears were wrenched from us on this terrible day. As we slowly walked back to the cars, Maddy drew level with me.

'I don't think I'll ever forget what you've done, Amanda,' she said in a hushed tone. 'But I do forgive you. It's what Max would want.'

I stopped and so did she. We faced each other.

'Well, thank you for that. I hate the way things are between us.'

She gave a quick, false smile. 'And you know, I realised that being angry at you was only hurting me, not you. So it's pointless. It's better for me if I simply forgive you.' She flashed her brief, phoney smile at me and turned away to catch up with Max's parents.

Only Maddy could offer an olive branch and give you a thorn.

In the days after the funeral, Finn and I found ourselves holding on to each other with a deeper certainty. Losing Max had made us both reconsider what mattered and how fragile and brief life is.

'I know we've not spent many weeks together, Amanda,' Finn said one night as we lay side by side after making love. 'But I just know what I know. And that means being with you full time, somehow.'

He rolled towards me and pulled me close.

'I know. I feel it too and it's so disconcerting because if a friend of mine said they were committing their future to someone they'd only known for such a short time I'd probably tell them they were nuts.'

We didn't need to say any more. We'd found our stride.

Finn would be going back to the island in a couple of days, travelling home with Robin and Brad and Rachel. The priorities for me were going to be keeping up the momentum of our new business until Rachel felt well enough to resume. And, searching for a way to make my relationship work with Finn while keeping Mum and Maddy and Sammy and Ben happy. It was a monumental task but it was everything to me and I knew it could be done.

Just as long as nothing happened to change the strength of feeling between Finn and me, anything was possible.

CHAPTER THIRTY

Amanda

You might want to check out your boyfriends timeline. Then tell me that the American lot aren't all totally toxic.

It was the first text I'd received from Maddy in a while. Communication between us was sparse and the only times we ever met face to face was at Mum's. I'd always ask if she was okay or if there was anything I could do to help but I'd get little more than a sneer in reply. If she initiated a conversation with me, it would usually be to make a sarcastic remark about Rachel or the rest of the Saxbys, or to laugh at me for having a long distance relationship with Finn. She said things like 'How's your pen pal this week? Isn't that sweet, it's just like when we were at school and we'd do student exchanges and stay with French families for a week.' Her face would become contorted and I wondered if she had any idea how ugly it made her. But Mum was always with us and she made it very clear that she thought Maddy had been through enough already and that I should suffer her attitude in silence.

I hadn't heard from Finn for a couple of days. Sometimes, if the diving centre was particularly busy, he wouldn't have time to call, but I'd most often get a text, even if it was just an 'X'. But I'd not spoken to or heard from him.

I didn't reply to Maddy's text. I wasn't going to be reeled into her games but I did log in and see what Finn had been up to. He was always tagged in lots of photos. Customers from the diving courses always wanted to thank the man who showed them an amazing new underwater world.

*Me, Stevie n' our main man, **Finn Alexander**—top dude* appeared under a photo of two bearded guys, holding up beer cans outside the Wacky Wahoo with Finn standing in the background.

Then there were some pictures Finn had taken of Parrot fish and a Barracuda, and a short video of some dolphins.

I scrolled down a little further and saw three photographs he'd been tagged in that made my stomach flip.

A very slim girl in a bikini, hair up in a messy bun, was leaning in to kiss Finn on the cheek. Her hands were on his thigh. Finn stared straight ahead. I guessed that Gary must have taken the photo.

***Anna Vane-Harvey** is with **Finn Alexander**—Feeling Happy. With this gorgeous man, so good to be back aboard The Deep Blue again enjoying some special time diving xxxxxx*

Heat flushed my face and my heart raced. Everything he'd ever said to me about wanting to be settled and not being interested in anyone else was now thrown into doubt. It *had* been difficult to trust again but I'd finally reached a point at which I could cope with the idea that girls he met while diving would not be a threat to us. But I hadn't reckoned on Anna making a return. Despite the way it was making me feel, I had to look at the other photos. I had to carry on with the torture.

The next shot showed the girl now without her bikini top. She was sitting on the dive platform and Finn was in the water, no diving gear on, just swimming. It looked as if she was splashing water at him with her feet. They were both laughing.

***Anna Vane-Harvey** is with **Finn Alexander**—missed this guy SO MUCH!!!! Nobody knows how to have fun like we do. Xxxxxx*

If someone had punched me in the head it would probably have hurt less and been easier to cope with. I looked up, glanced outside into the garden where life just continued as normal, with birds flitting around and spring flowers coming into bloom. I wondered how everything could carry on when to me it felt as if everything was an illusion. Trusting someone again had been like climbing a mountain and I was just in sight of the summit. Yet now I was free falling down the side of the rocks. I closed my eyes and took a deep breath before looking at the third photo.

Inside the Wacky Wahoo at night. Finn was sitting on a chair wearing the blue shirt I'd bought him when he was in the UK. He had his phone in his hand and looked as if he was sending a text. The girl was made up now and looked scarily beautiful. She was standing behind Finn, her hands resting on his shoulders. She wore a tight fitting white dress and she laughed into the camera.

***Anna Vane-Harvey** is with **Finn Alexander**—*
This time, the caption was not comprised of words. All that followed was a line of red heart emojis.

My hands shook. I hadn't felt this dazed and shaken since the day I'd discovered Dan's betrayal. I closed down the app, in case I was tempted to look again and make myself feel worse. Tears threatened but I couldn't let this happen again.

I switched off my phone, took myself upstairs and got back into bed, pulling the covers over my head and wishing I could sleep for a year and wake up to a new life and a new start.

* * *

After two hours of trying and failing to sleep, I gave in and decided I had to call Finn. Rage made my hands shake so much it took me two attempts to dial his number.

When he answered the phone, sounding relaxed and cheerful as if nothing untoward was going on, it only fuelled my jealousy more, wrecking any chance I had of discussing the situation with Anna as if I were a reasonable, mature adult.

'What the actual fuck are you trying to do to me? How can you make out you want me, make out you're loyal, and then casually take up with *her* again? And then let her plaster it all over the internet?' I didn't recognise my voice. It belonged to a snarling alley cat.

'Whoa there! Slow down, take a breath, Amanda. I don't know what the hell you're on about, there's no…'

'Don't tell me there's nothing going on. I'm not bloody stupid!'

'Look just calm down. I know you're not stupid and I know you are—you should be—smart enough to give the other person a chance to speak.'

'Chance to make excuses you mean.'

Finn remained silent. The first inkling that I had handled this very, very badly, took root inside my head.

I took a breath. I knew I sounded out of control. I was out of control. I did want to hear what he had to say but couldn't help thinking back to the days leading up to my split with Dan, to how stupid I felt afterwards for not facing facts, not seeing what was in front of my eyes. I wasn't going to be made a fool of again.

'Okay, so talk to me then. Tell me why you've stopped calling me. Tell me why this girl you were in love with is now back working with you every day, going out with you at night, putting up photos with you tagged in, all captioned with hearts…' My voice was getting louder. I couldn't help it. Saying these words brought the emotion back to the surface. I took another deep breath and licked my lips.

'Tell me the truth. Just tell me you're back with her. Tell me how you had a great time with me and I'm a great girl and all that bullshit and how you're really sorry, *but*. Go on, I'm listening.'

I sounded like a Mum talking to an errant child. I grimaced and leant forward, cringing at my own inability to speak how I intended to, to treat Finn at least with a little respect.

'Jeez Amanda.' Finn let out a long breath. I could imagine him shaking his head, probably wondering why he'd got involved with such an unhinged woman as me in the first place. 'I don't actually have time for this because I'm due out on the Deep Blue in fifteen minutes and I'm talking to you while trying to check the regs and tanks for the next dive, so I'll have to be brief. First off, I've been so flat out the last few days I've been too exhausted after work to call. I had planned to text you tonight, as it happens. Anna is working here again, not that I had anything to do with hiring her. We have to get along because we work together and people's lives are in our hands when we're thirty metres below the surface so that's pretty important, don't you think? I've no idea what she puts on social media. As you know, I only ever post pictures of fish and coral and don't look at what other people are doing. Anna being here has nothing to do with us. It's irrelevant.'

I so wanted to believe it. The desire to apologise for blowing my top was overwhelming.

But I kept thinking of what Maddy had said when she found out about Max. 'Men always want to have their cake and eat it. No matter what they say. If they think they can get away with it, with anything, they will. Women should never fall for the little-boy-lost, *I'd never look at another woman* act because that's what it is, an act.'

'Well, obviously you didn't think about me. It never occurred to you to mention that the woman you were once besotted with was now working alongside you, every day. What do you take me for?'

There was another long pause. I could hear voices in the background and arrangements being made to load the Deep Blue with equipment ready to take a group of divers out to sea.

'Amanda, I have to go.' His voice was low key. Defeated and flat. 'All I can tell you is that when Anna came back here, I realised that I felt nothing for her anymore. I mean nothing other than respect for the fact that she is a bloody great diving instructor. The customers love her and you know what, if I got into trouble underwater I'd feel a hell of a lot safer if she was there too. Gotta go, Amanda. Sounds to me like you've made your mind up already about us, so I'll wait to hear from you. Not going to hold my breath, though.'

The phone went dead. I stood with my eyes closed, holding my phone so hard my knuckles were white. Nausea swirled around the pit of my stomach.

I wished I hadn't made the call. I wished I'd given myself a few hours to calm down, to prepare what I was going to say instead of launching into a tirade of infantile abuse. Finn was a very different character to Dan. His outlook on life was to live honestly; it was the only way he could be stress-free.

I may have just handed him to Anna on a plate.

CHAPTER THIRTY-ONE

Amanda

I sent a brief text to Sammy saying that I wouldn't be around for a while and I'd be in touch as soon as I was back. Two hours later, there was still no reply. She probably didn't give two hoots what I was doing.

I told Ben to call me whenever he wanted to and made sure he had everything he needed so that Julia's primary job would be to feed him and make sure he got to bed at a reasonable hour. His school shirts were ironed and hanging up and I'd made Julia an easy to follow schedule for his after school activities, and a list of his favourite foods. Although, being such and easy going person, I'm sure he would eat whatever was put in front of him.

Julia arrived with a small suitcase and looked very happy at the prospect of a few days living here with only Ben for company. It was probably a relief for her to get away from the intensity of being a guest at Mum's.

Julia was also true to her word and kept quiet about my real reason for dashing off to The Bahamas at such short notice. At her suggestion, I told Mum and Maddy that I'd managed to find very cheap flights and so it was a great time to go.

Maddy, of course, questioned my motives and probably suspected that there was more to my trip.

'So, off to see lover boy even though he's got another woman on the go, are you?'

It was like a kick in the stomach, but I was determined to play it cool.

'Actually, that's not the case, Maddy, but I know you only see the worst in people so your reaction is hardly surprising.'

She let out a sigh, signalling to me that she continued to believe I was a wimp, a pushover.

'Look, now's a good time to go for all sorts of reasons. The flights were cheap and I'll only be gone a few weeks in any case.'

'Whatever. Have a good time, I suppose.' She put the phone down before I could say anything else. Since the funeral, she had barely been able to bring herself to speak to me and frankly, I felt the same way about her. Max's death had been a terrible shock to all of us but surely she must have understood that sympathy would be in short supply? I imagine she thought that I was somehow punishing her for having an affair, looking down on her from my high horse.

But it wasn't just the fact that she cheated on Max. It ran much deeper, but I doubt she'd ever see that because she's always been oblivious to chaos she's caused. She was certainly oblivious to the pain and distress she'd caused me over the years. The lies she told our parents to get her own way and the spiteful remarks when she knew my confidence was low. The humiliation she caused on my eighteenth birthday.

Maddy and Mum were still in their enchanted circle so I would let them get on with it. Thank God I had Julia.

As I finished packing my case, I heard a gentle tap on my bedroom door and Julia calling to see if I wanted a cup of tea.

'That would be perfect,' I answered. I was just about ready to go and my taxi for the airport wasn't due for another forty-five minutes.

I closed my case, checked my handbag for passport, money and phone and went downstairs where Julia waited with a pot of tea and a look on her face that I knew very well.

'All ready?'

I nodded. I was ready in that I was packed, ready in that I wanted to see Finn again, but not ready for the possibility of rejection. I didn't know what the future might hold long term and only time would tell if we could dovetail our very different lives and be together, somehow. Only time would tell if we were as well suited as we imagined ourselves to be. But allowing my past to cast a shadow on the present would have wrecked any chance of finding out and I wasn't prepared to let that happen.

Julia poured the tea and made small talk about how envious she was that I was about to enjoy some time in the sun because spring had barely made an appearance at home and it still felt like winter.

'You know Amanda, I do understand what mixed feelings you must have about this trip. It does feel rather *do or die*. And much as I hope that all will be well, we should be realistic.'

'Do you think I'm going to get there and discover that he is seeing Anna again?'

'Well, you absolutely can't rule it out altogether, but if I had to make a judgement call on whether he's that type or not, I'd say no. I think your biggest problem is that you may just have crossed the line when you started flinging accusations at him.' She gritted her teeth and flashed her eyes at me, looking concerned that I might react badly to her suggestion.

'Julia, I know. It's my worst nightmare. As painful as it would be if I found he and Anna were together, obviously it would push me backwards in my recovery from Dan cheating on me, but I'd have to take on the chin.' I shrugged. 'Anna is beautiful, he obviously loved her once and maybe she's shown how much she regrets leaving him. But if I get there and find we're over because I've been an idiot, well, that would be very hard to deal with.'

Julia answered with a wry smile and reached forward to squeeze my hand.

'You're doing the right thing by going to see him face to face. It's not going to be easy but the fact that you've galvanised yourself into booking a flight and getting over there tells me that you are very keen on Finn.'

I allowed myself a little smile. 'Keen is an interesting choice of word. But yes, it's all taken me by surprise. I thought after Dan that I'd be on my own for a very long time, maybe forever. Even when I first went over to see Robin and the rest of the family, it didn't occur to me that I'd meet someone. I just wanted to get away from here, to meet the other side of the family and break the spell everyone had put on me, to keep me away from them.'

'Sometimes you end up in the right place at the right time.'

Julia smiled and gazed into the middle distance. She thought I was completely unaware but each time I mentioned Robin, there was a faint blush to her cheeks and a softening of her eyes. I knew, of course, that they met briefly in London some years before and that they had been in touch intermittently since. I tried questioning her once about how much time they'd spent together and tried to persuade her to tell me what Robin was like. But she had blushed, turned away and closed the conversation down. I hadn't approached the subject since, so she probably thought I didn't have a clue that there was more to her meeting with Robin than she'd shared. But that was fine, she could have that. One day, truth will out. He may be older than me but I could absolutely understand that he would have charmed Julia and penetrated her tough shell in no time. I look forward to hearing the story one day.

We finished our tea and one last time, I ran through my list of instructions as to what Julia should do if Ben became ill, had problems at school, needed to talk to me. She rolled her eyes theatrically and muttered something about him probably not missing his 'smother.' I laughed but Julia didn't.

'Look darling, there's something I've been wanting to say

for a while now and I know you're under a lot of stress but perhaps if I say it now, you can think about it while you're away.'

I didn't like the sound of this. Julia licked her lips and seemed to be chewing the inside of her cheek as she struggled to put words together.

'There's a pattern in our family and I'm sure you've noticed it but sometimes we are all guilty of looking back to the past without using what we've learnt to improve the future. Your mother and I were brought up as if by two different women. Our mother treated us entirely differently for as long as I can remember.'

'Yes, I know that but it doesn't excuse the way Mum has been with Maddy and—'

'Please let me finish Amanda. My mother, your grandmother, would fiercely deny treating Diana and I any differently or loving one less than the other. Just like your mother truly believes that she has brought you and Maddy up the same. She has often said that if she appears to behave differently with you and Maddy it's because your characters and personalities are different, not because of anything she has done.'

'Okay, so, what are you getting at?'

'My love. What I'm driving at is that it happens in so many families, this favouritism, this preferring one child to another. No woman, or very few, would actually admit to it, but it does happen. Sometimes it's by such a small margin that it's barely perceptible but occasionally it's obvious and distinct and everybody suffers because of it. The parents *and* the children and it's often because the parents genuinely don't realise or they bury their heads in the sand because it's such a difficult subject.'

I felt the lens coming into focus again, a truth about to be revealed that I wasn't prepared for.

'And you are telling me this because you can see my relationships with Sam and Ben are following this pattern.' Julia nodded briefly, studying me, taking a deep breath.

It was a revelation in some respects but I don't think it was a new truth. Just a hidden one. I didn't love Ben more than Sammy but I did like him more. Sammy was difficult, prickly and perhaps a little too clever for her own good. Perhaps a bit too sassy, a bit too similar to Maddy and that meant I tarred her with the same brush. I had closed something off to Sammy. I'd stopped listening and made assumptions about her that were completely unfair.

I reached out and laid my hand on top of Julia's, nodding slowly. She relaxed a little and smiled. No more needed to be said. I knew I had work to do on my relationship with my daughter when I returned from The Bahamas,

Then we heard the *toot-toot* from the taxi driver.

Julia hugged, told me not to worry, to be brave, and to be true to myself. And off I went, to meet my fate.

CHAPTER THIRTY-TWO

Maddy

Julia replied to my text.

Yes, she told me, Amanda had arrived safely and Ben was fine and everything was under control.

I didn't intend to call my sister. She'd made it very clear that she now had other things going on in her life and that my attendance was no longer required. It was probably very convenient for her that Mum and I were both widows. We could console each other in our misery, away from her gaze, where she didn't have to deal with us. I doubt Amanda gave much thought to the depth of guilt and sorrow that I felt or considered that my behaviour, our behaviour, had been fashioned by events and people from the past. It may not always be pretty, but we are all the sum of the life we've lived.

It wasn't like I didn't know I'd screwed up. It surprised me though, that Amanda had never once asked me why, never talked to me like a friend. She saw me only as the annoying younger sister, spoilt and doted on, while she wallowed in her martyrdom. She thought she'd drawn the short straw because no one fussed around her as they did around me.

Of course I was the favoured sibling. I wasn't stupid, I'd always known and so had Amanda. What she failed to realise is that it wasn't my fault. She needs to stop thinking in terms of responsibility. I sometimes blamed our parents, Mum in particular. But as I grew older I couldn't help wondering if my upbringing was simply a replay of Mum's. And, of course, that would mean that Amanda's maternal relationship reflected Julia's.

Amanda called me a few days after I'd texted her about Finn.

'Just to let you know, I'm going to The Bahamas again on Tuesday. Julia's moving in to stay with Ben. Just so you know.'

I suppose she thought she was doing the right thing by not leaving the country without giving me the heads up but when she mentioned The Bahamas I had to shut my eyes. Even then, it didn't stop the image I had in my head of Max, on a boat I'd never seen, with people I didn't really know, falling to the deck like a felled tree as his life was extinguished in one, blood bursting, life changing second.

I thought she was a fool going back there. Her boyfriend, the diving instructor, might be honest and genuine but it concerned me that it was Amanda running off to see him and not him coming over here to reassure her. So, of course, I told her and unsurprisingly it didn't go down too well. She accused me of just seeing the bad in everyone. Bit rich really, as she's incapable of seeing any good in me.

That was always the difficulty with being the favourite child. Because I knew life was going to be made easy for me I took full advantage, of course. I watched my sibling being reigned in, moulded and guided so much more than me. I was free to do what I wanted because *doing what I want* was the mantra my parents brought me up with.

When I was in high school, not long after Amanda's eighteenth and the incident with the pregnancy test, I got friendly with a girl called Karen. I needed her friendship because some of my classmates were the younger sisters of the girls who'd been at the party. They'd been told not to speak to me anymore, but only after the ringleader called me a 'fucking parasite.' I never told anyone at home what had happened. I could never admit to becoming suddenly unpopular, and I didn't want Mum cooing around me like some demented pigeon.

Karen and I formed a bond for a few years. She didn't care that my name was mud because she had no friends and I think she saw a bit of a vacancy and decided to take the position. Karen, I discovered, lived in a household as messed up as my own. She had an older brother who'd had enough of the unspoken but toxic dynamics and would soon be off to join the army. He wanted to escape just as Julia escaped to travel endlessly, just as Amanda escaped into a marriage with the first man who showed any interest.

For Karen, being the favourite child shaped her life very differently to mine.

She was mollycoddled so intensely that the poor girl sank in the quicksand of her parent's good intentions, lacking confidence and never challenging herself. She made herself cosy in her bubble and I could see even at that young age that her parents were encouraging her to remain cocooned.

Inevitably, by the time we reached the end of High School, we'd drifted apart as she retreated further and further to safety. I did try to pry open her shell, let her breathe fresh air and see the world that awaited her. But as I was rebuffed at every turn, I began to suspect that some of her reticence was down to laziness and not just her overbearing parents.

I bumped into her at a wedding a few years ago. We chatted for a while and she told me she had never married, that her Dad had passed and that she still lived with her mother. She talked at length about her work at the town planning office and as she said goodbye and turned to go home, I realised that she had not asked one single question about me.

I wasn't angry about it. I know what being smothered can do and how it might have had the opposite effect on Karen than it did with me. I live up to the over-confident, strident persona that I created and Karen belly-flopped back into her mother's womb. She and I found different solutions to the same problem.

So when I lost Max, I didn't suddenly feel alone. I always have been, really. I've always been expected to cope with anything life throws at me because my tough exterior is impenetrable, apparently. No one is going to come to my aid. All I will ever get is Mum's simpering and I can't abide it.

I didn't think I'd ever be envious of my sister, but I'm starting to really see the appeal of running away and changing everything.

CHAPTER THIRTY-THREE

Amanda

It was very difficult making small talk with Thomas and trying to look as happy as I had on my first trip. I feigned tiredness and closed my eyes in the back of his cab, leaning my face against the cool glass of the window. I had a headache in any case, having mulled over every possible outcome in my head during the flight.

Each time I settled on the idea of asking for forgiveness for doubting him, Maddy's words of warning rang in my ears. Then, after changing my view and thinking I should stand my ground, be strong and insist that he give me a proper explanation, I also thought of Maddy. The woman who had been loved and adored, who was now defensive and lonely. Maddy's sneering view of men stemmed from her own deplorable behaviour, not from any man's.

I thought of Julia too. As she'd waved me off at the crack of dawn, she had hugged me while my suitcase was being put in the boot of the taxi. Then she whispered in my ear.

'If you see a chance of happiness, Amanda, you must grab it. Don't live in fear, don't follow anybody else's path. Do what your instinct tells you to and remember, nothing is guaranteed.'

She knew I was a much more confident woman that the one she helped prop up a year before. The woman with no self esteem who lived in a fog, unable to make the simplest of decisions. But she also knew that I still needed encouragement. I probably always would, when it came to taking a leap in the dark. I'd been cautious all my adult life. The road ahead looked foreign and strange, but this time it thrilled rather than terrified me.

I asked Thomas to drop me off at the diving centre. Gary was inside on the counter and shouted immediately out the back to Finn as I walked into the shop. There were a few customers around, trying on masks and browsing rash vests so it was hardly the private reconciliation I had been hoping for.

Finn emerged from the workshop out back and narrowed his eyes when he saw me, his shock at seeing me evident on his features. He went to say something but was pounced on for advice by one of the customers before he could speak. As he patiently explained the pros and cons of various dive computers, the curtains of the workshop parted again and a face I instantly recognised came through to the shop.

Oblivious, Anna smiled at me and asked, 'Can I help you? Are you looking to buy some equipment or did you want to book a dive?'

She was stunning. I'd so hoped she might be one of those people who didn't quite match up in the flesh, but she was a natural beauty.

I glanced over at Finn. He carried on talking to his customer but his arms were now folded across his chest and his eyes flicked over towards me and Anna constantly. Maybe he thought I was going to do or say something embarrassing.

'Actually, I'm here to see Finn. I've literally just stepped off the plane,' I said. Anna tilted her head slightly and still thinking I was a customer said, 'Anything I can do while you wait? I do have the diary here, so I can book you for a dive with Finn, if you'd like.'

'No, it's okay, I'm a friend.'

Immediately, I wondered why I'd said that. It was almost as if I was downplaying my role in Finn's life, in case he and Anna were back together. As if I didn't want to mess things up for him.

'Well, actually, I'm his girlfriend.'

I'd said it. I smiled and slowly filled my lungs with air, just as Rachel had taught me in Yoga classes, as a way of staying calm and controlling emotion. I studied Anna's face, keen to pick up any tiny changes in her expression. I was surprised. A huge smile spread across her face, lighting her eyes up as she took both my hands in hers.

'Oh, so you're *Amanda*! Why didn't you say!' She seemed so genuinely pleased that it took me by surprise. 'I've heard so much about you.' She leant towards me and lowered her voice, speaking in a conspiratorial but friendly tone. 'Put it this way, of course I've heard so much about you, he never stops telling me.'

This was an unexpected introduction to the woman I'd considered my nemesis. It didn't really tally with the girl who'd posted notifications that would make anyone think that she and Finn were a couple. That was something I'd have to take up with Finn later, when we had chance to be alone together and talk.

I took another look at Finn. He was trying so hard to answer the never-ending stream of questions from his customer but seemed utterly distracted by me and Anna. He watched quizzically the tableau of two women seemingly bonding. Both smiling, one holding the other's hands and talking animatedly. My heart surged with love for him. There may still be unanswered questions but it was clear I'd put him through a lot of worry and it had all sprung from another relationship, another man. Another version of me.

'Come through to the back, if you like,' said Anna. 'You're probably dehydrated after your flight. I'll get you some water,'

Still holding one hand she led me through the curtain to the dishevelled office where I sat on an old, beaten leather bench while she poured water from the cooler into a paper cup.

I could hear Finn's voice, stilted, drifting through from the shop. It didn't sound much like him. His answers were short and the usual enthusiasm was missing. I could imagine his heart pounding, imagine him trying to glimpse through the colourful strips of the fly curtain, checking up on me and Anna.

'Here you go.' She handed me the cup with long tanned fingers dressed in silver and turquoise rings that brushed against my hand. She reminded me of the models in the magazines I read in my teens. She had beach wave dark hair, long limbs, and looked no less than perfect. My white legs stuck out from beneath my skirt. I swiftly tucked them under the seat.

'Thanks Anna. Nice to meet you too, by the way.' I took a long gulp of water. 'Saw some of your posts, you know, the ones you tagged Finn in. Looks like you've been having fun.' My attempts to make myself sound totally unconcerned meant that my voice took on a different, slightly strangulated tone. As Anna didn't know me, I hoped she wouldn't pick up on it.

'Yes, being back has been so…' just then, she heard the door of the shop open again. 'Oh sorry, better go out front Sounds like we have another customer.'

I sipped the water and then heard Finn's voice, heard the cash register's jingle, and another voice thanking him for his time. The curtains parted and Finn walked through and stood in front of me.

Neither of us said a word. He looked down at me, unsmiling and wearing a slight frown.

I so wanted it to be fixed. I so wanted him to sit next to me, take me in his arms and tell me everything would be fine.

The old Amanda would have sat and waited for that and if it hadn't happened, she would have slunk away like a scolded Labrador and accepted her rejection. But not this Amanda.

I stood up, looking Finn in the eyes, my chest rising and falling with my breath.

'Finn, I don't know if I'm too late. I don't know if I've messed this up so badly that you won't be able to forgive me. I thought I was going to tell you all the reasons, make all the excuses as to why I said the things I did and treated you as if you were someone completely different. But now I'm here, all I want to do is ask forgiveness, ask for understanding. I just want to know if there is still a Finn and Amanda.'

His face was static. I held my breath.

Finn looked down at his feet and I couldn't see his eyes, couldn't read what was going through his head and connect with him.

He let out a long sigh. My heart took the elevator to the basement.

'I'm glad you're here. But I need to get some things straight with you because if I don't, I'm not sure we have a future together.' He lifted his head to look into my eyes. Were those tears he was holding back? 'I love you very much Amanda and I thought you knew that but that phone call the other day was a shocker. We're going to have a hard enough time working out how we're going to run a relationship that's long distance, but if there's going to be a whole load of other drama in the mix, I don't think we'll stand a chance. Sorry gorgeous, but I've got to be honest.'

I put my hands either side of his face and leant towards him.

'I know. I know that this is a mountain we have to get over

but Finn, I'm so determined to make this work and that's not me being blasé about it.'

He leant forward, closing his eyes, his forehead pressing against mine. The heat from him travelled through me, warming my soul but sounding an alarm that I must not let this man go, not because of another man, another relationship.

He reached up and took my hands, drawing back to look at me. A moment passed before he spoke.

'So explain it to me. Tell me where all that jealous rage came from because if that's going to be hanging between us in the future, we're doomed. I meet lots of women in this job and some of them flirt with me and often that's because they're on holiday and feeling light-hearted or because they're really nervous about diving and that's how they hide their fear. But it doesn't mean I'm going to be less than professional with them.'

He grimaced slightly and glanced away.

'And yes, I realise that didn't stop me where you were concerned but I was single then. I'm not now. At least, I hope I'm not.'

For the first time since our conversation had begun, I felt a little spark of optimism.

I studied his hands, calloused and solid, and caressed them in my own. I hoped I could help him see why and how I was damaged and persuade him that I would do everything I could to fix myself.

'Finn, the way I reacted to Anna was nothing to do with who you are. It was to do with who Dan is—was—to me. And that was totally unfair. I can see that. I need to sit down with you later and tell you what life was like for me being married to Dan. Not to excuse myself as such, but just in the hope that you'll maybe realise I've not felt what it's like to be in a real, loving relationship.'

He pulled me back towards him and wrapped his arms around my waist. I couldn't see his face, which was buried in my hair. But he said nothing, and I felt that I still needed to work to convince him.

'And from my point of view,' I continued, 'Anna's posts did look like you and she were a couple. All the hearts, all the lovey-dovey stuff.'

'That's Anna,' he replied with a shrug. 'She does like to be the queen bee. She always has. And whatever she does including friendships and work, she does with a bit of an over the top enthusiasm. Mostly, it's endearing but at times it's a bit of a nuisance. Like now. Thing is, she's actually been seeing a guy who crews on one of the yachts since she arrived back on the island. So I was never in the picture, not that I'd want to put myself through that again.'

* * *

Back at the beach house, I began to open up to Finn about my marriage, to help him understand that the damage I'd suffered was still affecting me. My biggest fears were that I would sound like a pathetic creature undeserving of the love of a man like Finn or that I would sound like I was self-involved, making excuses for my own bad behaviour when truly, there was no excuse.

'I don't get why a woman like you could have gone along with Dan being such a nasty piece of work. You seem so strong.'

He frowned and wouldn't look me in the eye as he fiddled with the bottle of Budweiser he'd opened uncharacteristically early.

I explained as well as I could, how even the strongest among us can be torn down by those people who are only out for themselves.

'Think of it like this. You look at an oak tree and think it's one of the strongest things there is. It's solid and immoveable, adapting to the seasons and living for hundreds of years. But when it's a sapling, a seemingly feeble bindweed can suffocate it. The oak dies but the bindweed thrives. That's how I see the action of a weak and needy person towards someone with quiet strength. Since Dan, I've had to do a lot of thinking and that's how I can best describe what our relationship was like.'

He listened while I told him some of the things that Dan had done, how I'd felt I should just go along with everything and how I'd become resigned to the way my marriage was. How I just wanted peace and would do almost anything to keep it. And as I went further back in time, I started to open up about my childhood, my teenage years and how I'd felt secondary to Maddy and inhibited from criticising. How I'd learned not to do or say anything to upset anyone, while others could say whatever they liked to me and I was permitted no voice.

'It's only now,' I said, sitting up to grab a tissue from the coffee table, 'that I can see how oppressed I was and it started as soon as I entered my teens. Maddy was the favoured one and I didn't stand a chance. I was doomed from the start.'

As I sat back on the sofa, the urge to expose all the events of my life that had made me so timid, made me feel so much less than I was, became overwhelming.

'My eighteenth birthday was a disaster,' I told him. 'Maddy ruined it for me. She was a spiteful little brat and humiliated me in front of my friends.'

Finn stroked my arm. My stomach knotted as I wondered if he just felt sorry for me or was perhaps beginning to understand what trapdoor I'd fallen into when I mistakenly thought the worst of him.

'Then Julia tried to stand up for me and it just got worse. It took me months to get over it and even now I feel sick to the stomach to think about it.'

'I never dared complain to Mum and Dad about the way I was expected to handle Maddy with kid gloves or to question why they did it. I found out years later that Mum suffered a couple of miscarriages between me and Maddy so maybe that explains it. And I'm not excusing my behaviour because of my past. We all have memories of incidents that have made us feel unworthy in some way, diminished perhaps. I'm well aware that there are lots of people far worse off than I am. I'm telling you all this to get it into the open, so that there are no surprises. Not to lay blame elsewhere.'

He placed his empty bottle on the coffee table and reached across and took my hand. Finally, he looked me in the eyes, and I could see the sadness in his own.

'Amanda, I really wasn't sure if we were going to move on from this. But I know how it feels to hit the buffers. I've been so caught up in finding someone I feel so connected with that perhaps I missed that you were still trying to get back to the woman you truly are. Now I know this; we're two parts of a whole. I want to be the cure, not another rock that's thrown at you to knock you off course.'

He pulled me to him and I nestled my face in the crook of his neck. Tears of relief began to flow as he stroked my back and gently placed a kiss on my head.

Finn said nothing more and I was grateful for that. I didn't want to be judged, or to be advised about what I should or shouldn't have done, how I ought to have handled things differently. I could see it all now. It was as if I'd been given a key to unlock a secret drawer and it was all laid out in front of me. I could never go back but now, with Finn, Julia and the American Saxbys in my life, I could make the future so much better than my past had been.

* * *

Over the next few days, I told Finn more details of what marriage had been like for me. I wanted him to understand and I definitely wanted no more secrets between us.

'Once, years ago, we'd had a huge argument and Dan had got very upset, taking himself off to bed early. He didn't speak to me for days. It frightened me because I didn't know quite what I'd done that was so terrible, but he clearly felt I'd behaved badly. I think the argument was about me forgetting to pay the credit card bill on time and we'd got some kind of late payment fee, and of course more interest the next month. We weren't hard up or anything. He'd just been really, really furious about it. He was red in the face and kept saying, "How can I trust you to do anything?"'

We were sitting on the beach after spending the morning in bed, feeling connected again and finding our place with each other. Finn shook his head.

'It sounds like he had serious issues. You actually kinda have to feel a bit sorry for the new woman he's with.'

I smiled up at him as I picked up a delicate pink shell, turning it over in my hands.

'Hmmm, in a strange sort of way, yes, I do feel sorry for her.' I put the shell back and brushed the sand from my hands.

'Anyway, I was so upset, that a day or two later, Eve asked me how I was and I started crying. I told her that Dan wasn't talking to me and told her why and she flipped her lid. She said, *"Christ on a bike, you forgot to pay a bill, so what? Bloody hell, if Marco did that to me I'd tell him to grow a pair and then I'd tell him he could start doing the household bills himself. Or I'd shove them up his arse."* So I back peddled. Eve's a feisty woman and Dan felt that she was quite bossy towards Marco and had a bit of a selfish streak which I suppose she did.'

We both laughed despite the seriousness of the conversation. I guess Finn, like me, was imagining Eve shouting the odds in her own unique way.

'I called her later that day. I told her things were fine with me and Dan. I said how I'd probably over-reacted because I was on my period and *he'd* over-reacted because he'd had a really stressful week at work. I said I'd made it sound worse than it was and that she should just ignore me. Eve didn't sound convinced but she never referred to it again. But stupidly, I did.'

I told Finn how, a couple of weeks later, when Dan was okay again and talking to me, he and I had gone out to dinner, just the two of us. We were talking about friends and their relationships and he mentioned Eve and Marco and as usual, went on and on about Marco being a bit of a 'wet weekend' and how he didn't know how any man could put up with someone like Eve telling him what to do.

'She can be a bit full on, that's for sure,' I'd said. 'I mentioned to her a little while ago, just casually you know, that you and I had had words and she immediately started telling me how she wouldn't let Marco "*get away with that!*"' I was chuckling slightly, thinking this would show Dan how I was always on his side, how I was prepared to handle his moods. Everyone has moods.

The restaurant was crowded and Dan would never make a

scene in public. But sometimes, words weren't needed. The waves of negative energy, of anger and resentment that came from him blanketed me and I couldn't finish my meal. We sat in silence until a waiter came. Dan smiled brightly and said, 'Can we have the bill please?' When the waiter returned and asked how the food had been, Dan smiled and said, 'Lovely food as always, wasn't it, Amanda?' and no-one would have guessed what hung over us.

We left the restaurant and sat in silence during the drive home. I was driving because Dan liked a drink when we went out. He worked so hard and paid for our social life so we'd agreed that I should be the driver. I didn't mind.

When we got home and went to bed, Dan told me how hurt he had been at my disloyalty. The children were staying at Mum's that night, so fortunately they couldn't hear him. But he was pretty savage. It made me feel such a let-down. I could see his point of view. I wouldn't like his friends knowing all our business. His raging wore me down and finally, through tears, I told him I was sorry and that he shouldn't worry. I don't like our private life being spoken about either and he calmed down. I kept saying I was sorry.

'I really hate it when we fall out like this,' he said. 'Sorry I went on. I didn't mean to make you cry, love. It's just something I feel very passionate about. Nothing should penetrate our little circle. What it is they call us? AmanDan?'

The next morning, everything was fine between us.

Finn reached over and brushed a sand fly away from my leg.

We could hear the sound of gentle waves and sat in silence for a while, watching a little boat glinting on the horizon as it made its journey out to sea.

'And that wasn't an isolated incident. Always, after I'd been cornered into apologising, I would feel enormous relief that he was talking to me again and everything was fine, so we could carry on. But there was this thin strand of something that went through me like sinew. A knowledge that it wasn't all right, it wasn't fine and I shouldn't allow myself to think that this was normal behaviour. But then I'd look at Sammy and Ben, and how my life just continued as usual and it was easier to ignore the doubts.'

When I'd finished the story, Finn let out a whistle.

'I'd like to get my hands on him, and no, before you say a word, of course I wouldn't do a thing, if we ever bumped into him. But honestly gorgeous, he deserves an ass whacking.'

I laughed out loud. I knew I could trust Finn to behave.

He was shaking his head again, picking up handfuls of sand and watching the grains sieve through his fingers. Then he turned to look at me.

'And do you know *why* I'd never do or say anything to Dan, if I saw him?'

I raised my eyebrows and gave a little shrug.

'Because he lost. He had you, and now he doesn't. He lost.'

That seemed to satisfy Finn and he gazed out to sea for a few moments before smiling and closing his eyes, leaning back on his towel and soaking up the sun.

CHAPTER THIRTY-FOUR

Maddy

Everyone was still so wrapped up in their own lives and thoughts that when I said I was going away for a while barely an eyebrow was raised. No one asked why, or what I'd be doing or questioned what had made me decide to take action. They perhaps made the usual presumption that *Maddy will be fine*. By then I'd come to the conclusion that I couldn't rely on support from anyone.

I think I started to unravel a few weeks ago. I was waking up in the middle of the night, heart pounding, gasping for breath and completely full of fear. It wasn't how I was after Max died. That was straightforward grief. No matter what everyone thought, it tore me apart.

This anxiety though was something different. I thought I might have some physical problem, a heart condition or worse. In a vicious circle, the more I worried about what might be wrong with me the worse the symptoms got. But deep down inside, I knew I wasn't suffering from a physical illness.

Then I went to see Mum. She had a different air about her, a calmness I hadn't seen before. I thought maybe I was so spaced out from lack of sleep that I was imagining things. Then she sprung a surprise on me.

'I think I should tell you that I spent most of yesterday starting to compose what might be a very long email. It's nowhere near finished yet, but when it is, I'm going to send it to Robin Saxby.'

I couldn't get my head around what she would want to say to the Saxbys. Was she letting out her frustration that my father had suffered from what Robin's Dad had done? Was she suggesting they keep away from us? Perhaps she wanted to point out the consequences of trying to blend the Brits and the Americans: I have lost my husband, twice, in effect, and Amanda had now become completely distracted by the Aussie.

I wondered if I should stop her. Whatever she wanted to say might be valid but she had a habit of droning on about herself and I wasn't going to stand by and watch her make a fool of us all.

'Look Mum, it's entirely up to you of course, but don't you think sometimes silence is a better way to get your point across?'

She looked at me quizzically and I realised we were talking at crossed purposes.

Mum sat down on the beige sofa and began picking at a tiny loose thread on the arm. She blinked several times in quick succession as she composed her explanation in her head.

'I've decided that enough is enough, Maddy. Whatever happened all those years ago has no bearing on Robin or the rest of the family. All he's ever done is offer his friendship, his kinship, to us. He is your father's half-brother. His children, and yes, I even mean Rachel, are family.' She stopped and looked at me, as if challenging me to argue, to throw a tantrum. I said nothing. I didn't even move. 'I doubt I'll ever visit The Bahamas. I've not wanted to travel much since your father died and I don't like the heat. But I would enjoy hearing about what they are doing with their lives. I want to feel as if we are all part of each other.'

I sat back, grateful for the coolness radiating from the wall behind me.

'But Mum, what about Dad's memory? You've always said he wouldn't like it. You've always said you'd have nothing to do with them.'

'I truly believed that and it doesn't change the fact that yes, John was eaten up with fury against his own father and all of the Saxbys. Sometimes though, life isn't as straightforward as that. There are things we don't always understand, facts we don't have at our disposal. But what I think I've come to realise now, is that admitting to myself that your father was wrong to harbour such feelings for so long doesn't diminish the love I felt for him.'

'But even if you want to leave the past behind, can't you see that they are just a selfish bunch? And doesn't what happened to me matter?' I leant forward, my arms folded across my chest as I fought the desire to burst into tears. 'If Max hadn't gone out to them, Rachel Saxby would never have got her claws into him and he'd eventually have fallen back in love with me. He'd probably still be alive!'

Mum looked at me aghast. 'That's nonsense Madeleine and I think you know it. Max wasn't taken from you. You pushed him away. You took him for granted in the most atrocious way and what on earth has being in The Bahamas got to do with his death, poor chap? On that day, at that time, the aneurism burst and it would have happened in The Bahamas or if he was sitting in his desk at home or if he'd been on the moon.'

It was so rare for my mother to call me out on something that her words took me by surprise. I sat up straight and hugged my arms a little tighter around me.

I had no answer to give her. Of course I knew that Max's death was sadly inevitable. I'd often wondered what would have happened if he had known he only had a limited time left. Would he still have gone to Rachel? Might he have stayed with me, safe in our damaged but familiar relationship?

I wanted to ask Mum what had happened to make her change her view of it all. I wanted to know why, after all these years, she finally felt she could issue me some home truths, now, when I least needed it as opposed to when I was growing up and was in dire need of restraint.

But at that moment, a seismic shift took place in me. All the talk of the past, of acceptance and being unable to change what had happened, overwhelmed me. The idea that had been swirling around my head for days like a distant moon around a planet, finally came into focus.

'OK Mum,' I said reasonably. 'You should do what you think is right. I'm not sure I'm going to want to hear very much about it so please don't give me chapter and verse about the marvellous lives of the other Saxbys. As it happens I'm planning on getting away for a bit. I'll tell you more about it another time but I should get going.'

After that conversation with Mum, I focussed on making arrangements for my trip. I needed to give myself space. I had some soul searching to do and that was going to be impossible while surrounded by memories and the accusing stares of locals.

I rented a house in Cornwall, in quite a remote area and difficult to access so I wouldn't be flooded by tourists. I negotiated the purchase of a small sailing boat. I'd always been confident sailing solo, and what better way to connect with nature and to slow down time than to be working with the elements, all alone, at sea?

I located a counsellor in the same village and I spoke to her a few times on the phone. I felt like I clicked with her. Perhaps I could get a lot out into the open though I didn't expect to 'recover' as such. But I did expect to find peace. I simply wanted to feel this enormous weight lifted from me, to grieve without my thoughts taking me down a rabbit hole of such darkness that I couldn't breathe.

I felt there had been something missing from my marriage to Max but then I realised, what had been missing was something inside me. I still feared that I'd never find out what that was but by going away for a while, I thought I might stand a chance of finding some form of contentment.

I needed to grieve for Max, for Paul, and for the relationships I'd missed out on with so many members of my family.

I needed to stop pretending.

CHAPTER THIRTY-FIVE

Julia

When Amanda came home from The Bahamas after what sounded like a very successful few weeks with Finn, I felt I was ready for the next stage of my life. Amanda seemed to be calmer and stronger somehow and more focussed on her future. I absolutely couldn't wait to see her finally blossom.

I also heard from Diana and felt quite pleasantly surprised at the small, but significant step forward she had taken with the Bahamian branch of the Saxbys.

The step forward she and I took to reconcile as sisters, I felt, was even more significant.

I called in to see her before preparing to set off to the south of France. A new luxury hotel head hunted me to oversee their first six months. I couldn't wait to get my teeth into it.

'Oh, it's such a shame you're off again,' Diana said, with that little pout that I always interpreted as her outward but fake expression of regret. 'I'll be all alone,' she continued.

'You'll be in Marsailles, Amanda is off to see her new man again next month, and Maddy is talking about going on some retreat or something. Sammy's down at University and Ben's going to stay with his father.'

I thought how lonely it must be, being Diana. In the past, I've felt quite angry at her. She knew of other single or widowed women of her age group, women who seemed to manage to carve out busy lives for themselves. But Diana, I feel, has never really learnt how to be a friend. She was fine when everyone danced to her tune but the moment the music stopped she was lost. When I visited, I must have been feeling particularly relaxed because the anger I usually felt was replaced by sympathy and a need to help her.

'You know Di, sometimes I think you cling too fiercely to the past. And I don't mean that unkindly.'

She placed her palms together as if in prayer and for the first time in years, she slowly nodded her head and signalled that she was ready to listen.

'You may be right, Julia.' She glanced out into the garden, lost no doubt in a memory of when she could lean on John and shield herself from the past and those aspects of life she found difficult. 'I had the most wonderful marriage. I could lose myself in domesticity and felt safe somehow, taking on John's values. I must be lazy I suppose.' She turned back to look at me. 'After what happened when we were younger, after...David, the guilt made me close my eyes to my own beliefs and absorb all of John's. It was a way of atoning for what I'd done.'

My throat was dry. We'd never spoken about David. To hear Diana mention his name made me feel a little faint. For a second, I was back in the doorway of that bedroom, staring at the figures beneath the sheets, my knees turning to jelly.

Diana stood and walked over to the big picture window overlooking the garden, her back to me.

'But I never made it up to you, did I?' Her voice was so low I had to strain to hear it. 'I think you loved David and I imagine you thought you were going to marry him. But all I could think about was how I might lose John, if it all got out. And that was unforgivable.'

I took in a deep, long breath. We had moved on, Diana and I. I had 'got over it.' I'd not told anyone about the baby, about the termination. I thought once about telling Diana, much later, after Amanda's eighteenth. It had worried me for years that Amanda might be David's, but by the time she was five, it was so glaringly obvious that she was John Saxby's daughter that my worries about that had evaporated.

'Di.' I shook my head, not knowing where to start. 'More than forty years have passed.' I stood and walked over to where she stood and perched on the low windowsill, my back to the garden. She looked down at me with a strangely calm expression. Perhaps it was a relief to open the lid on this taboo subject after all this time. 'I did love David. I had plans for us but they weren't realistic. I always knew I wanted to travel. I was always going to be ambitious and have a career. David was lovely. Kind, funny and good looking.' I chuckled a little. 'It was pretty naive of me to think that he could carry on working in construction while I swanned around the world. Even more naive to think I'd have been happy with that.'

I often wondered what my life would have been like if I'd had the baby, with or without David. It was always a regret of sorts. Whenever I saw or heard of someone having a child I always felt a little twist in the gut. But one thing I didn't regret was the life I'd had. There were men who had meant a lot to me and brought me joy. I'd never had to rely on a single one of them for money or self-esteem. How could I possibly know what life would have been like with a child? All I could know was that it would have been different.

Diana reached over and put a hand on my shoulder. 'Even so, at that time, my actions hurt you very badly. If I'd ever arrived home and found John with someone else...well. Well.' She closed her eyes, shook her head, and squeezed my shoulder.

I stood and hugged her to me. We're all guilty of clinging too fiercely to the past. It was time to take my own advice.

'Don't torture yourself with what might have been, Di. Don't worry about living up to other people's expectations, even John's.'

She drew back and studied me.

'Would you be very shocked if I told you I sent an email to Robin Saxby this morning?'

'Shocked?'

I was absolutely gobsmacked. My mouth fell open. 'You could say that, yes. What on earth brought that about?' I re-took my perch on the windowsill, mouth still agape. The sun was streaming through, warming my back and lighting Diana's face in a gentle glow.

'Everyone's moving on in life,' she shrugged. 'Except me of course. I've been thinking about contacting them for ages but I do feel disloyal to John. I can't help it. The thing is, whatever happened, they are a connection with John and that means they're a part of Amanda and Maddy's life too. Amanda's already made inroads and now of course, as well as feeling disloyal to John, I feel as if I'm betraying poor Maddy. But I sent the email anyway.'

'Hallelujah!' I clapped my hands together, feeling amazed and proud of my sister. 'So may I ask what the email said?'

'Just that I'd love to hear from him. I explained why I hadn't felt able to respond to his invitations and so on. Not that I intend going out there. I'm not like you Julia. I don't really have the travel bug. But I did say if he or any of the family were in the UK, they would be very welcome.' She gave a nervous little chuckle and a shake of the head. 'He'll probably read it and think me a silly woman,' she said.

'No, he won't, Di, I can promise you that. He will be thrilled to hear from you.' I stood up and gave her another hug. My sister had managed to surprise me, in a good way, for just about the first time ever.

* * *

Sitting with some afternoon tea in the frequent traveller lounge at the airport, I opened my laptop to confirm a few details with Jean-Jacques, the owner of the hotel I'm going to be working at. He came to London to meet before he hired me and flirted with me quite openly and continued to do this in his phone calls and emails. I smiled to myself when he did this. He was charming and charismatic but this was business as far as I was concerned so I planned to keep things friendly but professional. I was more interested in overseeing all the interior design and staff recruitment and so on. Making a complete success of a new hotel was what motivated me.

No, Jean-Jacques would not derail me. I'd met many interesting and attractive men during my life but the only one—apart from David back when I was a naive young girl—who had ever made me consider putting love before career was Robin Saxby. It seemed now that doors were finally opening between our families and that demons were being laid to rest.

I'd no idea what this might mean for me. I certainly wasn't going to rush off across the Atlantic on a mission to discover what sort of future we might have. If our paths were meant to cross again, they would. I couldn't imagine either of us wanting to be tied down to a traditional relationship.

While I was doing some last-minute packing in my hotel room, I received a text message from Robin.

Hey Julia. I received an email from Diana. May I call you?

I didn't hesitate. I called him instantly and smiled when I heard his drawn out, almost sleepy accent.

'Julia, what a perfect start to the day.'

He sounded half asleep but then he always did.

'Hello Robin, how are you? I did see Diana yesterday and she said she'd sent you an email. I'm so thrilled, at last, that this ridiculous stand-off is over.'

'It's great news Julia, really great. I'll see the kids and Jane and Brad at lunch today and tell them. They are going to think it's awesome. I've gotten so used to the cold shoulder from Di! I felt elated when I heard from her. When I get to the office I'll send her a reply. I'm still in bed at the moment, wishing you were here, *of course.*'

I could imagine him, the sun streaking in through a huge window, a view of the ocean no doubt from his bed. I could think of worse places to be.

'Yes, do! She'll probably think it was a mistake and that you're not really going to be interested in hearing from her so please bolster her, let her know she's done the right thing.'

'She absolutely has. And you? Are you doing the right thing? Diana mentioned in her email that you are off to Marsailles soon, is that correct?'

'Yes, it is. Today, in fact. My taxi will be here in an hour. I should be there for about six months, but it's all fairly fluid. It's a work thing so it will take as long as it takes.'

There was a moment's silence. Then I could hear him drawing in his breath.

'Well, maybe I need to look at flights to France. Maybe I should just show up and spend some time with you?'

I became flustered. The idea sent a little quiver through me but I would be busy and Robin was always busy and it would be a long way for him to come. Even so, the suggestion was delightful if unlikely to happen. I chuckled and changed the subject.

'Well, you may want to come over to the UK and see Diana. She did make it clear that she isn't interested in travelling but I'm sure you could persuade her. I doubt anyone who heard you describe the island and the people and how beautiful and relaxed the whole place is could possibly resist.'

'And you Julia? Can you resist? I think you should follow Amanda's lead and then maybe Diana will follow yours. How about you get this job in France finished toute-de-suite and then come over here and let me show you how to fall in love with The Bahamas? Or maybe, just how to fall in love?'

CHAPTER THIRTY-SIX

Amanda

I went into the bank to drop off a form for our new business. It had taken some time, but eventually Rachel had decided that she wanted to continue with our idea. She said that Max had encouraged her to work with me and that she would put her energies into it as well as into the marine conservation centre. Max had already produced initial designs for the building which would now be called The Max Emmerson Memorial Centre. The income from Saxby Health and Vitality would be split equally between me and Rachel. I would need my half to live on, while Rachel would donate her half of the profits and much of her time and passion to the conservation centre.

The bank was busy as usual and I had a million things on my mind as I took my place in line. It was not until the woman in front of me in the queue turned and spoke that I realised who it was.

Penny began wittering on immediately, talking about how lovely it was to bump into me, and how nice it was to hear my 'wonderful news.'

She congratulated me on finding love, which was decent of her, if you forgot the fact that she had taken a husband from me.

Dan's business had managed to survive somehow. I was glad for his staff that it had. I knew he had lots of contacts and so it was likely that he'd managed to get investment from someone. I knew better than anyone how persuasive he could be.

I'd also heard other rumours about Dan. From more than one source and I still found it shocking. The rumours that he was messing Penny around with a girl from the optician's in town, a girl not much older than Sammy. That part turned my stomach. It made me sick to wonder who else he'd slept with while he was married to me.

Eve told me one day that someone was talking about it in the bookshop. One of the old ladies in the village, the little clutch of women who poked their noses into everyone's business.

'She was tutting away like a good'un,' said Eve. 'Very holier-than-thou she was but enjoying every morsel of information she was telling Marco.'

I could imagine. Probably got the same thrill when she was talking about me.

'She made out how all the old lady mafia in the village were being considerate towards Penny, keeping the gossip to themselves. She said that apparently Sally Proctor is now quite good friends with Penny and she knows about it so she reckons it won't be long before Penny finds out. Sally never could keep her gob shut.'

As I stood in the queue at the bank with Penny, I had no desire whatever to enlighten her. And that may be a cruel thing because I could have saved her years of pain, years of a slow drip, drip, drip of her life being eroded like layers from a cliff face so that she wouldn't know who she was any longer. I could have caused her a heap of pain then, in that moment, to save her from her future. But that wasn't for me to do. That was for Sally Proctor or one of the old women, or for her to discover herself when Dan slipped up.

'We were truly delighted,' she went on, 'to know that you have met a man who completes you.'

I wanted to laugh in her face but I just smiled. 'Thanks.'

'Dan has always said, from day one, that he hoped you would find happiness and that you and the children would realise that he did what he did with the best of intentions. With the end game in mind of everyone being in a better place.'

She had her head tilted on one side, the unfaltering smile still on her lips. It was like a nurse telling you everything was going to be fine, you would recover from your road accident but without mentioning the fact that you had to have major surgery to survive, and that she was the one that ran you over. I couldn't say anything. To imply that Dan had acted in mine and the children's best interests was beyond belief.

An announcement rang out. *'Next customer to till number seven please.'*

'That's me, then,' said Penny. 'I'm so glad I ran into you. I hope we can continue being, well, nice to each other when we meet. After all, look how well you are now. And just think, if Dan and I hadn't got together, you'd never had met Finn and you wouldn't be so happy, would you?'

She turned and walked up to till seven. My mouth was open. My brain was jumbled as I tried to think through what she had said. Because yes, it was true. If Dan hadn't cheated, if she hadn't been a willing partner in his deception, I would not have hit rock bottom. And if I hadn't hit rock bottom, I would never have had to rebuild myself, would never have found a strength I hadn't even realised I'd lost. I would never have met Finn.

I would never have been Amanda Saxby again.

'Next customer to till number five please'.

I walked up to till five. I walked on past till five. The cashier looked perplexed as I made my way to till seven, just as Penny was putting her purse back into her bag. She didn't notice me at first. But she did when I grabbed her upper arm.

'Just so we're clear,' I said quietly, leaning close in, just millimetres from her ear, 'I'm happy *despite* what you and Dan did. Not because of it.' I remained still for a moment, my lips close to her ear, my grip still on her arm. Just so it sank in before I let go.

I didn't look back as I walked out of the bank, into the bright summer sunshine.

CHAPTER THIRTY-SEVEN

Amanda

I'm sitting on my suitcases, desperately trying to get them closed. I'll need a lot with me for three months in The Bahamas. Sammy and Ben fly out in the last week of July and will be travelling back with me at the end of August. Ben can't wait to go diving with Finn. Sammy's really keen to somehow get involved with my new business with Rachel and I think she might be quite good. She's more technically minded than we are and she has a good head for business.

Until then, Sammy will be at Uni for a while and then plans to stay with Ben and her father and Penny, until Ben finishes school and they're ready to come and join me. The thought of my children being part of a new family with Dan and Penny does still tense my stomach with panic. It's a reaction that serves no purpose except to torment me and it is nothing more than the distant echo of a pain I felt a year ago. They are perfectly entitled to see their father and he is equally entitled to spend time with them. Even Penny, I imagine, will be nothing but kind and generous to them.

Life keeps getting better. The real me was here all along, smothered under obligation and silenced by bullies. But no more. From now on there will be no hiding away, no doubting, no fear.

No more walking on eggshells.

THE END

ACKNOWLEDGEMENTS

Sincere thanks to my fantastic editor, Kirstie Edwards, for seeing what I couldn't see and for improving this book no end.

Also to Ray Lipscombe, a cover artist who is not only immensely talented but infinitely patient.

My gratitude goes to all those writers whose work has inspired and impressed me, and will continue to do so, judging by the size of my 'To Be Read' pile.

Thank you to my lovely new husband, Stuart, who encouraged me and engineered our lives so that I could do this. And just for being you—who knew it could be this good?

Thanks also to my talented and wonderful son, Andy for the technical help and for listening to me go on and on about writing. Keep your head up, keep your heart strong.

To my friends who have supported me through writing this book and through the ups and downs of life. So many of you, but special thanks to Jo, Lucie, Jill, Georgia, Sarah B and of course The Mermaids!

Finally, my thanks to all who have read this book. If you happen to be feeling like Amanda did at the beginning of the story, I hope that you can find strength and courage to carry on, move forward and become the woman you know you can be.

Printed in Great Britain
by Amazon